# THE MUSEUM OF
# THE FUTURE

## and other stories by
# ANDREW MAY

Typeset by Jonathan Downes,
Cover and Layout by SPiderKaT for CFZ Communications
Using Microsoft Word 2000, Microsoft Publisher 2000, Adobe Photoshop CS.

First published in Great Britain by CFZ Press

**CFZ Press
Myrtle Cottage
Woolsery
Bideford
North Devon
EX39 5QR**

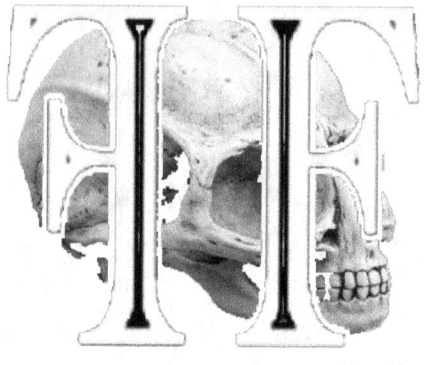

## ISBN: 978-1-909488-23-6

## Publishing history

# CONTENTS

THE GUARDIAN OF THE TOMB ............................... 5
THE BALLOON FACTORY ....................................... 12
THE CALL OF COOL-O ........................................... 18
FLOWERS OF THE FUTURE.................................... 25
THE GRAVITY ENGINE ........................................... 30
LOSS OF POWER...................................................... 38
A CASE FOR CRANE ............................................... 45
THE RENDLESHAM MAGI....................................... 76
THE CASE OF THE PURLOINED POE.................... 84
HOMICIDAL HOMEOPATHY .................................. 98
THE MYSTIC FAYRE AFFAIR................................ 112
MISS PERCEPTION ................................................. 119
THE MYTHOLOGIST ................................................ 127
PSYKICK KWEST...................................................... 135
THE MIND WHISPERERS ....................................... 144
SECRETS OF THE GREEN GOD............................. 154
THE ALCHEMIST'S CURSE.................................... 159
COLLECTOR'S ITEM............................................... 162
THE VANISHING CURATE...................................... 165
MUSEUM OF THE FUTURE.................................... 176
NOTES ON THE STORIES ...................................... 193

# THE GUARDIAN OF THE TOMB

I t has occasionally been remarked, by persons versed in such matters, that the modern-day legend of Rennes-le-Chateau displays striking parallels to the ghost story "Canon Alberic's Scrapbook" penned by Dr Montague Rhodes James. These parallels, however, fade to insignificance in comparison with those to be found in the following cautionary tale.

Whisperings of a mysterious discovery made in a remote French village percolated around the continent of Europe, eventually reaching Cambridge—in which town they fell upon the ears of our protagonist, an enthusiastic young antiquary whom we shall refer to as Soskin (although that was not his true name). Soskin was able to ascertain but a few firm facts in the matter: that the village was situated in the foothills of the Pyrenees and was named Rennes-le-Chateau, that the discovery concerned a purported relic of the Knights Templar, and that it had been found by the local priest, who went by the name of Abbé Saunière. Our protagonist determined forthwith to make the journey to Rennes-le-Chateau and investigate the matter for himself.

So it was that, one windy day in the Autumn of 189-, we find young Soskin taking the early morning boat-train from Victoria Station to the Gare du Nord, and thence on the slow chugging journey around the Petite Ceinture to the Gare d'Austerlitz. He was tempted indeed to spend a day or two visiting his old haunts in Paris (he had once passed the best part of a day in the Richelieu wing of the Musée du Louvre, where he had been particularly captivated by the symbolic paintings of Nicolas Poussin) but his impatience to proceed with his mission saw him ensconced on the overnight sleeper to Toulouse.

At Toulouse Soskin bought a ticket for Carcassonne, from which picturesque town he took a slow local train to the village of Couiza, situated at the head of the Aude valley. Alighting there in the early afternoon, and finding the weather agreeable, he proceeded to complete his journey on foot. The road to Rennes-le-Château wound its way up a steep hill, affording excellent views of the rocky, pine-clad scenery and the distant Pyrenees to the south.

As he turned a corner, the young man fancied he caught a sudden movement in a shady glade off to one side of the road. A fellow traveller, perhaps? But on entering the glade he saw no-one, nor any animal that might have been the source of the movement he had glimpsed. Yet for all that, there was something in the glade that took his attention: something he would never have expected to find in such an out-of-the-way place. It was a large stone tomb: a rather grand sarcophagus with a weathered and scarcely legible inscription. For some unaccountable reason the tomb seemed familiar to Soskin, and he spent many minutes trying to recollect where he had seen such a tomb before. But the memory proved elusive, and eventually he resumed his upward journey.

It was near to night-fall when the young man finally arrived in the tiny village... a place of just three hundred inhabitants, he discovered. He located an inn, which rather grandly called itself L'Hotel de la Tour, and booked two nights' accommodation. Then, exhausted after the long trip from Cambridge, he turned in for the night.

The next morning saw Soskin up bright and early, and enquiring after Abbé Saunière. To the latter's house he was directed, and there he found the priest just on the point of leaving for the church. On learning that the visitor had come all the way from Cambridge, Saunière readily offered to give the Englishman a short guided tour of the place.

Soskin was much surprised by his host's demeanour. In personal appearance there was nothing to remark on that was out of the ordinary, but his manner was quite peculiar, displaying a degree of nervousness for which there was no apparent cause. The man was perpetually half glancing behind him, with a curiously furtive or even hunted air—as if he were expecting every moment to find himself in the clutch of an enemy.

"It is dedicated to Saint Mary Magdalene," the priest informed him as they approached the small but attractive stone-built church. "The original structure was Visigothic, built in the eighth century, but the present building dates from the eleventh century... it is in the Romanesque style, you will notice."

As they passed through the round-arched door, Soskin glanced upwards and saw an inscription... it was in Latin, though judging by the lack of weathering it must have been of very recent date: *TERRIBILIS EST LOCUS ISTE.*

Observing the direction of his visitor's gaze, Saunière turned to him. With a visible shudder he said "I put that inscription there," but offered no further explanation.

Inside the church, Saunière dipped his fingers in the holy water and crossed himself. Automatically Soskin (who was high-church Anglican) did the same. Then he took a second look at the holy water stoup and gasped. Below it and supporting it was a small but frighteningly lifelike carving of Satan: luridly painted and making an obscenely onanistic gesture with his right hand.

"The devil, yes." Saunière shuddered a second time. "That statue is my work, too. A symbol of evil... yet it is not the most evil thing in this church. Let me show you what it is you have come all this distance to see."

The priest led the way into the chancel, and pointed towards the altar.

Soskin began to suspect he was in the presence of a madman. "The altar... a thing of evil? Surely you are joking."

Saunière knelt before the altar: it was supported on an ancient-looking limestone pillar. With trembling hands the priest touched the pillar and a concealed door swung open. He removed a dusty scroll from the hollow space within.

"This pillar formed part of the original Visigothic church," Saunière explained. "I discovered the secret hiding place within it by accident, and I wish to Heaven that I had not."

Soskin had no time for the priest's superstitious babbling. The antiquarian in him was brimming over with the excitement of discovery. "The scroll... what does it contain?"
"All in good time. First... what do you know of the Knights Templar?"

The question was one that, on any other occasion, Soskin could happily have spent all day answering. But in his present state of impatience he merely said "The Templars were crusading knights: a chivalric order that flourished during the twelfth century. They were known for their distinctive white mantles marked with a large red cross, and their headquarters in Jerusalem was built on the site of Solomon's Temple. But as time went on, according to certain accounts, the knights turned to..." He paused as he racked his brains for a suitable turn of phrase. "They turned to the dark side—indulging in heretical beliefs and pagan rituals. The Templar Order was abolished on the orders of the Pope."

"Yes, that is all substantially correct," Saunière assented. "It is, moreover, rumoured that the knights discovered a treasure of enormous value hidden in the ruins of Solomon's Temple, and that they brought it back with them to France. Many legends place the treasure here, in Rennes-le-Chateau."

"I have heard legends of this type," Soskin agreed. "As to the nature of the treasure, however, there seems to be much dispute. Some say that it is the Ark of the Covenant, others that it is the Holy Grail, still others that it is a mystical Brown Book which may earn a man a fortune overnight."
"It may be any of those things, or it may be something else entirely." Saunière gave another involuntary shudder. "Whatever it is, I have found its location, and I can tell you that it is an evil thing! I would not wish any man to seek it out... not even my worst enemy. Here, let me show you the parchment that I found..."

With shaking hands, the priest unrolled the dusty scroll he had taken from the hollow pillar. It was covered in crabbed Latin text.

"At a first glance, this appears to be nothing other than a passage from the Vulgate Bible: chapter twelve of the fourth gospel. But on closer examination, I noted a large number of misprints: specifically, the inclusion of numerous extraneous letters. I thought, perhaps, that by extracting these letters, and these letters alone, I would find a message directing me to the treasure. But the result was a meaningless jumble of letters."

"A cipher or cryptogram, perhaps?" Soskin suggested.

"Yes, yes—that was my thought precisely. And you may imagine how minutely I examined the text. Oh, the agonies I went through! At first, I felt sure the key would be found in some old book on secret writing, such as the *Steganographia* of Joachim Trithemius, or the *Cryptographia* of Selenius. But all that came to nothing. Then I tried analysing letter frequencies, taking first Latin and then French as a basis. That got me a little closer, and... but I am boring you, I can see. Suffice to say that after much mental labour I found that which I had been seeking: the true message of the parchment."

"And that was...?" The young Englishman was virtually dancing with impatience.

"I know it by heart," the priest whispered. "*Bergere pas de tentation que Poussin Teniers gardent la clef par la crois et ce cheval de dieu j'acheve ce daemon de gardien a midi.*"

"Shepherd, not of temptation, Poussin... er something." Soskin's face was screwed up with concentration as he endeavoured to translate what he had heard into his own language. "... guards the key by the cross and... oh, I forget the rest. Something about a demon guardian, I think."

"I suppose all this means nothing to you."

"I confess it does not. Or perhaps... yes! Wait a moment, let me think." Soskin's mind was racing. "Shepherds—Poussin... of course! It's a painting I saw in the Louvre in Paris. A picture of a tomb..."

"So you do understand." Saunière nodded. "The painting shows a tomb that lies on the road leading up to this village—perhaps you saw it on your way here?"

The tomb in the glade—of course! That's why it had seemed so familiar. It was the tomb in the celebrated painting by Poussin: *Les bergers d'Arcadie*!

The priest continued his narration. "I need not tell you that, late as the hour was (it was approaching nine in the evening), I hastened to investigate the tomb the very moment that my decipherment was complete. I snatched up an oil lamp and a few tools, and made my way down the hill. Strangely, as I approached the spot I thought I saw someone ahead of me, standing right beside the tomb. But when I finally reached it (breathless from excitement and unwonted exertion) the place appeared to be deserted. Immediately I set to work, placing the lamp on top of the tomb for illumination. You can imagine how I examined the structure with the keenest interest, but I could see no obvious way to gain access to its interior. I paused to think. Maybe there was a clue in the painting..."

"If I remember correctly, the shepherds are pointing to some detail on the tomb," Soskin suggested.

"You are right!" the priest exclaimed. "The same thought occurred to me. But at what, exactly, were they pointing? I racked my brains, and then it came back to me. The shepherds are pointing at one particular letter of the inscription. But which one? And the letters are now so worn as to be unreadable. But no matter... I could try each letter in turn. This I did, and before very long I had discovered the secret. A moderate amount of pressure on the correct spot, and the side panel slid open to reveal the interior of the tomb... and the lost treasure of the Knights Templar!"

"So you did find the treasure! But only a moment ago you said you had no idea what the treasure was!"

"And I spoke the truth. Because, you see, just as the tomb opened... all Hell broke loose. I mean that literally, not figuratively. A fiery blast of fetid, noxious smelling air blew out from the tomb and knocked me almost senseless to the ground. When the blast had subsided, I struggled to my knees and beheld, in the flickering light of the gas lamp (which stood miraculously unharmed on top of the tomb), a... figure. Human in form, but of gigantic proportions, it stood between myself and the now opened tomb. A seven-foot tall crusader, steel helmeted, clad in a tattered white mantle emblazoned with a large red cross. As it looked silently down at me, it slowly raised its hands and removed the helmet. What I saw paralysed me with terror. Dry, leathery skin of a dull leaden colour, a caved-in nose, eyes of a fiery yellow against which the pupils showed black and intense... there could be no doubt this was the demon guardian of which the parchment spoke. I can tell you no more, for at this point I mercifully lost consciousness. When I awoke the sun was up and there was dew on the grass. The tomb, thankfully, was once again closed. It is my earnest hope that it is never again opened."

We need not concern ourselves with the rest of Soskin's stay in Rennes-le-Chateau: suffice to say it was uneventful following the tour of the church and the priest's revelations. We resume our acquaintance with the young Englishman the next morning, when (it has to be said) he left L'Hotel de la Tour fully two hours earlier than was necessary to catch his train in Couiza. Now, it should not be supposed that our protagonist was an avaricious man, or one that would seek a fabled treasure for purely material gain. But he was a devout antiquarian, and any hint of undiscovered relics of the past presented him with an all but irresistible temptation. Furthermore (as he prided himself) he was not what could be termed a superstitious or otherwise credulous person, so his actions that morning were, I think, inevitable.

Arriving at the spot where he remembered the tomb to be, Soskin was mystified to find no trace of it. Yet there could be no doubt this was the correct glade: he remembered the exact arrangement of the trees. Puzzled, he went back to the road and surveyed his surroundings.

Surely he hadn't been mistaken? Looking back into the glade he saw, to his surprise, that there was a person standing there—one of the villagers out for an early morning stroll, perhaps. A stroke of luck! He could ask, in all innocence (after all, it was the sort of question a visiting tourist would ask), where in the vicinity he might find an old stone tomb...

He took a step into the glade, then abruptly turned on his heel and—in the firm conviction that discretion was the better part of valour—ran all the way down the hill to the railway station. "Of course, I'm not superstitious," he told himself. "It's just that I realize I'm not that keen on finding the old tomb after all. And the tall gentleman dressed up as a twelfth century crusader probably wouldn't have been able to help me anyway."

# THE BALLOON FACTORY

I descended from the upper deck of the omnibus, barely managing to alight before the impatient driver geed the horses and the 'bus clattered off towards the Edgware Road. Hunching my shoulders against the chilly London smog, I threaded my way along the crowded pavement towards my place of work.

Arriving at my wonted hour, I went through the gate at the side of Mr Dobson's haberdashery store and around to the rear entrance. As I reached the stairwell there was a low rumbling noise and the ground shook for a few moments. The disturbance was a rude reminder of the tunnelling work going on a hundred feet below—the burrowing machinery had nudged a few yards further toward its goal. The aim was to extend the Bakerloo tube line from Baker Street through to the main-line terminus at Paddington... or at least, that was the official explanation. Others detected more sinister motives for the tunnelling; secrets the government would prefer to keep to itself.

I ascended three flights of stairs—the first two floors occupied by Mr Dobson's shop and the third by a small architectural firm—and finally arrived, somewhat out of breath, at the door of my own office on the top floor. *CLARION OF THE TRUTH,* the sign read. *A Weekly Journal for Discerning Readers. Proprietor Quincy Solomon, Esquire.*

I unlocked the door and went in, shedding my hat and coat. I struggled for a few seconds with the window sash, finally persuading it to open. Cool, smoke-laden air wafted in from outside, carrying the busy sounds of trains puffing in and out of the main-line station below.

I opened the safe and transferred a pile of papers to the desk, eager to get started on the day's work. I had a great deal to accomplish in a short time. From the scribbled notes made the previous evening, I had to transcribe the substance of my interview with Madame Kaminsky, collate the resulting manuscript with the rest of the issue's copy, and take the whole lot to Mr Ramsbottom in Praed Street for typesetting and printing. What a joy journalism would be, if it were not for deadlines!

Anna Kaminsky enjoyed a deserved reputation as London's foremost clairvoyant, as well as being an accomplished astral traveller. She had recently been in contact with certain etheric intelligences on the planet Mars, and it was on this subject in particular that I had focused the majority of my questions. There were certain similarities and consonances between what she had to say, unearthly as it was, and mysterious events on our own planet that had been reported in the *Clarion of the Truth* over the last few months.

No sooner had I put pen to paper than a knock came at the door. Irritated, I hurried over to answer it, with the intention of getting rid of whoever it was as precipitously as possible.

I opened the door to see a bird-like little man, twitching from one foot to another with scarcely concealed anxiety.

"Mr Solomon, sir!" he exclaimed. "I'm sorry to impose on you like this, but I must speak to you as a matter of urgency."

"It's really not a very convenient time," I replied. "Perhaps you..."

The man glanced around to check that no-one else was listening. "It concerns the Martian sky-ship that crashed on Eelmoor Plain," he said, his eyes flashing with intensity.

"You'd better come in," I said, ushering him inside. I swept some papers off a chair and bade him sit down. As he did so, he handed me his calling card. Hand-written in smudged ink, it bore the name George Fripp, together with an address in Aldershot.

"It's an honour to meet you in person, sir," Fripp said. "I'm a regular reader of the *Clarion*, and have been so from the very beginning. It's a great service that you do—cutting through all the lies and hypocrisy of the so-called establishment."

I thanked him for his kind words, and urged him to proceed with his story as swiftly as possible. By way of a hint I removed my watch from my pocket and glanced at it meaningfully. My chief concern at that time was still to rid myself of Fripp and resume the business of the day as quickly as possible.

Once underway, Fripp's words came out in an excited rush. "Obviously I've taken a special interest in all your reports concerning the Martian flying vehicles, living down Aldershot way like I do. We've all seen them, buzzing around the sky like huge mechanical birds."

I turned to the filing cabinet and began rummaging through a drawer. After a few moments I pulled out a recent issue of the *Clarion* and placed it on the desk-top, facing Fripp. It was dated the third of August 1909, and the headline read: *Martian Sky-Ship Crashes on Eelmoor Plain... Army Denies Knowledge, Removes Evidence.*

Eelmoor Plain is the name given to a stretch of common land between the towns of Aldershot and Farnborough, in rural Hampshire thirty miles south-west of London. Although the event had gone virtually unreported in the mainstream press, I had uncovered ample evidence to prove that something very strange had fallen to the ground there three months ago.

"It makes me angry, it does," Fripp said. "The contempt our so-called government has for its own citizens. They tell us there's no such thing as Martians, that anyone who sees flying machines is either mad or lying. Well I've seen them, and lots of local people have seen them. So there must be Martians."

I nodded solemnly. "It's certain that no machine made on Earth will ever fly," I said. "Lord Kelvin has proved it scientifically."

"Unless it's made by our Mr Cody, of course." Fripp laughed without much humour, and I joined in. Sam Cody was an American entertainer, who had come over to England when his Wild West show fell on hard times. He'd established a small business in Farnborough making kites and other flying toys, but only the weak-minded believed his claim to have flown in one of them himself. At bottom Sam Cody was nothing but an illusionist, a clever showman, like his fellow countrymen the Wright Brothers that he strove to imitate.

"Anyway, I started to wonder what the army did with the wreckage they took away." Fripp felt inside his coat and pulled out a much-used map. Carefully he unfolded it on the desk.

"There's one obvious place." His finger came down on the north-eastern corner of Farnborough Common. On the map it was simply marked *Military Zone—Restricted Area*.

"The Balloon Factory," I said. "So-called, of course. Obviously a rather feeble cover-story for God-only-knows-what sinister activity they're keeping secret from the British public." It was a truly preposterous idea, that the Army should have any interest whatsoever in a childish toy such as a balloon.

"The story locally is that they're preparing for a big war against Germany," Fripp said.

"I've heard that story, and it doesn't hold water," I said. "The Germans have no grievance with us—if they go to war with anyone it will be the Froggies, looking for retribution after the thrashing they got back in the Franco-Prussian war. The Germans are our friends—after all, their Kaiser is our King's cousin. What fools the government takes us for, if they think we will believe that all their secrecy is motivated by an impending war with Germany."

Fripp looked thoughtful. "They must all be in league together," he said. "Our government, the Martians and the Germans. That Dr Einstein is German, and his ideas on space and time are beyond the capability of any human mind to think up."

I nodded in agreement. "Quite so—it is inconceivable that the theory of Relativity could have originated on our own planet." I thought about Madame Kaminsky, and what she had told me the previous day about Mars and its etheric intelligences. She had explained how they dwelt on a higher vibrational level than human beings, and the language she used to describe them was, to my mind, remarkably similar to that of Dr Einstein's theory. Suddenly there was no doubt in my mind that Relativity was a Martian concept.

Thoughts of Madame Kaminsky brought me back to the present, reminding me that I had a deadline to meet. I glanced at my watch and then looked up at Fripp. "But we are digressing—you were saying something about the Balloon Factory on Farnborough Common, I believe?"

"Yes. The place is surrounded by barbed wire fencing, and the whole perimeter is patrolled regularly by an armed guard. But by patient observation over many consecutive nights, I deduced that I had a clear period between one-thirty and two in the morning during which I could gain access with relatively minor risk. Even so, I had my share of heart-stopping moments, although I shan't bore you with the details now. The gist of the story is that I eventually succeeded in gaining a brief glimpse inside the cavernous building euphemistically referred to as Balloon Shed Number One. And as long as I live I shall never forget what I saw."

"You saw the wreckage of the Martian flying machine?" I asked with eagerness. This was starting to sound like the scoop of a lifetime.

"No, I saw no wreckage, but that is of little consequence in light of what I did see," Fripp said. Just at that moment there was a deep rumbling sound and the building lurched. Another few yards' progress had been made in the tunnel below—but the effect also served as dramatic counterpoint to Fripp's words.

"An unimaginably vast sky-vessel, shaped like a cigar and at least a hundred yards long. It appeared to be made from some unearthly silvery fabric, and had smaller side-pods that I can only describe as looking like windmills."

"Windmills?" I echoed.

"That's what they looked like. I can't even speculate as to their purpose. The whole thing defied terrestrial logic—there is no doubt in my mind that this was a ship from Mars."

I thought for a long moment, gazing out of the window. The sky was darker than it had been, and it had started to drizzle. "I can see only two alternatives," I said slowly. "Either the British government is indeed in league with the Martians, and their vessel is being harboured within the Army facility on Farnborough Common. Or else the machine you saw was genuinely made on this planet..." I waved aside Fripp's objection as I struggled to coin an appropriate phrase. "...*Reverse-engineered*, as it were, from the wreckage they recovered from the Martian crash site. Whatever the situation, you may rest assured this will be on the front page of next week's issue. The public have a right to know the truth."

I thanked Fripp again, and showed him out. Then I sat back and mused on what I had just heard. Crashed sky-ships, vast flying machines, feats of engineering beyond the wit of man...

To which could be added, of course, Madame Kaminsky's psychic insights into Martian civilization, Dr Einstein's strange unearthly theory of Relativity—and, to top it all, this infernal secret government tunnel-digging beneath the streets of London. What did it all mean?

Of one thing I was sure—something this big could not be kept secret indefinitely. Before long there would have to be an official announcement. I gave it five years at most—say until 1914.

And what would the announcement be? Contact with Martians, as I had been saying all along, or some Great War against the Germans, as the scoffers and sceptics would have it? Only time would tell.

# THE CALL OF COOL-O

Philip K. Dick meets H. P. Lovecraft

## 1. CLAY

Information is being beamed into my head, Hank Wilcox thought grimly. By some vast, timeless, impersonal entity. That was the only way to explain what had happened that morning. He speeded his pace, then, as he moved along the sidewalk clutching the small paper-wrapped package.

He came to the university building he was seeking and went inside, glad to be out of the hot sun. He ascended the wide stone staircase to the second floor, close behind a chick with a nice ass and fashionable Cool-O trainers. At the top of the stairs there was a soda machine. He felt in his pocket for change; he needed a Coke. But the machine was out of Coke, he saw; and out of Sprite and Dr Pepper also. The only cans left in the machine were Cool-O. He hated the taste but, hell, he was thirsty. He drank the Cool-O with a grimace.

Hank Wilcox inspected the directory and found the name he was looking for. Professor George of the archaeology department; an authority on ancient inscriptions, he'd been told. Hank went along the corridor to his left, found the right door, and knocked.

The dark-haired female behind the desk stood up to greet him as he entered the room.

"Hi, I'm Angel George," she said, eyeing him cautiously. "How may I help you?"

Jeez, Hank thought, the professor is a chick. No older than thirty, she was slender, with high cheekbones and a long neck. She wore black jeans and a man's style shirt, open to the third or fourth button. Her long brown hair was tied back in a braid.

"I need your help with some hieroglyphs," he mumbled, unwrapping the package and placing it on her desk.

---

As she leaned forward to look, he caught a glimpse down her shirt-front. Her breasts were tiny and braless. There was a ring piercing her right nipple, and a small tattoo just above the left. Christ, he thought, this is one kinky chick. She must need it real bad. He ought to offer to ball her, he realized, as a matter of Christian charity. But he didn't; somehow it didn't seem the right thing to say to a professor of archaeology.

Angel George looked up suddenly, fixing Hank with a penetrating stare. "What kind of joke is this?" she inquired fiercely. "There's nothing ancient about this object; it's an obvious fake of recent origin. Look, the clay isn't even dry yet."

"That's right. I only made it this morning," Hank said. "When I woke up."

"What?" She looked at him pityingly, as if he was a retarded child.

"I'm a sculptor," Hank said, solemnly. "That's my job. When I made this, I was in an altered state of consciousness. Under orders, as it were, from the avatar of a higher reality. Look, it's important. I need to know what these hieroglyphs mean."

Angel turned her attention back to the object. Observing it, really, for the first time. Before, she had seen only its newness; this time, she took in all the details.

The hieroglyphs ran all around the rectangular base of the clay sculpture. Above this squatted the figure of an alien creature, with a scaly, vaguely humanoid body, clawed hind- and forepaws, small leathery wings, and a bloated, tentacled, cephalopod-like head. The overall impression was of something ancient and unearthly.

Angel shuddered, then straightened suddenly. "I'm sorry—these symbols mean nothing to me. I'm sure they're nothing but a product of your clearly fertile imagination. Now, please excuse me. I have an important call to make."

Defeated, Hank re-wrapped the package and left. On his way downstairs he thought bleakly, I really should have offered to ball her. Look at all these nerdy college types. I'm probably the first real man she's seen this year.

Outside in the street, Hank stood at a crossing and waited patiently until the "Don't Walk" sign changed to "Walk". A Cool-O truck pulled up and he crossed in front of it, then started along the opposite sidewalk in the direction of his conapt.

A police air-car appeared from nowhere and landed right in front of him. Two cops got out.

"You're under arrest," the first cop said.

Hank was astounded, incredulous. "What for?" he asked.

"Jaywalking," the second cop said, after a pause.

"But I waited…" Before Hank could finish, the nearest of the cops shoved him bodily out into the traffic. A ground-car screeched to a halt, narrowly avoided hitting him, and sounded its horn. The other cop grabbed him roughly and pulled him back, punching him gratuitously in the stomach.

"You're busted, freak," he said.

"Yeah, goddamn long-haired hippie freak," the other said. "You're coming with us."

They bundled him into the back of the air-car, and seconds later it was climbing rapidly into the clear blue sky.

## 2. GRASS

At the police station, the first thing they did was confiscate the package containing his clay sculpture. Then they took his name and details, and seated him in an interview room. The cop there identified himself as Police Captain J. R. Grass. A big man, massively overweight, middle-aged, balding. He was dressed untidily and slouched back in his chair, with the manner of one who had occupied a position of power for so long that he no longer needed to impress people.

Captain Grass looked at Hank, assessing him. "So you're a member of the Cult. When were you recruited; how high up in the organization are you?"

"Cult …?" Hank echoed. He was stunned; events had overtaken him.

"You know what I'm referring to. The Cult of Cool-O, they call it." Grass sounded empty, like he was tired of life.

"Cool-O? You mean like the drink?" Hank asked.

"Like the drink, and the sportswear, the TV network, the intercontinental hypershuttle— you name it. Cool-O is everywhere. It's so ubiquitous people don't notice it any more." Grass steepled his hands, meditating. "But that's all above-board, a multinational commercial consortium. The Cult is something else—something sinister and threatening. Look—"

The police captain leaned down and took an object out of a cardboard box. He placed it on the table between them. The object was made from a strange greenish stone, flecked with gold. But apart from that, it was identical to Hank's clay sculpture. Even in its proportions.

Hank's eyes bugged out. He said "I don't understand."

Without speaking, Grass went over to a large video display and set the tape running.

"These events happened just over a month ago, here in Southern California; a combined operation by the Feds and ourselves. Watch."

The screen showed a group of sprawling ranch-style buildings; the view was unsteady, obviously taken with a hand-held recorder. Suddenly there was shouting, smoke and explosions, as uniformed men appeared from all sides, storming the building. The camera followed the troops in. Figures in long white robes appeared from the buildings, firing back at the attackers. But their old-style weapons were no match for state-of-the-art laser rifles, and most of the defenders fell quickly. The camera went through into the smoking compound itself, to an inner courtyard in which a group of the white-robed figures were kneeling before a central pillar. Panning up to the top of the pillar, the camera picked out the incongruously diminutive object there—the green and gold statue that was like Hank's clay sculpture.

Grass paused the video. "This creature with the wings and tentacles—the Cult freaks refer to him as Cool-O. In fact, they worship him as a god. We captured a group of freaks and interrogated them separately. They all told the same story, vis-à-vis Cool-O. They believe him to be a member of an ancient, virtually immortal race called the Great Old Ones, that came to Earth from the stars long before humans were here.

There was a clash with another set of space beings, the Elder Gods, and Cool-O ended up sedated and imprisoned in the depths of a parallel dimension beneath our own. But the Cult believe he will rise again, to reclaim his place as lord of this world. Which they see as his rightful place. Their rites are designed to speed up this process."

"I had no idea," Hank said. "I never heard of this Cult before, or of a god called Cool-O. I made the sculpture, sure, but I was in an altered state of consciousness—it was like I was receiving orders telepathically." He chewed on a knuckle, reflexively.

"You know, son, I'm inclined to believe you," Captain Grass said, placing his two great paws on the table between them. "The Cult freaks say that, even though Cool-O is sleeping, and imprisoned in another dimension, he has the ability to beam thoughts directly into the minds of certain individuals. That's how the Cult knows what it does about him; how they know what rites to perform. Some types of people are particularly susceptible to picking up Cool-O's mind-messages; by that I refer to schizoid types, specifically. Not that I'm saying you're crazy, of course. I'm not judging you, sanity-wise; I'm just pointing out certain facts to you."

"Thank you, sir, that's very generous," Hank observed, philosophically.

"Okay, interview over," Grass said, rising abruptly. "You're free to go."

# 3. MADNESS

*Some recent medical cases provide strong evidence in favour of the reductionist view. Human beings have a lower brain and two upper hemispheres, connected by a bundle of fibres. In treating a few people with severe epilepsy, surgeons have cut these fibres... The effect, in the words of one surgeon, was the creation of two separate spheres of consciousness.*

Derek Parfit: *Reasons and Persons*
Oxford University Press, 1984

A strangely dark mood came over Hank Wilcox as he walked back toward his conapt. He felt queasy and dislocated; the sickly Cool-O soda still sloshed around in his otherwise empty stomach. And the cop's talk about the bizarre cult had left him confused and uneasy. The high buildings pressed menacingly in on him, darkening and twisting into unfamiliar forms. Reality is changing around me, Hank realized. Shifting, in some indefinable way.

He found himself struggling up a steep slope, the buildings to either side of him now black and windowless, jutting at crazy angles. With shock, he saw that the walls were dripping with green ooze, and inscribed with hieroglyphs like those on his sculpture. He was alone, he realized; there were no other people on the weirdly sloping street. But there was a sound; a slow, rhythmic thudding, like immensely huge footfalls.

Hank stopped, and looked around at the insanely fractured landscape. Dark stone blocks, their geometry all wrong; shattered, slime-dripping towers of unearthly construction...

*"Ich bin der Welt abhanden gekommen,"* he thought. *"Mit der ich sonst viele Zeit verdorben."* Like most working-class Californians, his thought-patterns shifted at times of great stress to obscure German literature.

The thudding sound was much nearer now. He came to a corner and peered around the crazily-carved stone wall. And he looked upon the source of the sound; he saw the nightmare creature that was called Cool-O. It was huge, lumbering, of indeterminate size; it could have been anything from a hundred feet to a mile in height. In general outline the sculpture had been accurate—the scaly green bulk, oddly stunted bat wings, savage claws, and rubbery, tentacled head. But no image could have prepared him for the feeling of total, inhuman coldness that he perceived the instant he set eyes on the thing itself. In wave after wave it came upon him. The thing slowed its pace, fixing its glacial eyes on him, and the hideous feelers snaked down toward him...

Hank fainted, then.

"... I know this guy; leave this to me." A voice, as he drifted back to consciousness.

He opened his eyes to see Angel George leaning over him, a concerned expression on her face.

"You passed out—I saw the crowd gathered around you. They say you were babbling incoherently about an octopus and a soft drink, or something." She mopped the perspiration from his brow with a handkerchief.

"I looked on the face of God," Hank said, serenely. "He spoke to me, directly into my mind. He said this place—this world—it's nothing but an illusion. A fake. He's trying to help us, to break through and take us back to the real world. I was there with him, briefly."

"I'm sorry I had to turn you over to the cops," Angel said. "But your sculpture was identical to one they showed me last week. They said it came from some crazy cult. You can see the position I was in."

"Okay," Hank said, blinking at her. He meditated solemnly for a moment. "Can I ball you now?" he asked.

She slugged him, then.

# FLOWERS OF THE FUTURE

I t may seem strange to be reviewing a book that has been out of print for more than forty years, and one that attracted no interest whatsoever from the critical establishment when it first appeared in the early sixties. Indeed, if I'd encountered *The Flowers of the Future* at that time, or in the 1970s or 80s, it wouldn't have struck me as remarkable in any way. But it wasn't until a few weeks ago that I finally stumbled across it, as I was rummaging through a cardboard box full of old paperbacks in one of the West Country's countless charity shops.

I'd never have given the book a second glance if it hadn't been for the picture on the cover. I'd barely heard of the author—Melvyn Pettle—and what I had heard wasn't good. Of the book itself, *The Flowers of the Future*, I'd heard nothing at all. Yet the cover illustration grabbed my attention. It showed a long-haired guru sitting in rapt meditation while an impossibly baroque spaceship loomed on its launch gantry behind him. As it turned out, the picture had virtually no connection with the contents of the book (quite a common situation with mass-market paperbacks of the sixties) but it had done the trick. I'm a sucker for stories that combine arcane wisdom and high technology—so I took a closer look.

I turned the book over to read the short publicity blurb on the back, and that's when its tremendous significance first hit me:

> *On February 1st 2003 a returning spaceship bursts into flame and plummets to Earth. At the same time, the brave men and women of the free world are preparing for the last stand in the War on Terror... So begins Melvyn Pettle's chilling vision of a future just forty short years away...*

The coincidence left me thunderstruck: I thought of the Space Shuttle *Columbia*, and the invasion of Iraq. I hastily opened the book and looked at the copyright page: it was dated 1964, and appeared to be a first printing. The sorry state of the book—it was mildewed and dog-eared—was further testimony to its age.

I paid a pound for the book and returned home to give it further scrutiny. The first thing to say is that—despite being pigeonholed as SCI-FI by its publisher—the book presents itself as a work of non-fiction. The author, Melvyn Pettle (if that's his real name) claims to have been a student at one of England's newer 'red-brick' universities. While Pettle was experimenting with certain unspecified chemicals, he found himself translated forty years into the future, for a period of several months of his own subjective time. His descriptions of that time form the bulk of the book's narrative.

Before proceeding further I should point out that the book is absolutely dreadful—thoroughly abysmal in every way. I would certainly never have struggled through it if it hadn't been for the book's uncanny pre-echoings of our own time. The style is turgid to the point of unreadability, heavily overloaded with adverbs and multi-syllabic words that one looks up in the dictionary only to find they don't exist.

In several places the narrative is brought to a halt by rambling discussions of philosophy. Hegel, Schopenhauer, Gurdjieff and Ouspensky are mentioned quite often, but perhaps the most significant name-dropping is that of J. W. Dunne, the British amateur philosopher who claimed it was possible to dream about future events before they occurred. Dunne is probably best known to SF readers as the inspiration behind Robert Heinlein's novelette *Elsewhen*.

Long-winded, poorly constructed, pontificating... *The Flowers of the Future* is all of these things. But above all it is pornographic—relentlessly so. Every female character that is introduced is first described in great detail with her clothes on, then gradually stripped, then described in great detail (though not always credibly, from an anatomical point of view) with her clothes off. Finally, the woman performs a graphically described sex act on Pettle.

This rigmarole is gone through not once or twice, but a total of thirteen times during the course of the narrative, occupying in all perhaps a third of the book's 180 pages. The women come in all shapes, colours and sizes, but the final sex act is always identical, down to the last detail. Pettle's relentlessly obsessive style appears to be modelled on the work of his better known contemporary, J. G. Ballard.

I should repeat what I said earlier, that the book is presented as a work of non-fiction rather than as a novel. It has no coherent plot, no strongly drawn characters, no ups and downs of dramatic tension. It is little more than an episodic account of Pettle's monotonously predictable sexual encounters and philosophical ramblings. The sole interest for us today lies in the little snippets of background information that Pettle provides about his 'future' world: the world that, according to him, would exist in the year 2003.

Pettle finds himself in a Britain which has, along with the rest of Europe, been absorbed into the Soviet Bloc. Society is governed according to the principles of Communism, viz. peace, love, flower-power and freedom of expression. The people have collectively thrown off the yoke of the industrial revolution (these are all Pettle's terms, not mine), and chosen to live life at a slower pace, with back-to-nature, low-technology straightforwardness. There is no crime, no poverty, no unemployment, no pollution. Disease has become a thing of the past, ever since the outdated fascist concept of personal hygiene was joyfully cast aside.

This life of bliss prevails only in the Eastern hemisphere, for Pettle's world of 2003 is starkly bipolar. In the West squats the ugly dark empire of the United States, corrupt and decadent, whose inhabitants have surrendered their humanity to the false god of technology. Indeed, the incumbent US president, Nixon the Third, is nothing but a figurehead. The nation's real decision-maker is a near sentient electronic computer—a vast, subterranean monster that is all clicking relays and flickering vacuum tubes.

This may seem far-removed from the down-to-earth reality of 2003. But the name of that vast thinking machine—the name that Melvyn Pettle gave it in this dreadful forty-year old book— is INTER-NET. Uppercase, hyphenated, and lacking the definite article, but even so the resemblance is too close for coincidence. Pettle, in his confused and drug-addled way, was talking about the Internet.

The spacecraft that crashes at the start of the narrative bears little relationship to the ill-fated space shuttle *Columbia*. It had a crew of three—all American, and all male—and it was returning from a six month trip to Mars (not the first trip, incidentally: according to Pettle, the Americans set up their first bases on the red planet back in the 1980s). In the book, the crash of the spaceship is used as a clumsy metaphor for the collapse and decay of the 'evil' United States, and Pettle makes a laboured point about the symbolic significance of Mars as the God of War.

In the world that Pettle describes, war has ceased to exist, except in the twisted American mind. As far back as the seventies, the Soviet Union had unilaterally destroyed its entire stock of nuclear weapons. In contrast, it took years of negotiation and an ultimatum from the United Nations before the U.S. could be persuaded to follow suit. Even then, most people believed the U.S. was clinging to a small percentage of its originally huge stockpile of weapons of mass destruction. In effect, therefore, the U.S. was holding the free world to ransom. In outraged reaction, the Soviet Union and the United Nations declared a 'War on Terror' that would finally rid the world of these awful weapons.

Pettle's War on Terror isn't a war in the old fascist sense of a war to be fought with weapons—far from it. His version of the War on Terror is a Mahatma Gandhi style peaceful struggle, to be fought with Infinite Peace and Love. All around the free world, Communists were donning strings of colourful beads, putting flowers in their hair, holding hands with each other and radiating wave after wave of peaceful thoughts in a westerly direction. It was only a matter of time before the War on Terror would be won and the dark empire of the United States would crumble into the dust of history.

What are we to make of this dismal book? It contains a crashed spacecraft, which is certainly not the space shuttle *Columbia*, although the date—February 1st 2003—is right. It describes a War on Terror that is not history's War on Terror, although it does seem to be concerned with weapons of mass destruction. And INTER-NET is nothing like the internet, yet the name is chillingly similar.

My own feeling is that J. W. Dunne was right, and that it's possible to dream accurate dreams of the future. That's what Melvyn Pettle did in a drug-induced stupor back in 1963. But the thing is, he didn't understand what he saw. In the nineteenth century, when powerful telescopes were turned on Mars for the first time, people saw complex canals that simply weren't there. People distort what they see into what they expect to see, or what they want to see. Pettle saw the future, and his mind distorted it into something more comfortable— something that made more sense to his 1963 consciousness than the real 2003 did.

According to Greek mythology, Cassandra had the gift of prophecy—but no-one believed her predictions until they came true. Perhaps real-life prophets are doomed to suffer an even worse fate. No-one *understands* their predictions until they come true—not even the prophets themselves.

# The Gravity Engine

It was with some trepidation that I left my house in Gloucester Square that warm summer's evening in 1851. After all, it is not every day that one has an appointment with a madman. Yet the correspondence I had exchanged with Mr Faraday over the previous months had given birth to a profound curiosity in me; a curiosity that would only be satisfied by a personal meeting. I feared the man's enthusiasm was becoming infectious.

As I walked across the tree-lined square, I reflected on what little I actually knew of Michael Faraday. He had vanished from public view in the thirty-odd years since his ignominious dismissal from the Royal Institution. Yet at the start of his career he had been a rising star in the field of science; a potential genius by some accounts. Everything changed with his disastrous researches into magnetism. Faraday had become obsessed with the preposterous notion that magnetism and electricity were in some wise interchangeable; that magnetism could be generated by electricity and *vice versa*. He fostered some crack-pot scheme for a motor that would turn his "electro-magnetism" into rotational energy like a fantastic species of steam engine. In the space of a few brief years Faraday saw all his ideas discredited by experiment, and found himself ostracized by the scientific establishment.

Judging from his letters to me, Faraday's thoughts during his long scientific exile had turned from magnetism to gravity, the most ubiquitous and unchanging force in the world around us. Yet he spoke of harnessing its powers in the service of society. Surely this too was nothing but the continued raving of a lunatic?

I strove to ground myself in reality, as I made my way across the leafy spaces of Tyburnia. Like its sister Belgravia further south, this was among the first districts in London to be planned from the start on both aesthetic and functional principles. Elegant four-storey town houses, with their stuccoed facades and Doric porches, lined the broad squares and avenues. It all seemed a far cry from talk of anti-gravity and inertialess motion.

I arrived at the busy thoroughfare of the Edgware Road and hailed a hackney cab. I recognised the driver, a jolly fellow with a red waistcoat and a gap in his front teeth.

"Good evening, Mr Stephenson sir," said he. "And where might I take you today?"

"Waterloo Bridge, at the junction with Commercial Road," I replied, for such was the location of my planned *rendez-vous* with Mr Faraday. I climbed into the cab, and we moved off into the traffic, joining the general mass of cabs, carts and carriages clattering southwards.

In a few minutes we were heading down Park Lane, and for the hundredth time that year I found myself peering through the trees to my right to catch a glimpse of the vast wonder occupying a sizeable acreage of Hyde Park. Officially known as 'The Great Exhibition of the Works of Industry of All Nations', it was a veritable Crystal Palace of steel and glass, more than a third of a mile in length, and a fitting tribute to the great Industrial Revolution in which my father, and more latterly I myself, had been privileged to play a modest role.

"Ain't it a marvellous sight, Mr Stephenson," my driver said. "Have you visited inside it yet?"

"Indeed I have," said I. "And for my sins, I was asked to contribute a little to the exhibit concerning railways."

"Really, sir?" The cabbie looked impressed. "I wouldn't have thought you had any time for that sort of thing these days, what with you being a Member of Parliament and all."

"On the contrary," I exclaimed. "I consider myself to be an engineer first and last. The country already has more than enough politicians. I view my seat in the House of Commons as an opportunity to further the interests of my fellow engineers, and to do my best to ensure that this great country of ours remains at the forefront of industrial progress."

We turned into Piccadilly, and then slowly made our way along the Haymarket, around Trafalgar Square, and into the Strand. If such a thing is conceivable, the traffic became even denser and more chaotic as we travelled east. In common with many such journeys, we experienced several near accidents as the driver, cursing under his breath, narrowly averted collisions with other vehicles.

It has been suggested that all traffic should be made to drive on the left-hand side of the road, thus avoiding dispute as to who has right of way. But the sharply cambered roads, and the manure and other detritus piling up towards the gutters, mean that in reality anything but the middle of the road is treacherous for the horses. Perhaps Mr Faraday had the right idea indeed with his gravity-defying machines; a horseless carriage flying above the streets would be the perfect solution to London's traffic problems!

From the Strand we turned off down Wellington Street and then onto Waterloo Bridge. Below us, the Thames was as busy with barges, steamboats and sailing yachts as the streets were with carriages. The tide was low, and the water was a dirty pale brown. The stink was atrocious; the same rank odour that comes up from the sink-holes in the street. Instinctively I covered my nose with a handkerchief. I glanced at the cabbie; he seemed oblivious to the smell.

Ahead of us, on the south bank of the river, the building work for the great new southern rail terminus was visible on the upstream side of the bridge. On the downstream side rose the enormous spire of the Surrey Shot Tower, dwarfing everything around it. At a hundred and eighty feet, it was equal in height to Nelson's Column on the more fashionable north side of the river, and to my mind much more attractive because it was functional as well as decorative.

At the far end of the bridge I alighted and paid the driver a shilling. As I watched the cab turn round and disappear into the traffic, I suddenly felt rather foolish. A solitary, smartly-dressed, middle-aged gentleman, alone on an unfamiliar street corner in Lambeth, waiting for an excommunicated scientist with a reputation as a charlatan and a lunatic! I took out my watch and flipped it open. It was only twenty past seven, still ten minutes before the time I had agreed to meet Mr Faraday.

A few minutes later I espied a figure shuffling purposefully towards me along Commercial Road. Dressed in rumpled grey clothes and with straggling white hair, the intensity of his gaze nevertheless convinced me that this was the man I had come to meet.

"My dear Faraday, it's so good to make your acquaintance at last," I greeted as he came up to me.

"At your service, Mr Stephenson," he replied. "I cannot tell you how grateful I am that you have agreed to see me tonight. Please, follow me. There is much that I wish to show you, and I have no desire to take up more of your time than is absolutely necessary."

Faraday started to lead me back the way he had come. I warmed to his straightforward manner immediately. He had a noticeable Yorkshire accent, which endeared him to me still further. Although my work kept me in London most of the time, I was and always will be a Northerner at heart.

"My theories on electromagnetism were wrong, and I paid dearly for that mistake," said Faraday. "Since then I have conducted many more experiments, and I believe I have now made the breakthrough I was seeking. Yet my reputation is such that no-one in the scientific establishment is prepared to give me so much as a hearing. It is my fondest hope that you, with your practical knowledge of engineering and your position in Parliament, will be able to take my ideas forward in a way that I myself never will. There is a chance, and I believe it is a fairly good chance, that a machine will come of this that is every bit as revolutionary as your late father's invention."

I said nothing. I had become accustomed, as indeed my father became accustomed in his later years, to hearing him referred to as the inventor of the steam locomotive. It served no great purpose to point out that what my father had actually done was to refine and develop a machine that had already been invented by the Cornishman Trevithick.

We turned off Commercial Road down an alley leading to the waterfront. I realized then that our destination could be nothing other than the Shot Tower itself.

"I needed a tall building for my experiments," Faraday explained. "To this end I secured a menial job for myself at this place. During the day I polish newly made shot and sort it into bags. I have been fortunate enough to gain the sympathy of the superintendent, and he allows me use of the building in the evenings on the condition that everything is back in good order by the next morning."

We arrived at the entrance to the tower, where a large ornately lettered signboard left one in no doubt that these were the premises of the Patent Shot Manufacturing Company. Faraday produced a large iron key and unlocked the door.

The inside of the tower was as impressive as the outside. About thirty feet across at the base, it tapered upwards to the top of the tower, where there was located a metal grille. During the normal course of operation, molten lead would be poured through this grille to plummet the hundred and eighty feet to ground level. In the middle of the floor was a large vat of water, designed to break the fall of the by now almost perfect spheres of molten lead, and cause them to cool and solidify into pieces of shot.

Looking up, I could see some sort of object suspended beneath the grille, attached by a rope which passed over a pulley arrangement.

"That is a pig of lead, weighing a hundred and seventy pounds," Faraday said. "Wound around it is an insulated copper wire, the two ends of which are then twisted around the rope supporting it. The rope passes over the pulley, then descends down to ground level where it passes around this winch."

Faraday indicated a large drum with a crank handle near the wall of the tower. The rope, with the two wires wrapped around it, was wound several times around the drum. The free ends of the two wires then passed through the hub of the drum, and a length of twisted wire protruded from it.

Faraday wheeled over a small table on which was placed an instrument made of brass and polished wood. I recognised it as an electro-calorimeter, a device commonly used for measuring electric current. I have a very similar thing in my own collection. Invented by a brilliant young gentleman from Salford by the name of James Prescott Joule, it works on the principle that a measurable amount of heat is generated whenever an electric current is passed through a resistance. The instrument makes use of a precisely known resistance, the heat capacity of which is also precisely known, together with an accurately calibrated thermometer which can measure temperature changes of small fractions of a degree.

Faraday picked up the free ends of the wire and clipped them onto the electro-calorimeter. "For the first experiment, I will simply release the brake on the winch. This will allow the weight to fall freely under gravity, pulling the rope and wires after it. What I have discovered is that some of the gravitational energy that is lost by the weight as it falls can be converted into electric current. Observe the meter carefully."

I glanced nervously up at the pig of lead, and then at the vat of water far below it.

"Oh, there is no need to worry," said Faraday, sensing my discomfort. "We will not get very wet if we keep close to the wall."

Faraday released a lever on the winch, and the lead weight began its descent. It took just over three seconds to make the journey to ground level, unravelling the rope from the winch with increasing speed as it fell. It landed in the vat with an enormous splash, emptying quite a quantity of water onto the surrounding floor in the process. But as Faraday had predicted, only a few spots reached us where we stood.

Il this went on behind my back, for my attention was focused on the scale of the electro-calorimeter. As the weight descended, the mercury level jumped up by a significant fraction of an inch, then subsided back to its original value soon after we heard the splash. The fall had indeed produced a sizeable electric current.

Faraday turned to me, his eyes sparkling. "This was the first of my discoveries; that it is indeed possible to convert mechanical motion into electricity," he said. "Previously, the only method we have had to create electricity is the chemical cell, which is expensive and cumbersome. The generation of electricity will be revolutionized."

"That is a remarkable discovery indeed," said I. "But you implied that it is just the first of two that you have made."

Faraday disconnected the electro-calorimeter and pushed it away. He wheeled up a second table, on which stood a large battery of electrical cells. "The conversion of gravitational energy into electricity is reversible," he said, clipping one wire to the negative terminal of the battery. "Observe what happens when I close the circuit."

Faraday connected the other wire to the positive terminal. I looked anxiously at the vat of water, somehow expecting to see the pig of lead shoot up out of it and ascend heavenward. Nothing happened.

"Try pulling gently on the rope," Faraday said.

I took hold of the rope just above the winch, and gave a small tug. I felt a slight resistance as the lead weight rose up out of the water, but then all resistance vanished. I let go of the rope in surprise, but the weight continued its ascent. It appeared to rise at constant speed until it clattered against the pulley at the top of the tower, finally arresting its motion.

"Good Heavens," I exclaimed. "Anti-gravity!"

"I believe it is not just gravity that is neutralized, but inertia itself; the resistance of a body to any change in its motion," said Faraday. "This experiment used a lead weight, but it might just as well have been a steam engine. Just imagine; a locomotive flying through the sky as light as a bird."

I was suddenly put in mind of some lines by our new poet laureate. "What is it that Mr Tennyson says in Locksley Hall? How he *saw the heavens fill with commerce, argosies of magic sails…*"

"*…and the nations' airy navies grappling in the central blue,*" continued Faraday. "Yes, anti-gravity will shape the future of commerce, and war, and everyday travel; everything will shift from the Earth's surface to the skies above us."

My mind filled with visions. "We are standing on the brink of a revolution which will make the steam engine look old-fashioned," I said. "Who can guess what the world will be like a hundred and fifty years hence?"

"By the start of the twenty-first century, even the crustiest old professors will be preaching anti-gravity as if it is the most obvious thing in the world," Faraday said. Suddenly his mood darkened. "But if some creative young thinker ever makes so bold as to suggest a connection between electricity and magnetism—ah, that will be a different matter entirely. Then the guardians of scientific orthodoxy will foam at the mouth like mad dogs, and damn him as if he were possessed by demons."

# LOSS OF POWER

**T**he expectant darkness that precedes the creation of the world.

Distantly, on the threshold of perception, a low triadic chord. Ponderously growing, filling empty space, tentatively breaking up into rising arpeggios, a slow primeval crescendo.

Then, bursting through, the first leitmotiv, the inexorable flow of the ancient river.

The world had begun again.

Gradually, the darkness around him seemed to give way to a pale blue mist. Of course, his environment remained unchanged, but he was isolated from it by the machinery of the helmet covering his head. Sophisticated electronic circuitry projected the sounds and images of the opera directly onto the sensory cortex of his brain.

The mist cleared to reveal the first scene. The waters of the Rhine lapped against a narrow gravel bank, at a point where the river encroached so far into the mountainside that its whole width was virtually enclosed by a rocky vault. A sudden shaft of sunlight broke through the narrow gap on the far side, and at the same time the invisible orchestra swelled into full chromatic splendour. The cavern awoke to the sound of splashing, singing and laughter, as the three Rhinemaidens greeted the new day.

He became aware of a personality not his own. The machine was programmed to project the scene through the mind of Alberich, one of the Nibelung dwarfs who inhabited the mountain. So he saw through Alberich's eyes, thought Alberich's thoughts, felt Alberich's feelings as he witnessed the water nymph's games. He was only distantly aware of the music now, as a subconscious flow of complex symbols and intercorrelations.

As Alberich watched the nymphs, his shock turned to anger, and his anger turned to lust. The aggression of their beauty, the challenge of their nakedness, stirred memories of an unsatisfiable desire he had long since tried to extinguish. But it was too late; the desire was rekindled.

With a mixture of fear and excitement, he shambled forwards to greet them. How amused they were! Their giggles, jokes and teasing—the same as a thousand times before. One girl would flirt with him and then mock him, another would allow a brief touch before darting away, the third, swimming this way and that, would offer tantalizing glimpses of succulent pinkness before diving beneath the waves. And his obvious frustration only filled them with greater glee.

Suddenly, there was a sparkle of light at the back of the cave. The sun's rays had momentarily caught a gleaming object among the rocks, towards which the Rhinemaidens, pausing in their antics, gazed reverently.

"What was that?" Alberich asked, puzzled.

Amused by his ignorance, the Rhinemaidens were only too pleased to explain the legend of the Rhinegold—the magical treasure they were entrusted to protect. Forged into a ring, it would endow the bearer with unimagined power—but it could be wrested from its place only by one who had renounced forever the love of women. So the gold was safe, the Rhinemaidens stated with giggles, since no man would ever do that!

For the first time, Alberich was gripped by hope.

"Arrogant fools," he sneered. "Are you not afraid? What do you think love means to me, who has never known love? I will take the gold and forge the ring, for I do most surely curse love!"
Alberich stumbled towards the gold, wrenched it from the rocks, and held it aloft, triumphant in the Rhinemaidens' woe.

Then, at the very moment of victory, he was plunged into darkness and silence. No longer could he feel the gold in his hands, or the rocks beneath his feet. Confused, his mind reeled uncontrollably for a moment, until awareness came flooding back.

Of course, he was not really Alberich—the dwarf only existed as a character in a work of fiction. In reality he was who he was: Ludwig, of the house of Wittelsbach, Count Palatine, king of Bavaria. The second of that name. He had been viewing the first scene of *The Rhinegold*, by his friend Richard Wagner—the greatest music-dramatist of the 19th century.
Gingerly, Ludwig removed the delicate interface device from his head. The simulations were so realistic, time after time, that he found it impossible to retain objectivity once the opera began. The illusion became more real than reality.

He rose from the massive throne of gold and ivory, and crossed to the console at the side of the raised apse. He replaced the helmet in its niche and switched off the machine.

*The beginning of the great story*, he mused—*a loveless man, renouncing love in favour of supreme power*. The symbolism was precise. Replacing the natural with the unnatural, changing nature's rules to beat nature's system. The essence of all human endeavour.

Thoughtfully, he descended the white marble steps to the tessellated floor of the main chamber, idly examining the splendour around him—the double rows of Corinthian columns, red porphyry below and blue Lapis Lazuli above, the long barrel vault with its Byzantine-style ceiling paintings, the magnificent golden chandelier in the shape of a gargantuan crown.

*Changing the order of things to suit oneself*, he thought. *The human way, my way, Ludwig's way*. Moving over to one of the small Roman-arched windows, he looked out onto the Bavarian summer afternoon. Below the castle were the familiar wooded hills with their picturesque lakes and villages; in the distance the jagged grey backdrop of the Alps. A small bird flew past the window and landed on a parapet below.

He had been called mad, he knew—'Mad King Ludwig'—by Doctor von Gudden and others. Why? Mad for building this castle, for valuing the past, for patronising the Arts? For daring to be different?

He turned from the window and pressed the intercom button on the wall. The screen lit up with the face of an attendant.

"I wish to dine," Ludwig said. "Prepare the Banqueting Hall."

"Very good, sir." The servant bowed slightly and the screen went blank.

Swirling a rich crimson cloak around his shoulders, Ludwig swept through the doorway into the grey stone passage outside. He ascended two flights of the echoing spiral staircase and entered the main suite of state rooms. Everywhere was rich with carved oak, polished marble, inlaid stone, golden ornaments. Huge tapestries and frescoes decorated the walls, depicting scenes from Wagner's operas: *Tristan and Isolde, Lohengrin, Tannhäuser, Parsifal*.

Ludwig arrived at the Banqueting Hall, where his guests were already seated around the long dining table, with its glittering silver centrepiece and tableware. As he entered, the guests stood and waited for him to take his place at the head of the table. He greeted them and bade them sit down. He knew them all well: Hans Sachs, Konrad Nachtigall, Fritz Kothner, a dozen others. They were good men, trusty friends—the Mastersingers of Nuremberg.

A procession of servants began serving the food. After several generous preliminary courses the main dish was brought in—a huge wild boar, killed by a local hunting party that morning.

"Of course, my opinion differs from Herr Wagner's on one vital point," Ludwig said, eating hungrily. The guests looked up with interest. "As you know, Wagner is an ardent disciple of the late Herr Doctor Schopenhauer. It was Schopenhauer's belief, and also the belief of some of the most learned oriental sages, that the world of everyday perceptions is an illusion, and that this is a bad thing because it engenders desire for illusory goals, leading to inevitable suffering. So, according to these people, the only way to end suffering is to banish desire, by striving to coexist with the reality that lies beneath perceptions. Such is the thesis of Herr Doctor Schopenhauer, and of the Buddhists, and of Wagner's story of the Nibelung's Ring."

"More wine, sir?" A servant bent close to Ludwig's left shoulder. Ludwig nodded and resumed speaking.

"For my part, however, I say that if the world is a bad illusion then one should replace it with a better illusion, more to one's liking. Eh?"

Ludwig looked up, and realized that something was very wrong. All around the table, the guests were frozen—unnaturally frozen, in awkward postures of eating and drinking. And the servant at his shoulder remained bending, frozen in the act of pouring the wine.

Gripped by sudden alarm, Ludwig pushed at the man with his hand. Without uttering a sound, the figure toppled, spilling the wine while keeping a grip on the silver flagon, falling to the ground in the same frozen posture. The face remained passive, the eyes open and attentive.

The light in the room had faded. The windows no longer showed the blue summer evening, but only blackness. The candles had flickered out. Only the dim emergency lighting remained on.

And there was silence—no hum of air-conditioning, none of the other soft electrical sounds that had passed unnoticed until they ceased.

*Power failure*, thought Ludwig in horror. Long unneeded memories began to return— memories suppressed for how long? Strange, half-understood concepts: the guests and servants had been robots, the views from the windows mere projections. All had been illusions.

But something had gone wrong—the power had failed; the illusion was over.

Dimly, instinctively, Ludwig knew what he had to do. Leaving the Banqueting Hall with its bizarre frozen tableau, he began to run through the lifeless castle. He searched for what seemed like hours, through rooms and passages made unfamiliar by darkness and silence. Finally he came to a part he knew he had not seen for years, the air stale and dusty with disuse. He stopped at the end of a darkened passageway, facing a heavy iron-studded door. He could not remember what lay beyond the door, but he knew he had to go through it now. With an effort he drew back the rusty iron bolts, and cautiously pushed the door open.

He was outside. But it was not the outside he had seen through the castle windows. Dark sheets of rain descended from a slate-grey sky, driven against the walls by an angry, howling wind.

Wrapping his cloak tightly around him, he took a few steps out onto the asphalt driveway. Yes, there was a forest—but it was denser and more threatening than the pleasant Bavarian woods he had looked at so often. And the castle itself was a huge concrete mass, weather-stained and windowless. An empty service truck stood idly at a loading bay.

He saw the reason for the loss of power. A massive tree, felled by the storm, had crashed down across the main supply cables.

As he looked around, long-suppressed memories began to filter back into his thoughts. It was the 21st century, not the 19th, and he was not King Ludwig of Bavaria—although he had been a king of sorts; enough of a king to build this castle, and to retreat forever from—from what? What kind of world had prompted such an escape? Still there were gaps in his memory; even his true name eluded him.

Confused and disoriented, he wandered away from the castle and into the woods. He walked aimlessly for hours, his mind battling with unfamiliar thoughts and conflicting images. Gradually the rain stopped and the wind eased. He continued walking, not knowing where he was going, or where he could go. Exhaustion and hunger crept up on him; his vision began to play tricks. The forest shimmered in and out of focus; his eyes struggled to make sense of his surroundings.

He came to the edge of a lake, and stood blinking as his mind registered the new image.

"Can I be of assistance, sir?" A man's voice, coming from nearby.

He turned around in alarm, searching for the source of the voice. He could only see the forest, the grassy bank, the lake. Nothing moved. His confusion was growing worse; it was harder than ever to focus his eyes.

Then he thought he saw a figure detach itself from the trees and move towards him. It seemed to be a middle-aged man, wearing a dark dress coat and carrying a tall hat and cane.

He blinked, and suddenly he recognized the figure. It was Doctor von Gudden, his personal physician. Memories grappled with memories, as the figure approached. Doctor von Gudden—the man found drowned with King Ludwig in Lake Starnberg, in 1886. Two centuries ago. Impossible, of course—so what was happening? Was he hallucinating?

He stumbled a few steps backwards, and felt the cold water of the lake around his ankles. Like his surroundings, his thoughts were swaying in and out of focus with a dizzying effect.

He seemed to feel gentle hands take hold of his arms and legs, pulling him down into the water. Horrified, he cried out.

Suddenly, the scene crystallized. The triumphant figure advancing towards him, holding aloft the tiny golden ring—it was not a man at all, nor even a human being. It was one of those accursed Rhinemaidens! And the other two water-nymphs had him by the neck and arms, giggling as they dragged him out into the flowing waters of the Rhine.

"Give back the ring!" he cried, before a soft hand closed over his mouth. It all seemed so clear now. He was not a man of the 21st century, nor of the 19th. He was Hagen, only son of the Nibelung Alberich, and the Rhinemaidens had seized the ring of power from his grasp.

His head was pulled under the water, and gradually he became aware of the music again—the Rhine leitmotiv, followed by the Fate leitmotiv, followed by the Death leitmotiv.

# A CASE FOR CRANE

**J**erry Vincent sat down in his favourite armchair as the TV set warmed up. First the speaker came to life—a familiar theme tune—and then, with a flicker, a picture appeared. Jerry settled more comfortably in his chair: this was his favourite cop-show, *A Case for Crane*. The title of the episode flashed up on the screen—'Names and Addresses'—followed by the name of the screenwriter: Steven G. Mitchell.

As the title sequence finished, the picture faded into a night-time scene: a shabby tenement building on a city street intersection. Several police cars and an ambulance were clustered in front of the building, their flashing blue lights illuminating the scene. A small crowd was gathered near the entrance.

The camera panned in and more details became visible. The crowd, held back behind a cordon of yellow and black police tape, seemed to be a mixture of journalists and inquisitive onlookers. On the police side of the cordon, five or six plain-clothes detectives were searching the area thoroughly, taking photographs and questioning possible witnesses. Near the steps leading into the building lay what appeared to be a human body, covered by a sheet and presumably dead.

The camera zoomed in on the person supervising the proceedings—Police Lieutenant Alex Crane, the eponymous hero of the show. Crane, played by Dick Sylvester, worked in the homicide division at the Northwest precinct of this fictional city. He was tall, broad-chested, sober, dedicated: a typical TV hero.

The camera angle changed again. At the kerb, a car screeched to a halt. The door flew open and the driver jumped out: a small, tough-looking woman with short dark hair. She stood for a moment, hands on broad, denim-clad hips, and surveyed the scene rapidly. She spotted Crane and headed over towards him.

This was detective Kanefsky (first name never revealed), the female lead of *A Case for Crane*. Kanefsky was the perfect foil to Crane, his opposite in almost every respect. She was young (26), while he was middle-aged (48); she was impulsive and hot-headed, he was level-headed and methodical. But both of them were dedicated to the pursuit of law and order.

As Jerry sat watching the show, something strange began to happen to his vision. The room and everything around him—including the TV—began to fade from sight. Blurrily in their place he could see vague moving shapes. He blinked, annoyed, and the room and the TV set reappeared, solid once more. But a moment later they faded again. The other blurry scene—whatever it was—gradually became stronger, until it was the only reality he could perceive. He was no longer aware of the room he was in; he could no longer see the TV; he could no longer hear the background music coming from its speaker.

His new surroundings were dark and unclear: things appeared flat and grey and lacked fine detail. But the scene was unmistakable. He was looking at the small, stumpy figure of Detective Kanefsky—a fictional character!—as she approached him. He was Alex Crane.

Kanefsky stepped over the tape barrier, and Jerry felt his legs carry him across to meet her.

"What's going on?" Kanefsky asked. "I was just heading back to my digs when I got the call to come here."

Jerry's mind raced: he didn't know what was going on either—the show had only just started. He had to think quickly. It was the beginning of the episode, and it was obvious that some crime had been committed. But what? And what were the details? Of course—there was the body over by the steps: it must have been murder. It could hardly have been anything else, since Crane and Kanefsky worked in Homicide. "Murder," said Jerry. Then he tailed off, not knowing what to say next. He thought rapidly, trying not to let his discomfiture show on his face.

Suddenly, memory came to him.

"The victim is male, Caucasian, around 35," he said. "No identification. The murder weapon was a knife—it was a professional job: one clean stab through the heart. No signs of robbery or a struggle. All the indications point to some kind of ritual killing—the work of one of those secret societies or eastern cults you hear about."

"It could be, at that." Kanefsky swept a stray lock of hair from her eyes. "Any leads on the killer?"

Jerry noticed that his surroundings were becoming clearer and more substantial. "Nothing at all so far," he said, again recalling unfamiliar memories. "But something's bound to turn up soon—I've never come across a murderer who left absolutely no trace behind."

The two of them watched as the body was loaded into the ambulance.

Without warning or any sensation of motion, Jerry was displaced. He found himself sitting at a desk in a brightly-lit office. His immediate instinct was to shield his eyes from the suddenly bright light, but his hands wouldn't respond. He was holding some documents and examining them carefully. After-images of the dark street he had just been in still flitted through his mind; he had no intermediate memories. This was the next scene.

Slowly, the feeling of disorientation left him. He inspected the room with the corner of his eye, and saw that objects now appeared quite solid and real. Seeing the cluttered desk, the many filing cabinets and the stacks of reports scattered around the floor, he realized he was in Crane's office, at the police station. And he was Crane.

There was a knock at the door. He looked up to see detective Kanefsky enter, holding a sheaf of papers.

"Are you busy?" she asked.

"No, I can get back to this later," Crane replied. "It's briefing material about the nuclear safety conference this weekend. They're expecting trouble and some of us may get drafted in to help.

What did you want?"

"It's about last night's murder." Kanefsky consulted the sheaf of papers she was holding. "The victim has been identified as one Philip Schwartz, a middle-income marketing manager. Unmarried... lived in lodgings on the Southside."

"You've got a lot a paper there," Crane observed when Kanefsky stopped talking. "Fire away—what else is there?"

Kanefsky frowned. "A connection, but one that doesn't make any kind of sense." She flicked through the papers. "Another murder, exactly 24 hours earlier, with the same MO. But that victim was from the other side of the tracks—name of Pasquale Bianco, a part-time cook and a complete nobody. Same clean stab to the heart, and same time of death—eight pm— although on different days. The two bodies were found within a mile of each other: Bianco at the corner of 6th and 25th, and Schwartz at 4th and 27th. But there's nothing to connect the two victims."

"Maybe they were members of the same secret society," Crane suggested. "There must be something—we just have to look for it." He pondered for a moment. "You said Schwartz rented a place—has anyone spoken to his landlady yet?

Kanefsky shook her head. "No, there hasn't been time—the identification only just came through."

"Then let's go and do it now." Crane rose to his feet. "Have you got the address?"

Kanefsky consulted her notes. "Schwartz lived in apartment six at 1350 East Third Street."

They left Crane's private office and went into the large open-plan outer office. The room was full of activity: typewriters clattering, telephones ringing, people rushing about...

As they crossed towards the exit, Crane heard someone shout "Hey, Lieutenant!"

He looked around and saw detective Creeley waving a newspaper at him. Creeley was a regular but minor character in *A Case for Crane*: a small, chubby desk-worker whose purpose was to move the plot along and/or provide comic relief. His distinguishing characteristic was that each episode he had a brand new enthusiasm for a brand new subject.

"Lieutenant," repeated Creeley, having got Crane's attention. "Can you think of a word that means 'Glow with anger about messed-up raid'—nine letters beginning with I?"

"IRRADIATE," Crane said, with hardly a pause for thought.

"Okay—I guess 'irradiate' means glow. But how do you figure the rest of it?"

"Irate means 'with anger', and then inside it you've got an anagram of raid," Crane explained.

"But what's with the crossword puzzle? I thought you were into wildlife photography these days."

"Oh, that was last week." Creeley waved his fat hand in dismissal. "There ain't no wildlife in this part of the city worth photographing. Puzzles, on the other hand—crosswords, chess problems, logic puzzles—now that's something you can do any place, any time."

"Even sitting at your desk when the city's paying you to do police work?"

"Hey, Lieutenant, would I do that? I'm on my lunch break." Creeley picked up a half-eaten sandwich to prove his point.

Crane shook his head wearily. He followed Kanefsky's broad, denim-clad bottom out of the room.

Suddenly Jerry was displaced again: another scene change. He was walking down a plushly carpeted corridor with detective Kanefsky.

"Smart apartment house," Crane commented. "Nice for those who can afford it."

At the end of the corridor they stopped in front of a door labelled E. VAN HOOSEN, and in larger letters below that, ENQUIRIES.

Crane knocked the door. After a moment it was opened a short way, held by a security chain. A female voice from within asked them what they wanted.

Crane presented his badge. "Police—My name's Lieutenant Crane, and this is detective Kanefsky. Can we speak to you for a minute?"

The door opened and they found themselves face-to-face with a large, fleshy woman. "Betty Van Hoosen at your service," she announced. "I'm the proprietor of this establishment. I take it you've come about Mr Schwartz in number six?"

Crane blinked at her. "What makes you say that?"

"He didn't come home last night. That's not like him—not at all like him. He's always so regular about everything—even pays his rent on time, which is more than I can say about some of my tenants."

"Um, may we come in?" Crane asked.

"Of course—what am I thinking of?" She led them into a nicely furnished lounge, where Crane and Kanefsky sat on a wide sofa while the landlady sank her weight into a well-used armchair facing them.

"It's bad news, I'm afraid," Crane told her. "Mr Schwartz is dead—he was murdered last night."

"Oh my God." She buried her face in her hands and began to sob. Crane glanced at Kanefsky, who raised her eyes to the ceiling.

After a while the landlady pulled herself together and looked up, her eyes still red. "I'm sorry... but he was such a good tenant. Is there anything at all I can do to help you find his murderer?"

"Would you mind if we asked you a few questions?" Crane asked.

"No, go right ahead," she said. She was still sniffing slightly.

Kanefsky started with the obvious question. "Can you think of anyone—anyone at all—who might have wanted Mr Schwartz dead?"

She shook her head.

"The body was found on West 27th Street—have you got any idea what Schwartz might have been doing there?"

"No, none at all."

As the questioning continued, Jerry noticed something strange about the room they were in—something he hadn't noticed when they first entered it. Instead of having four solid walls and a ceiling, as he had originally supposed, the room had only three flimsy walls and no ceiling at all. Outside the room was a dark and cavernous space; the room itself was illuminated by brilliant arclights suspended from gantries overhead.

In the gloom beyond where the fourth wall should have been, Jerry could make out dim shapes—sound booms, movie cameras trundling backwards and forwards, people moving about.

Then the room was solid again.

"Did Mr Schwartz ever have a visitor named Bianco?" he found himself asking. "Or did you ever hear him mention that name?"

She thought for a moment. "No, I don t think so."

"Okay, that's all for now," Crane said. "Thank you for your help—I'm sorry we had to be the bearers of bad news."

She nodded distractedly. Crane and Kanefsky left the room.

Then Jerry was back in his sitting room, watching TV; it was a commercial break. He realized he had to work quickly, while he had time—there was a crime to solve. He ignored the inanities blaring out of the TV and began to think things through.

The situation was this: two similar murders had been committed, both with the appearance of a ritual killing. No clues had been found as to the murderer. There were no obvious connections between the two victims, and there did not appear to be a motive for either murder. Jerry had to find the killer. So what did he have to work on?

First of all, he reflected, the show was fiction—so there had to be a good reason for every element of the story. It was likely that any apparently casual reference early on was actually very important—an essential piece of information that would be needed later. So, working backwards, it ought to be possible to anticipate how the plot would develop by considering any such casual references. So what had there been? He racked his brains.

He remembered that something had been said about an upcoming nuclear safety conference— that was bound to be important later on. But how would it fit in? Neither of the victims had any connection to it. Perhaps the life of someone to do with the conference would be threatened at some point... that seemed a definite possibility.

Then there had been Creeley and the crossword puzzle. Maybe the murders had something to do with puzzles of some kind. But then again, solving a crime was like doing a puzzle—so maybe the incident was simply intended to show Crane's skill as a detective.

Suddenly, Jerry recalled the title of the episode: 'Names and Addresses'. That must be significant in some way. But whose names, and whose addresses? The victims, or the killer (s)?

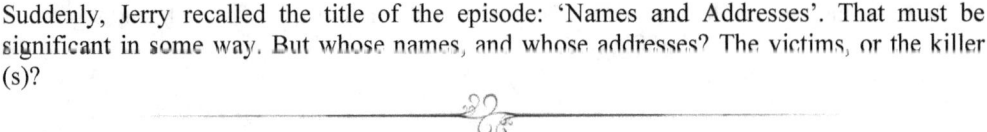

Just as Jerry's thought process arrived at that point, *A Case for Crane* came back on the TV. He had no time to follow the train of thought any further. The picture showed Crane and Kanefsky in a car, driving along a city street. Crane was at the wheel.

Instantly, Jerry was in Crane's mind again.

Kanefsky glanced at a signpost. "West 26th Street," the young female detective observed. "You know, I've lived in this city for three years and I still need to look at the signposts. Everything looks the same—there are nine parallel avenues running north-south, and a lot of parallel streets running east-west... all making a regular pattern of square blocks. One intersection looks just like another."

Before Crane could reply, they were interrupted by the car radio. An emotionless female voice said "Foxtrot Delta Three, proceed to the intersection of 3rd and 29th. Witness reports possible homicide in progress."

That's us—let's go!" Kanefsky picked up the radio microphone. "This is Foxtrot Delta Three, responding. Ten-four."

Crane forced the car into a U-turn and accelerated back the way they had come. Kanefsky leaned over and flicked on the siren, and then slapped a flashing light onto the roof of the car. As they drove along, Jerry pondered Kanefsky's words about the arrangement of the city streets. That was gratuitously spoon-fed information, if anything was! Surely it was another reference that would be needed later on in the story. He added it to his mental list.

They came to an area of old tenement buildings similar to that in the first scene of the episode. They drove along an almost empty road towards a street intersection; the traffic lights were on red.

Up ahead, past the intersection on the right hand side, Crane spotted a body lying near the steps of a building—exactly the way they had found Schwartz.

As they approached the crossroads, a figure on the sidewalk turned round, saw the police car bearing down, and began to run.

"There's our man!" said Crane.

He drove through the red lights, swerved to miss a truck, mounted the sidewalk, and screeched to a halt just behind the running figure. Crane and Kanefsky bailed out of the car and began to run after their quarry.

"Stop, police!"

The man dropped something he had been holding—a knife—and fumbled for a moment inside his jacket. He produced a gun and began to fire over his shoulder at them. Crane and Kanefsky fired back.

As he ran down the street, Jerry had the strange feeling that he knew what was going to happen an instant before it occurred—almost as if he had already done this once, a long time ago. That was odd, he thought, because he was sure he had never seen this episode before. The fugitive ducked off to the right into a side-street. Crane and Kanefsky followed in hot pursuit.

Running up the side-street from the other end were two uniformed policemen, their guns held out ready to fire. The man stopped short and looked around wildly.

"Okay, drop it. We've got you surrounded."

After a second's hesitation, the man threw his gun to the ground and raised his hands in surrender.

Then Jerry was displaced again: he was entering the large open-plan office at the police station. He went up to Creeley's desk.

"Have you got anything on the perp we found by the body at 3rd and 29th yesterday?" he asked.

Yesterday! So a day had passed since the previous scene, which to Jerry had only been a moment earlier.
"We certainly do." Creeley glanced at a report on his desk. "The guy's name is Melendez—a real lowlife with numerous previous convictions, several of them stabbings." He indicated a door marked INTERROGATION ROOM. "He's in there now, with Kanefsky."

"Okay. Has the body been identified yet?" asked Crane.

"Yes—the victim was one Bernie Blackwell, a newspaper reporter."

Crane nodded and went into the interrogation room. It was small and plain; the only furniture consisted of a wooden table and two chairs. Sitting at the table was Melendez: small, wiry and coldly hostile. He ignored Crane.

Kanefsky was leaning against the far wall, looking tired and frustrated. Crane went over to her.

'It's no good." Kanefsky rolled her eyes. "It's like trying to get blood from a stone."

"He denies murdering Blackwell?"

Kanefsky shook her head, a puzzled frown on her face. "No, he admitted to that murder pretty quickly. But he denies the other two—Schwartz and Bianco—and they were exactly the same MO. Says he knows nothing about them. I give up—see if you can make him come clean."

Crane went over and sat opposite Melendez. "Why did you kill Blackwell?" he asked.

After a moment, Melendez looked up sullenly. "Who? Oh, the guy yesterday. Well, you see— this joker came to see me, out of the blue, like. He gave me five hundred bucks right there and then, and told me what I had to do. It was a cinch—and besides, I needed the dough."

"And you know nothing about the other two murders?" asked Crane.

"No, like I kept telling that little guy with the fat butt." Melendez nodded towards Kanefsky, who glared at him with a face like thunder. Kanefsky—who had a small bosom and rarely wore make-up—was, nevertheless, difficult to mistake for anything but a woman.

Crane tried another tack. "Okay then. So who was it that paid you?"

"I don't remember," Melendez sneered.

Kanefsky took two steps forward, grabbed Melendez by the lapels and pulled him to his feet. "Okay, squirt," she growled. "This little guy with the fat butt has got bigger muscles than you. So for the last time—who paid you?"

Melendez scowled. "It was Christopher Robin."

"Why, you..." Kanefsky drew back her fist.

"Wait a minute," said Crane. "There is someone around who calls himself Christopher Robin... a real weirdie. He started something called 'The Church of the Undying Underlying Reality' a few years ago. It could be the truth."

Kanefsky released Melendez reluctantly, pushing him back into his chair. "Then I guess we've got all we're going to get from this loser," she said.

As he got up to leave, Jerry was displaced: somehow he was no longer in Crane's mind. He was sitting at the table in the Interrogation Room, watching Crane and Kanefsky leave the room. He was Melendez,

Melendez was thinking that—although he had answered all the cops' questions—he hadn't told them everything he knew. It wasn't his problem if the cops were too stupid to ask the right questions. Intrigued, Jerry looked deeper into Melendez's mind to discover what he was concealing. He located the relevant memories in the form of pictures.

He saw that when Christopher Robin had been instructing Melendez about the murder, he had given him something which seemed to have great symbolic significance; it was essential that Melendez should have it on his person when he killed Blackwell.

Jerry could see a vague picture of the object, and he tried to focus on it. It was a small white thing, carved out of wood; a charm or token of some kind. It was shaped like the head of an animal—a dog, perhaps, or a horse.

Jerry was sure he had seen something like it before, but where? On TV? And in what context? He couldn't remember.

Whatever it had been, Melendez had thrown it away as worthless.

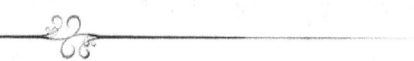

Then Jerry was in Crane's mind again; he was standing outside the Interrogation Room, talking with Kanefsky. "Do you believe him, about not knowing anything about the other murders?" the female cop asked.

"I'm not sure," Crane said slowly. "He might be telling the truth—maybe Christopher Robin hired a different person to commit each murder."

Kanefsky nodded. "Hey, what was that you said about the church of the—what was it?"

"The Church of the Undying Underlying Reality," Crane told her. "It was a phoney religious cult—mind over matter, you know the sort of thing. Promised to bring you closer to the true nature of the world. It started out as a bit of a joke, but then it began to take itself more seriously. It turned into a small, close-knit society, with its own rules, secret handshakes and so on. But nothing illegal, until now."

"So you think the murdered men were members of the cult—transgressors of some kind?"

"Could be," Crane nodded. "Anyway, it's easy enough to find out. I think I know where we can find Christopher Robin."

"Then it looks as if this investigation's finally getting somewhere," Kanefsky observed.

Suddenly Jerry found himself outdoors again. He was walking down a crowded sidewalk with Kanefsky. They came to a small, cheap bar and Crane looked up at the neon sign. The bar was called *Benny's*.

"This is the place," he said.

Kanefsky scratched her head. "You mean this is where the high priest hangs out?"

"He's unorthodox," said Crane.

They entered the bar.

Suddenly Jerry had a flash of memory—it was a page of writing, part of a script:

That was all; the page ended there. Jerry wondered briefly where the memory had come from. But what was that at the end about a gun? He didn't like the sound of that at all.

Inside the bar it was hot and crowded, filled with tobacco smoke and the smell of beer. They went up to the counter and Crane called over the bartender.

"Police. We're looking for Christopher Robin..."

A tall, thin man who had been sitting further down the counter got up hurriedly and left by the rear exit. Kanefsky shouted and ran after him. Crane followed a moment later. Emerging into the alley at the back of the bar, Crane saw that the tough little policewoman had caught the man and was holding him.

The man looked scared, darting his eyes about wildly.

"Christopher Robin," Crane addressed him. "We've got a few questions we'd like to ask you."
"Okay, but let go of me first—I'm not the fighting type, you know."

Kanefsky released him.

*No, don't let him go—he's got a gun,* Jerry thought.

Despite his inner turmoil, he found himself carrying on as if there was nothing wrong. "First of all, did you hire a man named Melendez to kill Bernie Blackwell?" Crane asked the tall man.

"Kill?" Christopher Robin looked more scared than ever. "No-one was supposed to get killed. It was meant to be a game. Yes—I hired him. I'll tell you anything you want to know."

"What about the others—did you set them up, too?" asked Crane.

"What others?"

"Schwartz and Bianco. What did the Church of the Undying Underlying Reality have against them?"

"What? Oh, the church—that broke up months ago," Christopher Robin said bitterly. "There was a rebellion among the brethren and the church funds were ripped off. I've been struggling to pay the bills ever since."

Crane was puzzled. "Then why have Blackwell killed?"

Jerry froze in alarm—he recognized the words as he spoke them. It the was the first line on the page of script he had glimpsed. And in a minute: *Chr. Robin pulls a gun out of his pocket, and fires...*

Christopher Robin was answering Crane's question. "I didn't know he was gonna be killed, honest. The guy told me it was all a big game. He paid me—told me what to do. I hired Melendez and passed on his instructions, then phoned Blackwell to set him up at the right place and time." The exact words from the script.

"The guy who paid you—who was that?"

*Pulls out gun ... fires*, thought Jerry. Somehow he had to stop Christopher Robin before he could do that.

"I don't know, I swear. The money came through the mail—there was no return address or anything. I got all my instructions over the phone—the final details only hours before. I didn't know there was really gonna be a murder."

Jerry tried to move, but his legs wouldn't respond. He tried to warn Kanefsky, but he couldn't form the right words. He was scared—he began to panic.

"So you don't know anything about the other murders?" he found himself saying.

"No—like I said, I've told you everything I know."

Crane turned to Kanefsky. "What do you make of it?" he asked.

*It's too late—that's the cue*, thought Jerry. He made one last desperate attempt to move.

Suddenly, Christopher Robin pulled a gun out of his pocket and fired wildly. Crane dodged the shot instinctively, then Kanefsky kicked the gun out of the man's hand.

Christopher Robin began to run, and Kanefsky dived after him. The small female detective landed squarely on the tall, gangling man and brought him to the ground, unconscious. She deftly snapped a pair of handcuffs onto the inert body. Breathing heavily, Kanefsky looked up at Crane. "Do you think he was telling the truth?" she asked.

"He was too scared to do anything else," Crane replied. "We're up against a powerful organization—one that's so big we've only seen the edges of it so far. People like Melendez and Christopher Robin are small fry—they have no more idea who's running this thing than we do. We're not going to get anywhere working our way up from the bottom—the whole setup's too complicated."

"Then what do we do now?" asked Kanefsky.

"We need to look more carefully at the connections between the three victims," Crane answered. "That way we'll discover the motive behind the murders and get straight to the people at the top."

Then Jerry was back in Crane's office at the police station. Crane was standing by a whiteboard, addressing a group of detectives crowded into the small office. The group consisted of Kanefsky and a handful of others, including Captain Stanton—Crane's immediate superior. Stanton, white-haired and close to retirement, was looking harassed and overworked. He always did.

On the board was a hastily drawn sketch map of the North-side of the city, from 22nd Street to 30th. The name of each victim was written by the street intersection where the body had been found.

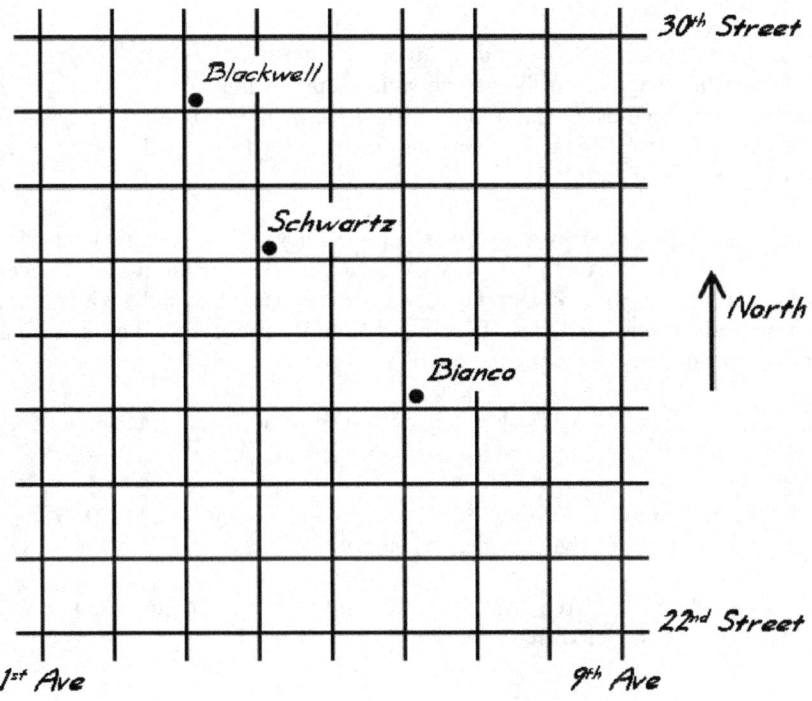

"Okay, let's start by summarizing the case so far," Crane was saying. "Over the last few days there have been three connected murders..."

The situation was becoming urgent, Jerry realized: the episode was more than half over and the investigation wasn't getting anywhere. It was almost certain that there would be other victims if the crime wasn't solved soon. As he continued to speak to the group of detectives, his inner thoughts returned to his own investigation.

He tried again to fit together the various clues he had collected. There was the strange object in Melendez's mind, the title 'Names and Addresses', Creeley's reference to puzzles, and the layout of the city in squares, like a chessboard. Chess—that was one of the types of puzzle Creeley had mentioned! And Melendez's object—he remembered now: it had been a chess-piece. Chess—the connecting factor had to be chess!

"Lieutenant, forensics have just found this..." The chubby figure of Detective Creeley entered the room, holding something small in his hand. He stopped in mid-sentence, looking at the whiteboard. "Are you doing a crossword puzzle of your own now? Or is that a chess problem?"

"What do you mean?" asked Crane.

"Just my little joke, Lieutenant. The eight by eight square, like a chessboard... What are you staring at me like that for?"

"Chess! That could be it—that could be the connection we've been looking for!" Crane looked again at the diagram on the whiteboard. "Suppose this area of the city represents a chessboard, and the victims.... wait a minute, their names! They're all variations of Black or White: Blackwell—black; Schwartz—German for black; Bianco—Italian for white... I think we're finally getting somewhere."

"If you want another chess connection, I've got one for you." It was Creeley again. He held out the small object he was holding—it was the thing Jerry had seen in Melendez's mind. "This is a chess-piece: a white knight. Forensics found it when they did a wider search around the area where Blackwell was killed. They weren't sure if it had any connection to the crime, but it was so out of place they thought it might."

Crane was pacing up and down, thinking rapidly. "It must do. There's a game of chess behind all this—I'm sure of it now. Suppose someone is playing a game of chess—slowly, say one or two moves a day. Every time a piece is taken they find someone—using the phone-book say—with a name like Black or White, whichever colour piece was taken. They find a way of making that person to go the right square, and have him killed."

Creeley looked dubious. "There's more to a chess-piece that its colour, you know. There are different types of pieces, with different moves."

"Okay, let's think that through." Crane paused, frowning. "If the colour of the piece is given by the victim's surname, maybe the type of piece is given by the first name—the initial, say."

*Of course!* Jerry thought. *The title of the episode!* 'Names and Addresses'—the name of the victim represented the piece that was taken, and the address where the murder took place represented the square...

Crane was flicking through his notes, looking for the full names of the victims. "Pasquale, Philip and Bernie—P, P and B. Could that mean anything?"

"Pawn, pawn, and bishop maybe," said Creeley. "But, what's the point of all this? Killing strangers at random, just because of their name..."

"I know—it's a grim thought," Crane agreed. "We must be up against a pair of madmen. Perhaps they're the rich, decadent types—always looking for new kicks, new and more outlandish ways to keep themselves amused."

"Sounds a bit far-fetched to me," Kanefsky broke in. "But if what you're saying is correct, then anyone with a surname like Black or White could be the next victim."

Captain Stanton looked up suddenly. "Whitman! Kent Whitman, the pro-nuclear campaigner—he's one of the delegates expected at the big conference tomorrow. I saw his name on the list of key speakers."

"Kent Whitman," Crane pondered. "Initial K, colour white... the white king! It makes sense... and I'll bet the game's near to checkmate."

"But the king isn't taken in checkmate," Creeley protested. "The object of the game is to..."

Crane shook his head. "I might not be a chess expert, but I think I understand the kind of people we're up against. This is what it's all building up to—they're going to try to kill Whitman."

Kanefsky indicated the clock on the wall. "The three murders so far have taken place at eight pm," she pointed out. "That means we might have less than two hours to locate this Whitman guy."

Crane turned to Stanton. "Do you know if Kent Whitman has arrived in the city yet?"
"I think so," Stanton replied. "I'll find the name of his hotel."

Immediately Jerry found himself in the lobby of a large, modern hotel. He followed Kanefsky's broad rear as she made rapidly for the front desk.

*I'm dead beat,* Jerry thought. *I'm falling asleep on my feet.* He wondered how long it would be before he started to miss cues and forget lines.

Jerry was confused—a moment ago he had believed he actually was Crane, solving a crime—but now it seemed he was just playing Crane's part in a TV show. He looked around him: the spacious hotel lobby was gone—he was on a stage set. He was Dick Sylvester, the actor.

Sylvester was worn out by the constant bickering of his co-star, Joanna Ross, who played the part of Detective Kanefsky. Ross was a talented young actress, but she was also a horrendous primadonna who never stopped arguing with the director and the other cast members. Wistfully, Sylvester's thoughts strayed to the peace and quiet of his large house in San Fernando. He would be back there in just a few short hours, able to relax and forget about work... but first he had to finish shooting this scene. He had to go up to the desk clerk, and say (he struggled to get the simple line straight in his head): *Police. Has Kent Whitman arrived yet?*

Then Jerry was Crane again, and the hotel about him was solid and real. He walked up to the desk clerk.

"Police. Has Kent Whitman arrived yet?" he asked.

"The nuclear guy? Yes, he checked in a few hours ago." The desk clerk glanced at the rack of keys on the wall behind him. "But he went out again and hasn't come back yet. He didn't say where he was going."

Kanefsky frowned. "The chess move?" she speculated.

Crane shook his head. "No. It's too early. But we've got to get to him before they do." He turned back to the desk clerk. "How did Whitman leave here—by car?"

"No—he took a cab.... a CPT cab, I think."

Kanefsky reached for the phone on the reception desk. "Okay if I use it?" she asked.

"Sure, go ahead," the desk clerk said.

Kanefsky picked up the receiver and said: "Hello, operator? Get me the CPT cab company, please..." She spoke for a few seconds, then put the phone down and turned to Crane. "They'll get in touch with the cab driver and find out where Whitman was headed. It shouldn't take long. They'll call police headquarters as soon as they know anything."

Then Jerry found himself sitting in his armchair at home, watching TV. It was another commercial break

He was tense from all the excitement—his heart was beating quickly and his palms were sweating. Dimly, he realized it was just a story, and that it was bound to end happily, but the thought gave him little comfort. It all seemed so real.

*We're going about this investigation the wrong way,* Jerry thought. *We'll never get anywhere simply by looking for Whitman: that's too straightforward.* The story had to be properly balanced, he reflected: each element of the story had to be woven into the plot. There had to be a way of using their new-found knowledge about the chess-game.

But how? What was there about the chess game that would enable them to save Whitman? Subconsciously, Jerry searched through the key details: the series of murders, the game of chess, the taken pieces, the names of the victims, the city chessboard, the murder sites...

Suppose the police were to finish playing the chess game themselves, Jerry mused. Surely that would tell them the square on which the white king would be checkmated? Then they could go to the corresponding street intersection and prevent Whitman's murder...

On the TV, *A Case for Crane* had started again; the commercials were over. The picture showed Crane and Kanefsky entering the large open plan office at the police station. Immediately, Jerry was inside Crane's mind.

"Lieutenant, over here!" It was Creeley, waving a newspaper at them in a replay of his first appearance this episode.

They went over to Creeley's desk.

"What's this?" Crane inquired. "Another crossword puzzle at the City's expense?"

"I told you—I was on my lunch break," Creeley insisted. "But this is work... read that." He handed over the newspaper.

Crane saw that a paragraph had been circled with a ballpoint pen. He glanced at it, then read it out loud for Kanefsky's benefit. "*Passionate about his beliefs, Kent Whitman has never shied away from controversy. When a critic accused him of treating people like pawns in a chess game, Whitman replied that being treated like a pawn was preferable to being dead—which, he claimed, would be the inevitable consequence if his proposals were ignored.*"

"A motive at last," Kanefsky observed, flicking the hair from her eyes. "But a pretty flimsy one—and why carry out three random murders first? It doesn't make any sense."

"We're up against psychopaths," Crane said grimly. "This quote of Whitman's may have appealed to their twisted sense of irony—but the idea of the chess game came first. They originally devised it simply to provide themselves with an amusing pastime, like the ancient Romans watching gladiators kill each other. That's my theory, anyhow."

Kanefsky shook her head. "It beats me. A political assassination I could understand, but not this arbitrary killing to self-imposed rules."

Crane pondered for a moment. "These rules of theirs—the rules of chess, and their method of choosing victims and murder sites... the way they stick so rigorously to the rules is their weak point. Now that we know the rules, we can break in on the game."

Jerry remembered the idea that had occurred to him during the commercial break. He tried to push it into Crane's consciousness.

Crane turned to Creeley, who had been listening intently to the conversation. "You're the precinct's chess expert. Based on what we know about the game so far, could you predict what the next moves are going to be? Specifically, on what square checkmate will occur?"

"Not me," Creeley admitted. "I'm just a promising beginner. The person you need is Professor Hoffler."

Crane blinked. "Who?"

 "Professor Hoffler... he used to teach math at City U. He's retired now, but he still produces a daily chess problem for the newspaper. He's the best chess player in the city."

"Then get him here."

"I'm on it." Creeley left the room.

Crane turned to speak to Kanefsky, but before he could open his mouth the telephone on Creeley's desk rang.

Kanefsky picked up the phone. "

Hello, this is police headquarters, homicide division..."

Without warning, Jerry was displaced again. His new surroundings were unfamiliar: he was in a small apartment room, sitting at a table facing a battered typewriter. In the typewriter was part of the script of 'Names and Addresses'; it was unfinished. He was Steven G. Mitchell, the writer of the screenplay.

Mitchell leaned back and looked at the sheet in the typewriter. There were no more important plot developments until the very last scene, he thought, when the cops found the two bad guys on the top floor of the Beckerman Building. Until then, he had to pad the action out with plenty of excitement and suspense: another wild goose chase followed by the mandatory race against time. He resumed typing.

Then Jerry was Crane again, back at the police station.

Kanefsky replaced the phone. "That was the cab company. Whitman went to the City Museum."

The scene changed. Crane and Kanefsky were walking up the broad stone steps of an imposing building with a classical-style portico: the City Museum. A large sign said OPEN TILL 9 PM EVERY DAY.

"What do you suppose Whitman's doing here?" asked Kanefsky.

"Maybe he's just relaxing while he can," Crane suggested. "From what I gather he's going to have a pretty hectic day tomorrow."

"If he's still alive, that is," Kanefsky murmured. She went through the revolving door into the museum.

Crane followed her, then looked around the bustling entrance hall. It was a large, ornate space with a vaulted ceiling, and archways and staircases leading to other parts of the vast building. Crowds of people were moving in all directions. Crane spotted a uniformed museum attendant and went over to him.

"Police—we're looking for someone. Do you recognize this man?" Crane held out a photograph of Kent Whitman.
The attendant studied the picture. "Sure—I've seen a face like that this afternoon." He looked up. "At least two hundred people with a face like that, in fact. Do you have any idea how many people we get in here every day? And how many of them look just like that photograph?"

"Thanks, you've been a great help," Crane said with irony. Then he turned to Kanefsky.

"Okay, you search this floor and I'll look upstairs."

Kanefsky nodded and headed for a long gallery marked NATIVE AMERICAN ARTIFACTS.

Crane hurried up the staircase to the second floor. The first room he came to was labelled THE CIVIL WAR. Dozens of people were milling between the rows of display cases, peering at the objects inside. Crane began a frantic search for Kent Whitman.

As he moved rapidly through the gallery, Crane thought he could hear faint music coming from somewhere—the kind of music that was played on TV when nobody was speaking—but when he listened harder it went away. He decided he must have imagined it.

Suddenly he caught sight of someone he thought could have been Whitman, right at the far end of the gallery. He pushed his way through the crowd mumbling "Excuse me" and "Police"—then he saw that the man wasn't Whitman, after all. He went through into another gallery and resumed his search.

Some time later, in EARLY 20TH CENTURY INVENTIONS, Crane saw the short, stocky figure of Kanefsky heading towards him from the other direction.

"We'll never find him this way," Crane told her. "There are too many people and the place is too big."

"It's even bigger than it looks," Kanefsky replied. "Some guy just told me there's another wing that's not generally open to the public."

"Do you know what's in it?"

"Documents, apparently," she made a vague gesture. "I guess that means rare books, manuscripts..."

"Legal records, maybe?" Crane suggested.

"Of course!" Kanefsky snapped her fingers. "Whitman must be doing research for his speech tomorrow."

Crane looked around and spotted a uniformed museum attendant, standing next to a bust of Thomas Edison. He went over to him. "We're police officers. Where are the legal documents kept?"
The attendant pointed down a corridor. "You go straight along there and turn left at the end. It's the second door on the right."

"Thanks," said Crane. They hurried off.

They found the room marked LEGAL RECORDS—PRIVATE, and went in. It was smaller and less brightly lit than the other rooms they had seen, and was filled with racks of dusty, musty-smelling books. Near the entrance a young, bespectacled woman was working at a desk. She looked up when they entered.

"Excuse me—we're the police. Has this man been in here?" Crane showed her the photograph of Kent Whitman.

"That's Mr Whitman," she said without any hesitation. "Yes, he came in here around five o'clock. I had to help him find what he was looking for—he might be a VIP but he didn't know anything about the Dewey decimal system. He was here for a couple of hours, but then he had a telephone call and had to rush off. He looked rather worried—he isn't in any kind of trouble is he?"

"He might be." Crane turned to Kanefsky. "The call must have been from the chess-players—or more likely from some menial agent of theirs, like Christopher Robin. They're still one step ahead of us. On some pretext or other they've persuaded Whitman to go where they want him... wherever that is. Professor Hoffler's our only chance now."

Another scene shift: Crane and Kanefsky were entering Crane's office at the police station. Detective Creeley was in there, and a flustered-looking old man standing near the whiteboard. The old man was writing rapidly in a small notebook and muttering to himself.

Crane went over to him. "Professor Hoffler? I'm Lieutenant Crane. How are you getting on with our chess problem?" He glanced at the clock on the wall; it was 7.40.

Hoffler blinked at him through thick lenses. "Let me make sure I've got this straight. There's a chess game you want me to reconstruct, but the only information available is the pieces that have been taken and the squares they were taken on. In other words..." He consulted his notebook. "First, a white pawn taken on black king's bishop five. Then—and we have no way of knowing how many intermediate moves there may have been—a black pawn taken on white queen six. Finally, a black bishop taken on white queen's bishop eight. Is that right?" Crane glanced at Creeley. "Well, is it?"

"Right as far as it goes," Creeley acknowledged. "But we know one other thing. We know that the piece that took the black bishop was a white knight. Forensics found the piece at the scene, remember?"

Hoffler tore a page out his notebook and threw it in the bin, with a glare at Creeley. "Well, detective—you failed to tell me that the first time. This new information changes the problem—but it should make it easier to solve."

Suddenly Crane was displaced; he was no longer in his office. He dimly recognized his new surroundings: the small room, the typewriter—but where was he? Surely he hadn't been here a moment ago? His mind was in confusion: he couldn't remember anything. Who was he? For a moment he had thought he was the detective, Crane. But no, he was an actor playing Crane, and his name was Dick Sylvester—or was it? He shook his head to clear it. The disorientation left him; he had been dizzy for a second there, but now he was all right again.

He was Steven G. Mitchell, and he had a story to finish.

*Now, what happens next?* he wondered. *Professor Hoffler mutters something about the chess game, Crane asks if he's found the solution and Hoffler tells him which is the correct square. No, that's not quite right,* Mitchell thought. *It doesn't happen like that—Hoffler has to make a mild protest first.* He wondered why he was so certain of the way the story had to go. It was as if he had already seen the show on TV and was simply writing it down... or else he was remembering something that had actually happened to himself. *I guess I'm just good at visualizing plots,* he decided.

Then Crane was in his office again.

Professor Hoffler was muttering to himself. "Bishop to bishop seven, king to bishop square, knight to king six, checkmate..."

"Well, professor, have you found the solution?" Crane asked impatiently.

"*The* solution? No, I can't claim that," Hoffler protested mildly. "There are so many variations, and I have had so little time to study the problem. But I have found *a* solution."

"And the square on which checkmate will occur is..." Crane prompted.
"King's bishop—sorry, I mean..." Hoffler glanced up at the whiteboard. "The junction of 6th Avenue and 22nd Street."

"Thanks, professor!" Crane turned to Kanefsky. "Let's go—that's less than two miles away."

The scene shifted.

Crane and Kanefsky were driving through heavy traffic in a bustling, brightly lit part of the city. Despite their siren and flashing light, they were only making slow progress.

"Not the best place for a quiet assassination," Kanefsky commented.

"Don't forget the rules," Crane told her. "The location of the murder is decided by the chess game. It was sheer luck that the first three murders occurred in quiet streets."

The traffic ground to a halt and Kanefsky swore under her breath.

Crane looked anxiously at his watch. "It's one minute to eight o'clock—we're not going to make it. Pull in here and we'll carry on by foot; it'll be quicker."

They leapt out of the car and began to thrust their way along the crowded sidewalk.

Up ahead, Crane spotted a man standing in a doorway, looking about uneasily. Crane recognized him from his photograph. "There's Whitman," he said. They made a beeline for the man.

Then someone broke away from the crowd and began to move purposefully towards Whitman.

"Stop, police!"

Their quarry turned around, startled. He saw Crane and Kanefsky pushing their way towards him. He hesitated, looking around wildly, and then stepped back into the flow of people. As he tried to get away he ran into a grossly overweight passer-by and was knocked to the ground.

Kanefsky hurried up to the fallen man, pulled him to his feet, and handcuffed him.

Crane went over to Whitman. "Are you all right, sir?"

Whitman nodded, looking shaken and bewildered.

At that moment, sirens screaming, several police cars pulled up. Whitman was helped into one of the cars, while the would-be assassin was thrust into another.

Crane and Kanefsky made their way back to their own car.

"So Whitman is safe and the chess game is over," Kanefsky remarked. "But we're still no closer to locating the real villains—the chess-players themselves."

A sudden memory popped into Crane's mind: *the two bad guys on the top floor of the Beckerman Building*. That was where they would find the chessplayers. But it couldn't have been a memory, of course—just a strong hunch.

"I've got a strong hunch I know where they are," Crane told Kanefsky. "If I read these people correctly, they'll be somewhere they can see the whole chessboard at once—and there's only one place where that's possible." He pointed to a huge skyscraper a few blocks away, rising high above the surrounding buildings.

"The Beckerman Building? But those offices must be the most expensive in the city."

"So? The people we're up against—I don't get the impression they're short of money. No, that's where they'll be, all right—on the very top floor, if my hunch is correct."

There was no perceptible passage of time, but now they were entering the lobby of the Beckerman Building. They were accompanied by three uniformed police officers.

"Get all the exits sealed off," Crane ordered.

The uniformed policemen nodded and hurried away.

Crane and Kanefsky went over to the bank of elevators, and Crane punched the call button. After a few seconds the doors of one of the elevators slid open and they stepped in. Crane pressed the button for the top floor.

As they ascended, Crane was suddenly overwhelmed by an irrational feeling that none of this was real. There was no point searching for any homicidal chess-players because there hadn't really been any murders. He shook his head to clear it, but he couldn't quite rid himself of the feeling.
The elevator doors opened, and they stepped out into the top floor foyer. There was no-one in attendance at the reception desk. According to the sign, the whole floor was given over to one company: BLACK AND WHITE ENTERPRISES, UNLIMITED.

Crane glanced around the foyer. Behind the empty reception desk, there was a large potted palm and a double door—presumably leading to an inner office.

The feeling of unreality was still there. Crane noticed how flimsy everything seemed. The walls, the desk, the door—they all looked so thin and insubstantial that he felt he could put his hand through them. But the place couldn't be that poorly constructed—it was the prime piece of real estate in the city. The unreality must be inside his head, he realized—not in the external world.

They went past the desk to the double door. Crane knocked, and then listened: there was no answer. He knocked again, louder, and shouted "Open up, it's the police!" There was still no answer. He tried the door cautiously—it was unlocked.
Crane felt strangely detached from the world around him—as though this wasn't really happening to him but to someone else, while he looked on from a safe distance. Once again he shook his head to clear it.

He glanced at Kanefsky and she nodded, taking out her sidearm. Crane did the same, then silently mouthed the words "One—two—three!" They burst through the door into the inner office, their guns held out ready to fire.

Then they lowered their weapons and looked about them in astonishment.

The room, originally designed as a vast open plan office suite, had been completely transformed. It was extravagantly furnished in a bizarre mixture of styles, and filled to overflowing with artworks from all countries and all periods. Victorian England clashed with ancient Greece and Renaissance Italy and tribal Africa.

At the far end of the room, easily a hundred feet away, a floor-to-ceiling window overlooked the city chessboard. In front of the window was a raised dais, and on the dais two men sat silently on either side of a small table. Their bored-looking faces were turned towards the two startled police officers.

Crane and Kanefsky walked slowly towards the dais. As they got closer, they could see what was on the table: an ornate oriental chess-set, with the pieces arranged in the final positions of the game. The taken pieces—a white pawn, a black pawn, and a black bishop—lay on their sides next to the board. The white king was still standing.

Crane scrutinized the two men sitting at the chessboard. Behind the black pieces was a white man—fat, balding, impeccably dressed in a pinstriped business suit. Behind the white pieces was a black man—tall, dreadlocked, wearing a long silk robe.

Crane stopped a few feet away from the dais.

Suddenly he realized he was four distinct people at the same time:

He was Alex Crane, confronting two psychopathic killers in a bizarrely furnished penthouse at the top of a skyscraper...

And he was Dick Sylvester, finally shooting the last scene of this episode of *A Case for Crane...*

And he was Steven G. Mitchell, typing rapidly as he finished off a TV screenplay....

And he was Jerry Vincent, sitting at home watching TV.

In Crane's world, the white man blinked lazily. "Ah, Lieutenant Crane, I believe. What can we do for you?"

"Let's start with the little matter of murder in the first degree—three counts, and attempted murder—one count," Crane said. "And then there are all those assistants you must have hired. We know about Melendez and Christopher Robin, but there must be many others—we'll be wanting a list of names and addresses."

Then he was sitting at home, watching TV. The Crane theme music was playing, and the closing credits were rolling up the screen. The show was over. He leaned back in his chair.

He wasn't Alex Crane, detective.

He wasn't Dick Sylvester, actor.

He wasn't Steven G. Mitchell, screenwriter.

He was Jerry Vincent, unemployed... a chronic loser with no prospects, no talents—and nothing to do all day except watch TV.

# The Rendlesham Magi

**C**hristmas 1980: a day I will always remember. St Dunstan's College was almost deserted. The students were on vacation, of course, and the married fellows were at home with their families. That left just four of us in the Senior Common Room that evening: the three wise men and myself. At that time I was the youngest 'don' at the college, having been appointed to the post of Teaching Fellow in Asiatic History the previous summer. The next in age was more than a decade my senior—Don Hunter, a lecturer in Astronomy, with whom I was engaged in a game of Fortean supercheckers.

The other two sat by the open log fire, smoking cigars and talking earnestly to each other: Arthur Dodson, the ancient and venerable professor of Theology, and Otto Ziegler, a German professor who was visiting Cambridge for a couple of semesters during a sabbatical from his own university. I had never quite made out what Ziegler's specialism was—some kind of abstract mathematics or higher physics. He was small and round, with a bald head and goatee beard—pretty much what you imagine when you hear the term 'mad scientist'.

"Oh do hurry up, Justin!" Don Hunter ran a hand through his long, prematurely grey hair. "If you don't make a move soon we shall be here all night." He looked impatiently at his watch—the third or fourth time he had done so that evening. He said a few other things, muttering under his breath, that I didn't catch. I got the general impression he wanted to get away and do something he considered Very Important.

It was true that I was having difficulty concentrating on the game. Part of the reason was the sheer effort (not made any easier by the imbibing of several festive brandies) of focusing my mind on a board with 1600 squares and hundreds of pieces. By this stage, if I remember correctly, I was down to less than 200 men while Don still had most of his original 360.

I shrugged and moved a piece at random. Don grunted in disgust and proceeded to take another fifty or so of my men.

There was another reason for my lack of interest in the game. I was listening with more than half my mind to the animated conversation over by the fireplace. They were talking, of all the hackneyed subjects, about the Star of Bethlehem.

"It's all nonsense, of course," old Dodson was saying. "The Star in the East is purely symbolic. A theological necessity, to demonstrate fulfilment of God's prophecy in the Book of Numbers. To a good Christian, that is all that is needed. But materialists like yourself—and countless others going back to Johannes Kepler in the sixteenth century—refuse to be satisfied with the beauty of religious symbolism. You insist on looking for comets and supernovas and planetary conjunctions. But these theories are all discredited—totally discredited."

"*Nein—nicht so.*" Ziegler puffed excitedly on his cigar. "Not my comet—nobody discredits him."

Dodson looked amused. "And what's so special about YOUR comet, Herr Professor?"

"Ah, my comet—he travels backwards in time. Backwards! It is *sehr unheimlich*—it is very strange—but it is what the equations tell me. And equations, they never lie."

"A comet travelling backwards in time? Where from? And why?" Dodson seemed mildly intrigued in spite of himself.

"These things the equations tell me. My comet, he is one of a pair—a time-symmetric pair created by a Fanthorpe singularity in the year 988 AD. One comet travels backwards in time, the other forwards. The two orbits are like mirror images, with aphelion in the Kuiper Belt and perihelion here, on Earth. For the backward travelling comet, perihelion was 4 BC..."

"4 BC?" Dodson looked up. "The year that Herod the Great died—generally accepted as the year of the Nativity. Well, that fits your theory, I suppose. What about the forward-travelling comet?"

"From 4 BC to 988 AD it is 992 years," Ziegler said slowly. It was clear that he was building to something in the nature of a climax. "And from 988 AD another 992 years is... 1980! Christmas Day, 1980! Today!" He beamed triumphantly.

Whatever response Dodson was about to make was cut off by a cry from Don Hunter. I had made another disastrous move and he had promptly taken all my remaining pieces.

"Finished at last!" Don looked at his watch and jumped to his feet. "Sorry, gents—I've got to go now. Must keep my appointment with that new star in the East, you know."

We all gaped at him.

"New star in the East?" Dodson and Ziegler spoke almost simultaneously.
"Yes—I'll have to leave young Justin here to tell you about it. I've been chattering away to him all evening. First saw it through the telescope a couple of days ago—much brighter yesterday—should be visible to the naked eye by now. Rises just before midnight. I'll have to rush off to the Observatory if I'm going to catch it."

I have to admit this was news to me as much as to the others. Now I came to think of it, Don had been mumbling about something or other, but I hadn't been paying much attention

"We know all about your new star," Dodson said. "Or rather, the *Herr Professor* here knows all about it. It's a backwards travelling comet, previously known as the star of Bethlehem. If you can believe a word he says, that is."

"*Nein, nein*—this is the forward-travelling one," Ziegler said. "But the rest—*ja*, it is essentially correct." He turned to address the astronomer. "You have a physics background—you know the theoretical possibility of a Fanthorpe singularity. I say it is more than a theory—it is a reality which occurred in 988 AD. Your so-called new star is nothing but the inevitable mathematical consequence of this."

Don shook his head uncertainly. "A Fanthorpe singularity? But that's impossible—such a thing could only be produced artificially, using an immensely powerful nuclear reactor. It's not possible today, and it certainly wasn't possible in 988 AD."

A sudden thought flashed into my head. "Maybe it was," I said.

Now it was my turn to be gaped at.

"988 AD," I stated flatly, "was the year that Zhang Tsu disappeared."

There was a long pause in which they continued to gape at me.

"Let me explain," I went on. "Zhang Tsu was the original rocket scientist. The Chinese had just invented what they called 'fire arrows'—simple rockets that they used in warfare. But Zhang Tsu tried a series of experiments in which he replaced the black powder in the rocket with red mercury. Many scholars believe this resulted in a primitive form of nuclear propulsion. The first few experiments seem to have been successful, but then there was a huge explosion and Zhang Tsu was never seen again."

This time the pause was so short as to be imperceptible.

"For what are we waiting?" Ziegler demanded. "To the observatory, *schnell!*"

Don Hunter needed no further encouragement—he had been itching to leave for several minutes. And I was all for it—it sounded like a great adventure. Only Dodson seemed reluctant to forego his place by the fire, but I managed to persuade him by pandering to his ego: "After all, we're just an astronomer, a mathematician and a historian. We have our limitations. There are some situations that only a theologian can rise to."

So the four of us were in it together. We rushed downstairs and piled into Don's battered old Austin Mini. We decided he should drive because... I was about to say "because he was the least drunk", but what I mean, of course, is "because he was completely sober".

He hadn't a drop of liquor all evening, you know. Which was a good thing, because if none of us had been fit to drive we would have missed the adventure of a lifetime.

We pulled up at the observatory just on the stroke of midnight. Don let us into the deserted building and opened up the huge dome. The bright yellow star on the Eastern horizon was clearly visible.

"It's altered significantly in the last twenty-four hours," Don said, frowning as he adjusted the giant reflecting telescope. "There's been a significant course change—there's no doubt now that it's headed for Earth. Let's see if George can compute an impact point for us."

'George' turned out to be the observatory's state-of-the-art VAX-11/780 mainframe. It chugged and clicked as Don fed it the data.

"Impact point, eh?" Arthur Dodson chuckled to himself. "My money's on Bethlehem, if history is anything to go by." It was clear that he thought the whole thing was a load of hooey.

"Bethlehem? *Nein*—I think not." Otto Ziegler, in contrast to Dodson, was taking the matter very seriously indeed. He bent over a globe and studied it carefully. "Theory predicts impact point is one hundred-eighty degrees from starting point. Starting point was somewhere in China, I believe?" He looked at me expectantly.

"Um, yes—I see what you mean," I said. "Let's see—Zhang Tzu's experiments took place near the town of Huangshi in Hubei province, I believe."

"You show me." Ziegler indicated the globe.

With a bit of difficulty I located the place and pointed it out to the earnest-looking mathematician.

"*Ach, ja*—approximately thirty degrees North, hundred-fifteen degrees East. So we subtract hundred-eighty degrees to get..." He rotated the globe carefully. "Thirty degrees North, five-and-sixty degrees West. *Jawohl*! Right in the middle of the Bermuda Triangle. It surprises me not."

"Bermuda Triangle, my foot!" Dodson scoffed. "You mark my words—this comet is heading for Bethlehem."

A heated argument ensued, and might have gone on all night if it hadn't been interrupted after a few minutes by a cough from Don Hunter.

"Sorry to disappoint you fellows, but George disagrees with you." Don was standing at the computer, a slip of paper in his hand. "The impact point isn't Bethlehem and it isn't the

Bermuda Triangle. It's much closer. Just on the coast about sixty miles east of here. A place called Rendlesham."

"And the time of impact?" Ziegler looked anxiously at his watch.

Don glanced at the paper. "0140 hours—just over an hour from now."

"Can we make it in time?"

"We can if we're lucky. Let's go!"

Cramming ourselves back into Don's little car, we tore off eastwards along the A14. All the time the yellow star grew brighter and brighter ahead of us.

"Follow that star!" I shouted.

The new star in the East!" Dodson added, chuckling.

"We're just like the three wise men following the star," Don observed.

Ziegler, the great mathematician, grunted. "Except that there are four of us," he pointed out.

"Ah, but only three of us are wise men," Don said. "Justin doesn't count—he's only 28. You can't be a wise man at 28. It would be a contradiction in terms."

I ignored the insult. "Maybe we'll witness the Second Coming," I speculated.

"Poppycock," Dodson snorted. "The Second Coming is a purely symbolic concept, just like the Star of Bethlehem. Theology is about the world of the Spirit, not the world of superstitious nonsense."

We drove at hair-raising speeds past Newmarket, Bury St Edmunds and the sprawling lights of Ipswich. Just as we were passing through the village of Woodbridge we saw a huge, silent burst of brilliant yellow light ahead of us.

"The star's gone!"

"It came down in the woods over there!"

We drove a bit further and came to a gate into the woods. A sign informed us that the place was called Rendlesham Forest, that it was the property of Her Majesty's Forestry Commission, and that we were welcome to enter so long as we didn't light any fires.

We left the car by the gate and went into the woods.

"I should have brought a flashlight," Don muttered. "So much for foresight."

"It doesn't matter," I said. "There's a light over there in the forest. Let's head towards it."

The light turned out to be an eerie yellow glow with no obvious source. We crept towards it and came to an unnatural looking clearing.

"I think this is where it came down." Dodson was looking upwards, and our eyes followed his. There was an gap in the canopy of trees that was open to the sky. The ground beneath was littered with freshly broken pine branches.

"Some of the wood looks scorched," I observed.

"You're right," Don agreed. "There must have been intense heat here."

Ziegler was standing at the edge of the clearing, looking thoughtful. "Intense heat, *ja*—or intense radiation."

Our thoughts were interrupted by the clamour of voices approaching. With a start we realized we were not the only ones in the woods that night.

"What the blazes?" Dodson looked around. "They sound like Americans. A large number of them! What are they doing here?"

Don snapped his fingers. "Americans—of course! We're right next to a US Air Force Base. Woodbridge, I think it's called. Top Secret atomic stuff—we don't want to be caught snooping around here!"

The voices were getting closer.

"There's someone out there, Sir!" one of the voices shouted. "What should I do? Finding that thing out here has made me mighty nervous."

"Take no risks, man!" another voice barked. "Shoot the commie blighters!"

Actually the word he used may not have been 'blighters', but we weren't paying much attention by that point. We were running as fast as we could back to the car.

Well, that's more or less the end of the story as far as my involvement is concerned. The 'Rendlesham Forest Incident', as it's now known, has become quite notorious among conspiracy theorists. Many people are convinced that a UFO crash-landed in the East of England that Christmas Day more than thirty years ago—despite consistent denials by the UK and US governments. Another theory is that it was a Soviet nuclear powered satellite that came down. But an artificial comet created by a tenth century Chinese rocket scientist... a time-travelling twin of the Star of Bethlehem? Who knows? I may be the only one left who's in possession of the full facts. Old Dodson died years ago, and Don Hunter is in a retirement home. I've no idea what happened to Otto Ziegler—he must be either dead or a very old man by now.

There is one curious postscript to the story. It appears that the remains of the reactor core—or whatever it was the US airmen recovered—was transported back to the States on board an aircraft carrier. It was then ferried by helicopter, slung underneath a giant Chinook, to NASA headquarters in Houston, Texas. And late at night, a few miles outside Houston on the 29th of December 1980, this strange phenomenon was witnessed by two local women returning from an evening out. The women—Vicky and Betty—were both born-again Christians, and when confronted with this huge glowing apparition in the sky they could only draw one conclusion.

This was the Second Coming of Jesus, and they promptly went on record to that effect.

And maybe, in a sense, they were right.

# THE CASE OF THE PURLOINED POE

S aturday, 10.15 am. Holywell Street.

"Ah... I believe things are about to get interesting." Pierce Stormson was looking out of the window of his book-lined and distinctly Victorian living room. "When I observe a personage of marked obesity hurrying at an undignified pace along Holywell Street, it is a fairly safe deduction that a prospective client is eager to consult us."

"Let me see..." I went over to the window and looked out. "Why, that's Roy Burlington—one of the Eng Lit professors. He sometimes helps me with my research."

Stormson glanced at me. "English Literature? Surely not—I thought you were studying the work of some American hack writer whose name escapes me."

"H. P. Lovecraft," I reminded him. "Who wrote in the English language, so it counts as English Literature. Professor Burlington is an expert in... but there goes the doorbell. I'll go and let him in."

"Hello, Melvin—didn't expect to see you here. Of course—I remember now..." The overweight Burlington, red-faced and dishevelled-looking, paused to catch his breath. "You rent the top floor flat here, don't you? Is Professor Stormson in? I need to see him... it's rather urgent, you know."

I showed Burlington into the living room, where he plopped down gratefully on one of the ancient but well-upholstered sofas.

"Can I get you something to drink?" Stormson asked.

"No—no time for that," Burlington panted. "There's no time to lose. And it's a long story... I'm not sure where to begin."

"Why not begin at the beginning of the story?" Stormson sat down, crossing his long legs and steepling his fingers in his favourite Sherlock Holmes manner.

"Ah yes... the beginning of the story. That's what it's all about, you know—the beginning of the story. The beginning of the detective story, in fact."

"*A Study in Scarlet,*" Stormson said.

"Pardon?"

"*A Study in Scarlet,* by Arthur Conan Doyle. Originally published in *Beeton's Christmas Annual* in 1887. The first Sherlock Holmes story... the beginning of the detective story, in other words."

Burlington shook his head vigorously. "Not at all, not at all. *The Murders in the Rue Morgue,* by Edgar Allan Poe, was the first published detective story by a long stretch. It made its first appearance in print as far back as 1841, yet it contains all the classic elements: the careful analysis, the deduction, the tracking down of the perpetrator. Poe was a genius—the American Shakespeare. He wrote poetry, philosophical discourses, fiction of all types. Not only did he invent the detective story, but he effectively invented science fiction and the modern horror story as well. I might even go so far as to state that he invented the short story itself, as a literary form..."

"It is clear that you are a great admirer of Poe," Stormson observed dryly.

"I certainly am! The central character in *Murders in the Rue Morgue,* C. Auguste Dupin, is the archetype of all the great fictional detectives that came after... including Sherlock Holmes. Dupin appeared again in two other published stories: *The Mystery of Marie Rogêt* in 1842, and *The Purloined Letter* in 1844."

Stormson leaned back and sighed. "All this background is very interesting, but perhaps it is time now to get to the point. When did the manuscript go missing, and under what circumstances?"

"B-but... how could you know about that?" Burlington was aghast. "Hardly anyone knows of the manuscript's existence, let alone its recent disappearance. The only person besides myself who is aware of its loss is my graduate student, Miss Sparkes."

"Oh, but it was a simple deduction." Stormson waved his hand dismissively. "Hardly worthy of C. Auguste Dupin, I'm sure. But I couldn't help observing how you were careful to qualify a couple of your statements with the word 'published'. You said *The Murders in the Rue Morgue* was the first 'published' detective story, and that Dupin appeared again in two other 'published' stories. Statements qualified in such a way indicate that you know of at least one other story that was not published... in other words, one that exists only in manuscript. And the fact that you have come here to consult SOLVED, the Secret Oxford League of Volunteer Extracurricular Detectives, strongly suggests that the manuscript has now disappeared "

"Well, yes—I suppose it is obvious when you put it like that. It's true that there is another Dupin story which is known only in manuscript. The facts relating to its existence have been in the public domain for almost eighty years—and yet scarcely anyone has given any credence to them. You see, the source is a work of fiction... a work of detective fiction, in fact. It's a novel by John Dickson Carr called *The Mad Hatter Mystery*. I don't know how Carr got hold of the information, but the plain fact is the details he provides about the Poe manuscript are correct in every detail."

"Perhaps you would be so good as to enlighten me," Stormson prompted.

"The manuscript was found by an English book collector named Sir William Bitton early in the twentieth century. He was on a visit to Philadelphia, and went to look at a house where Edgar Allan Poe had lived on Spring Garden Street. When he arrived at the place he found it in the middle of a major renovation, and while the builders' backs were turned he had a wander round to see what he could find. He discovered the manuscript tucked behind the dusty framework of an ancient closet. Scarcely daring to look at it, he spirited it back to England, where he scrutinized it carefully. There could be no doubt it was a genuine Poe, and moreover that it was a Dupin story that predated *The Murders in the Rue Morgue*. Sir William told very few other people about the manuscript, and on his death he bequeathed what remained of it to Oxford University. He stipulated that its existence here should be made known only to persons he referred to as 'academics of the highest standing'. Ahem." (That last 'Ahem' was directed at myself, for reasons I failed to discern).

"Just a moment," Stormson interjected. "Did you say 'what remained of it'? Do you mean to say the manuscript was incomplete in some way?"

"Very much so, regrettably. Soon after the manuscript arrived in England, and before it could be fully examined by Sir William or anyone else, the manuscript was set alight. Only a small fragment of the first page escaped the flames. The exact circumstances of the accident are unknown—they were certainly nothing like those described in Carr's novel. Carr does, however, accurately record the few words that remained legible. I know them by heart: *'Of the singular gifts of my friend the Chevalier Auguste Dupin, I may one day speak. Upon my lips he has placed a seal of silence which must, for fear of displeasing the eccentricities of his somewhat outré humour, I dare not at present violate. I can, therefore, only record that it was after dark one gusty evening in the year 18-- that a knock sounded at the door of my chambers in a dim, decaying pile of buildings of the Faubourg St. Germain, and...'*—and that is all. Nothing else remains."

"Not even a title?"

"Not even a title. By convention, those few scholars who know of its existence refer to the fragment simply as 'Detective Story Number One'. And now..." Burlington paused, a desolate look on his face. "And now, as you correctly deduced, even this small fragment has disappeared."

"Perhaps you could describe the circumstances of its disappearance," Stormson suggested.

"What? Oh, yes, of course. Well, the manuscript is normally kept in a safe in my office. It comes out only if it is required for research by myself or one of my colleagues, or if we want to show it to a visiting academic, and on those rare occasions when I have to take it away from Oxford for one purpose or another. One such occasion took place this past week, when the manuscript accompanied Miss Sparkes and myself on a brief trip to another university. We returned early this morning, when I placed the manuscript on my desk with the intention of putting it away immediately. But I was tired—jet-lagged after the long flight, you know—and I must have dozed off for a few minutes. A few minutes only: certainly no longer than that. But when I awoke, the manuscript had gone. You can imagine how frantic I was. I searched everywhere, but to no avail. I fear some opportunistic thief must have taken advantage of my brief period of inattention and... well, as you can see, I came straight here. I had no wish to involve the police."

"A very wise decision," Stormson said. "I sense that there is scope here for some, ah... shall we say embarrassment—and to bring in the police would only accentuate that embarrassment. SOLVED, on the other hand, may be relied on for discretion: our clients' secrets always stay secret. We will start immediately. I believe a visit to the scene of the crime is called for."

"Then let's go," I said. "SOLVED is on the case—the Case of the Purloined Poe!"

*Saturday, 11.45 am. Department of English Literature.*

Roy Burlington's office was a small one at the best of times, and with four people crammed into its interior it seemed even smaller. Burlington flopped down into the chair at his desk, apparently exhausted in both body and spirit. Stormson and myself had to remain standing, as the only other chair was already occupied by a dejected-looking figure curled up in a rather gangly foetal posture.

"My research student, Carmella Sparkes," Burlington panted, waving his arm rather feebly. He was suffering visibly from the exertion of walking the short distance from Holywell Street to the English Faculty.

I had seen Carmella around the faculty before: a tall, ungainly girl with glasses and short hair, and a permanently serious expression. She was looking more serious than ever now—distinctly miserable, in fact.

"So this is where the mishap took place," Stormson said, his eyes sweeping around the room.

"What? Oh, yes... right here." Burlington thumped the desk. "Just a couple of hours ago. Feel free to take a look around." He lapsed into a melancholy silence.

Stormson spent several minutes examining the small room and its contents, glancing along the packed bookshelves, rummaging in the overflowing in-trays, and even looking inside the waste bin under the desk. Carmella remained curled up in her chair, frowning and occasionally biting on a fingernail.

Stormson turned his attention to the steel safe in the corner. "An excellent design... and very secure, I imagine."

Burlington gave a humourless laugh. "It certainly is. No thief could get inside that. But the thief didn't have to. The manuscript was laid out in plain sight on the desk. It was a mistake to take it out of the safe, of course, but I was determined to flaunt it in front of old Nordstrom." "Nordstrom? An American academic, I presume? You said you had just returned from a trip to the other side of the Atlantic."

Burlington glanced up sharply. "Did I say that?"

"You said as much. You said you got back to Oxford two or three hours ago, and mentioned that you were suffering from jet-lag. A transatlantic flight was strongly indicated."

"Oh, I see. You're right, of course. Clarence Nordstrom is a professor at Penn, and a big-headed, arrogant show-off. A typical Ivy Leaguer... thinks he knows everything. And because he's on the spot in Philadelphia, he imagines he knows more than anyone else about the works of Edgar Allan Poe. Well, he's wrong, and I was determined to put him in his place."

"You showed him the manuscript?"

"I did. And do you know what? He had the cheek to tell me it was a fake. A fake! That was tantamount to calling me a liar. He wanted to have it tested in their labs, so I told him to go right ahead. I knew what the result would be. And of course the test came back positive... that really took the wind out of his sails!"

After Burlington's outburst, the room once again lapsed into silence—a rather awkward silence.

There was a sudden stirring as Carmella Sparkes unravelled her long legs and stood up. Frowning, she pulled out a mobile phone and glanced at the screen. Then without saying a word she left the room.

I noticed that the chair she had been sitting on was an old-fashioned wooden one. A thought occurred to me, and I went over and picked it up. I turned it upside down and carefully examined the foot of each leg. But no... my hunch was wrong. There were no gimlet-holes drilled in the chair legs.

Suddenly the silence was jarred by the ringing of the phone on Burlington's desk. The sound made him jump, but before he could pick up the phone Carmella reappeared in the doorway, darted into the office, and grabbed the phone.

"Hello? Yes, he's right here. An urgent delivery, you say? I'll let him know. Goodbye."

Putting the phone down, Carmella turned to her supervisor. "That was the mail office. They've received a package for you. Apparently it's marked urgent."

Burlington's eyes flickered with a brief hope. "I wonder... You hear sometimes about thieves returning stolen property when they discover it's unsaleable. I'd better go and see what it is." He hurried from the office.

Carmella waited a few seconds, then spoke up. "We've only got a few minutes. The mail office is right at the other end of the faculty, but he'll be back again when he discovers there's no package waiting for him."

Stormson chuckled. "I begin to see. You called the professor from your mobile, then picked his phone up before he could answer it himself. There was no-one at the other end—just a clever subterfuge to get him out of the way while you impart some delicate information you don't want him to hear."

"If you want to put it like that." Carmella frowned, looking more worried than ever. " I think I know who took the manuscript fragment. Have you ever heard of Harry Sparkes?"

Stormson shook his head slowly. "I can't say the name rings any bells, no."

"THE Harry Sparkes?" I said. "The world-famous author? Of course I've heard of him. And you have the same surname. Are you related?"

Carmella lowered her gaze and shuffled her feet. "I'm afraid I am. He's my Great Uncle Harry. He's always been a bit of an embarrassment to the family."

Stormson glanced from one to the other of us, looking faintly amused. "World famous author? Embarrassment to the family? I confess I'm getting a bit lost."

"Really, Prof, you must have heard of Harry Sparkes," I told him. "He's one of the top writers on paranormal subjects. His first bestseller hit the shelves a couple of years ago—it was called *The Stone Tapes*. Then there's a new one just out, called *The Glass Tapes*. I can't believe an educated person like yourself has never heard of it."

"I have to admit *The Glass Tapes* rings a faint bell. I've seen the phrase somewhere recently, I think. But please enlighten me... what are these modern masterpieces all about?"

Carmella gave a quick nervous glance over her shoulder, then said: "It's Great Uncle Harry's big theory, you see. He thinks old things—inanimate objects—retain an imprint of the past, which he says he can retrieve with some weird mechanical contraption he put together in his garden shed. As far as anyone can see it's just a battered old eight-track tape deck, with a food blender bolted onto it. He keeps it in an old leather suitcase, and takes it with him wherever he goes. At least it keeps him quiet—that's what the family has always said. Only now he isn't quiet about it... he's started writing these books, which are squirmingly embarrassing." She squirmed, to illustrate her point.

"But what are stone tapes and glass tapes, exactly?" Stormson was developing an interest in spite of himself.

"Well, he started off with old stones... just pieces of rock he dug up around castles and prehistoric tombs and that sort of thing. Then for the second book, the one he's plugging at the moment, he moved on to old bits of broken glass that he found lying around. And now..."

There was a sound out in the corridor and Carmella almost jumped out of her skin. She peeped out, then breathed a sigh of relief. "It's not the professor, but he'll be back any second now. I don't think it would be a good idea if we were still here when he gets back. Let's go outside and I'll tell you the rest of the story."

<hr>

*Saturday, 12.30 pm. Parks Road.*

Once we were out on the street, Carmella, leaning forward earnestly as she walked, resumed her narrative. "I haven't seen Great Uncle Harry for months. But I saw him this morning. He's in Oxford to promote his new book—the one about glass tapes. He popped in to see me just as we got back from the airport."

"Now we are getting to it!" Stormson rubbed his hands. "So Great Uncle Harry was there in the office around the time the manuscript went missing?"

"Yes, he was. But it's really not accurate the way people keep referring to it as a manuscript. It's a tiny fragment of burned paper. But that's the whole problem. It's just the sort of thing Great Uncle Harry would be on the look-out for. You see, his next book, the one he's working on at the moment, is going to be called *The Paper Tapes*."

"So you think he pinched the Poe manuscript—excuse me, the Poe fragment—when he visited you in the office this morning?"

"I'm certain of it. The professor and myself were so knackered after the flight, Great Uncle Harry could have plucked it from right under our noses without our noticing."

81

Stormson pondered for a moment. "Hmm... It sounds very much as though a chat with Great Uncle Harry would not go amiss. Have you any idea where he might be found?"

Carmella pointed straight ahead. "We're heading in the right direction. He's doing a book-signing at Brickwell's bookshop... from noon to one o'clock, I think he said."

"Brickwell's, of course!" Stormson snapped his fingers. "That's where I saw the phrase *The Glass Tapes*. They had a large poster in the window the last time I walked past."

As ever, the Prof was right. The poster was there in the window when we arrived at the shop a few minutes later, together with at least a hundred hardback copies of the book.

"And you say people actually buy these books?" Stormson asked, peering dubiously at the garish display.

"In their millions," I assured him.

"It's clear that I'm in the wrong business, then," he observed dryly. "Come, let us enter."

There was a fair-sized crowd inside the shop, if not quite the millions I had confidently predicted. There was no doubt the event would prove lucrative for Carmella's Great Uncle Harry—who obviously wasn't one of those writers who had to struggle to make ends meet, like... well, like Edgar Allan Poe, for example.

Harry Sparkes, from what I could glimpse of him through the mass of people queuing up for the book signing, was a fairly well-preserved seventy-something. He was tall and bony like his great-niece, but whereas she had a permanently sombre expression, he had what can only be described as a maniacal glint in his eyes.

"He'll be signing books for another ten minutes," Stormson murmured, after a glance at his watch. "You two wait here and speak to him when you get the chance. I'm feeling a little guilty about leaving my client in the lurch. I'd better go back and see how he's getting on."

Carmella darted an anxious glance at him. "You won't tell him I faked the telephone call, will you?"

"Certainly not, my dear. I wouldn't want to add to the troubles the Sparkes clan has already got itself into today." And with that parting shot, the Prof left the bookshop.

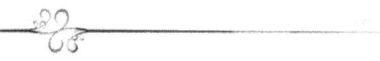

*Saturday, 1.10 pm. Brickwell's Bookshop.*

After the book signing, we managed to negotiate our way into a back room where Harry Sparkes was, to put it crudely, counting his money.

"Four hundred and thirteen books sold in that session," he gloated. "At a royalty of two pounds twenty per book, that's, erm—well, it's a lot of money "

"Nine hundred and eight pounds sixty pence," I said. I've always been good at mental arithmetic.

"Like I said, a lot of money." Harry fixed his vaguely maniacal gaze on me. "And who are you? Are you a friend of Carmella's?"

"I'm a detective," I said (because it sounded better than "I'm an amateur detective").

"You're not from the Inland Revenue, are you?" Harry asked suspiciously.

"No... nothing like that. I work for the University. I'm investigating the theft of a priceless manuscript."

"You took it, Uncle Harry, didn't you?" Carmella interjected. "When you visited me this morning. You pinched the manuscript just so you could analyze it with your silly machine."

Harry gaped at us. "Manuscript? Priceless? All I took was an old scrap of paper that someone had thrown in the waste paper bin."

"It was in the bin?" Carmella was incredulous.

"Well, it was on the floor next to the bin. Right there under the desk where the large gentleman was having a nap. I assumed he had meant to throw the paper into the bin, but missed his aim."

Carmella looked at me, horrified. "Professor Burlington must have knocked it off the desk onto the floor when he fell asleep!" She turned back to Harry. "Look, Uncle Harry, this is important. Where is the paper now? We need to get it back as quickly as possible."

Harry blinked at her. "But I put it into the tape machine to be analyzed. It was obviously an old piece of paper, with old writing on it, so it was ideal material for my forthcoming best-seller *The Paper Tapes*... for which, I might add, I have already received a six-figure advance. So it's too late to renege on the deal. Any old paper I find goes into the machine. At the moment it's in my hotel room. I started it running this morning and it will be going through the program as we speak."

A memory came back to me—something Carmella had said about a food blender. I had a sudden premonition of disaster. "This analysis procedure... what does it entail, exactly?"

"Well, the sample is dropped in the hopper on top of the machine, where it is pulverized, and then... What's the matter? Why are you both looking at me like that?"

"Pulverized?" Carmella wailed.

"Pulverized?" I echoed.

"Pulverized, that's right. And then..."

"Never mind 'and then'. There's no 'and then' to it. Uncle Harry, do you realize what you've done?"

Harry was starting to look a little bewildered. "Not exactly, no. Perhaps you could explain."

"Harry, you've pulverized the last surviving fragment of Detective Story Number One," I told him. "A priceless handwritten manuscript by Edgar Allan Poe—who, although he never received a six-figure advance, was a writer of no small..."

At that point we were interrupted by the entrance of a surprisingly cheerful-looking Pierce Stormson.

"Prof, it's a complete disaster!" I informed him. "Harry here fed the Poe manuscript into his crazy food blender contraption. He's just told us it's been pulverized!"

Stormson shrugged. "These accidents happen, I suppose."

Carmella looked at him anxiously. "How will we ever explain it to Professor Burlington? He's probably still seething after his visit to the mail room."

"Oh, I think he's calmed down now. In fact he's taking the whole thing very philosophically, all things considered. He was, however, rather taken aback when he first opened the package."

"What package?" I asked, deciding I must have missed something.

"The package marked urgent, that was waiting for him when he got to the mail room."

"But I made that up!" Carmella said. "There never was any package. It was just a ruse to get him out of the room."

"Well, call it a coincidence, then." Stormson perched on the corner of a table, looking very pleased with himself. "The mail room staff were certainly surprised when Burlington showed up, because they hadn't even sent for him yet. But they did indeed have a package for him, which was indeed marked urgent. It must have run you a close race across the Atlantic last night."

"The Atlantic?" I was getting more and more confused. "You mean the package came from America? Who sent it? What was in it?"

"It was sent, as anyone who was paying close attention would guess, by Professor Clarence Nordstrom of the venerable old University of Pennsylvania in Philadelphia. The package contained a photograph and a short message."

"A photograph and a message?" I echoed.

"A photograph of a new display cabinet in the English department at Penn, proudly exhibiting the surviving fragment of Detective Story Number One. The accompanying message read, if my memory serves me correctly: *'With gratitude to Roy Burlington for returning what was taken from Philadelphia to its rightful home. I trust that Oxford will be content to possess the good quality facsimile we made for that fine city'.*"

"Good quality facsimile?" Carmella's face broke into what could almost be described as a smile... a very serious smile, of course. "Uncle Harry—this means you're off the hook! It was only a good quality facsimile that you pulverized."

Harry was the only one who didn't look pleased. "Are you telling me that piece of paper was fabricated a few days ago? What use is that going to be in a paper tape analysis? I want historical material, not something made yesterday."

Carmella patted him on the shoulder. "I'm sure you'll make something up, Uncle Harry—you usually do."

I was busy trying to keep up with events. "So it was just a fake that went missing? You mean the Purloined Poe wasn't purloined at all?"

"Oh, it was purloined all right," Stormson chuckled. It was purloined by Sir William Bitton almost a century ago, from a house in Philadelphia. And now it's safely back in Philadelphia again."

"Great," I said. "Then that's the Case of the Purloined Poe—SOLVED!"

# HOMICIDAL HOMEOPATHY

I stood in the foyer of Casterbridge public library, scrutinizing a large corkboard labelled *LOCAL SERVICES*. I'd got my own local service lined up, but first I wanted to see if I was going to face any competition. Nope—there was nothing in the line I was thinking of. The only thing that came remotely close was a small pink card advertising the services of one *"Jessica Peace-Lily, Clairvoyant and Tarot Reader"*. I pictured an overweight, middle-aged hippie and shook my head. No competition at all.

I carefully pinned up my own card: *Byron Bland, investigator of the paranormal, the unexplained and the generally weird. No job too small, rates negotiable...* followed by my mobile phone number. I stood back for a better view—yes, that looked very professional. All I had to do now was return to my flat and wait for the first phone call.

I speculated on what my first case might be. Perhaps someone would report seeing a UFO, or a ghost, or an out-of-place puma. Or it might be a mysterious crop circle, or a bizarrely mutilated farm animal—you hear about such cases occasionally. Or maybe a sinister religious cult, or a coven of naked witches…

As it turned out, when the call came a few days later, it was none of the above. It was a double murder.

Casterbridge isn't what you'd call a hotbed of crime, and when there's a double murder—or even a single murder—you generally read about it in the newspapers. But the first I heard about this one was when the woman, Mrs Millet, phoned me. I was intrigued, to say the least. I got out a map, found the address I'd been given, and cycled there as fast as I could. It turned out to be one of a row of small Victorian cottages on the outskirts of the town. I propped my bike against the stone wall and knocked on the door.

"Mrs Millet?" I said to the birdlike old lady who opened the door. "I'm Byron Bland, the paranormal investigator."

"Ah, yes, I saw your advertisement in the library. Do come in." She led the way into the small, over-furnished and slightly mouldy-smelling front room. "Would you like some tea? I've just made some." She disappeared into the kitchen.

I sat down on a sofa that had seen better days, and presently she returned carrying the tea and biscuits. "No-one else will listen to me," she said, perching on the chair opposite me. "But it's all too much of a coincidence, really it is."

"Perhaps you'd better start at the beginning," I said, sipping my tea. I sounded just like a professional investigator, I thought.

"Well, it started with my Len—he was the first," Mrs Millet said wistfully. "He was sitting drinking his tea, right where you are now, when suddenly he had this seizure and dropped down dead. A heart attack, old Doctor Warren said, although Len didn't have a history of heart problems or anything. At first the doctor thought it might be poisoning..."

I coughed and splurted out a mouthful of tea, spilling half the remainder in my lap. "Sorry, it went down the wrong way," I croaked, fumbling for a handkerchief.

"... it could have been digitalis poisoning, going by the symptoms, Doc Warren said. But then he had some tests done and they didn't find anything. So the death certificate says heart attack—but I still have my doubts."

"Why?" I asked. "I mean, I assume Len was getting on in years, and..."

"Oh, he was," she said. "But it's the coincidence, you see. A couple of days later exactly the same thing happened to poor Mortimer."

"Mortimer?" I asked.

"My cat. One minute he was lapping up his milk, the next he jumps two feet in the air and lands with his paws sticking up, stiff as anything." She started sobbing. "Len's death I could handle, but I really adored that cat—he meant the world to me."

I nodded sympathetically. "But if the deaths weren't natural, and they weren't simple poisoning—what do you think they were?" I took out my notebook and pencil; I was beginning to see why she'd called in a paranormal investigator.

She dried her eyes on a tissue. "It's that Stanley Badd next door, you mark my words." She made a vague gesture at one of the walls. "He's some kind of mad scientist or inventor or something, always tinkering in that workshop he's got in his back yard."

"Sounds innocent enough to me," I said. "Why do you suspect him?"

"He was always arguing with Len—they never got on with each other. Mind you, my Len never got on with anyone... but Stanley Badd was the worst. They almost came to blows a few weeks ago."

"I guess that's a motive," I nodded, scribbling in my notebook. "But what about Mortimer, the cat?"

"Now that I just can't understand," she said. "He was such a lovable creature. And very territorial—all these gardens round here, Mr Badd's lawn and his flower beds—they were all part of Mortimer's territory."

"Ah, cat shit!" I said, with sudden understanding.

"I beg your pardon?" Mrs Millet looked up, startled.

"Um, I said *I'll catch it*... or him. Or her, or them," I extemporized wildly. "Whatever or whoever was responsible for these dreadful killings—just leave it to me."

I departed from the Millet residence, and went to check out the house next door. It was a similar stone-built cottage, set back slightly from the road. There was a narrow path leading past the house to the back garden, and I could just see the large corrugated iron workshop that Mrs Millet had mentioned. But there was no chance of getting a closer look, at least not in broad daylight—the path was overlooked by several windows in the cottage. But maybe from the field at the back...

I went the long way round and located the high stone wall at the rear of Stanley Badd's garden. After much clambering, I managed to struggle onto the top of the wall—but then a stone came loose, and I tumbled in a heap on the other side. I landed on a pile of refuse sacks, which was fortunate for two reasons. Firstly, because it broke my fall, and secondly, because I'd been intending to look through the suspect's garbage anyway.

One of the bags had a tear in it, and among the chicken bones and banana skins I could see a screwed-up piece of paper. I retrieved it and flattened it out. It was a receipt from an organic health store called Nature's Wayz—with an address in the centre of Casterbridge—and it was clearly made out in the name of Mr Stanley Badd. It was for just one item: *"Digitalis Purpurea 30C, 25 doses, £4.99"*.

Digitalis... the exact same poison that had been mentioned by the doctor who examined the late Len Millet! I punched the air in triumph. I had the case virtually sewn up already!

After scrambling back over the wall, I returned to my bike and pedalled off toward the centre of town. Once there, it took a while to find Nature's Wayz: I finally located the establishment in a small side street, between a charity shop and an internet café. I went in and approached the bored looking woman behind the counter.

"My name's Byron Bland, and I'm a paranormal investigator," I informed her, flashing my Wessex County Library card by way of identification. "I understand you sell digitalis here."

"Yes dear, it's one of our homeopathic remedies," the woman said. "And you're in luck—our part-time homeopath is working here today. You'll find her upstairs in the Treatment Room." I ascended the narrow staircase to the upper floor, where the door to the Treatment Room was standing open. Inside, a diminutive female figure in a white coat was standing at a table, doing something with a rack of small brown bottles.

She had her back to me, but she seemed to sense my presence immediately. She turned and came over to me.

"Can I help you?" She blinked at me through her metal-rimmed glasses. "My name is Jessica Peace-Lily. I'm a homeopath, amongst other things."

Jessica Peace-Lily... the name rang a bell. Of course—she was the one whose card I'd seen at the library: the clairvoyant! She was nothing like the mental image I'd had of her. She wasn't middle-aged—probably in her late twenties, a year or two older than myself. And she wasn't fat—just a little chubby around the hips, perhaps. And she certainly wasn't a hippie. She looked prim and spinsterish, with short mousy coloured hair and—as already mentioned— steel rimmed glasses perched on her pert, upturned nose.

She looked, in other words, just like one of those geeky, smarter-than-thou females that needs to be shown who's boss. I wasted no time in getting to the point. "I'm a paranormal investigator, Miss Peace-Lily, and I have reason to suspect that one of your homoerotic remedies was used in the murder of one Len Millet."

"What?" She looked genuinely horrified.

I told her about my conversation with Mrs Millet, and showed her the receipt I'd found in Stanley Badd's garbage.

"But this wouldn't poison anyone," she said. "Where it says 30C—that means the digitalis has been diluted a hundredfold, thirty times over. So its chemical strength has been reduced by a factor of one hundred to the power of thirty. That's an enormous number—there would be very few digitalis molecules left in the solution, if any."

"A likely story," I sniffed. "Why on Earth would anyone want to do that?"

"Because every time the chemical strength is weakened, the homeopathic potency is increased by the same factor. Homeopathy is for curing ailments, not causing them. It works on the principle of similarity—Like cures Like. If a patient has an illness which exhibits symptoms similar to those of digitalis poisoning, then prescribing a homeopathic form of digitalis can act to alleviate the symptoms."

I said nothing. If she was really clairvoyant, she would pick up the fact that I didn't believe a word she was saying.

"Here, let me show you something." Jessica looked over at a bookcase on the far side of the room... but oddly she made no move towards it. "It's a monograph on the subject of 'Water Memory' by a French scientist called Jacques Benveniste. It gives a full scientific explanation of how homeopathy works."

She frowned slightly, and a thin booklet worked its way loose from the bookshelf and flew across the room into her hands. She passed it to me, but it dropped through my fingers onto the floor.

"Wha...? How did you...? I mean... the book, how did it...?" For the moment, I had lost the ability to form a complete sentence.

"Psychokinesis." Jessica shrugged. "It's one of my talents."

I was impressed, in spite of myself. "You mean you're a mutant? Like in the *X-Men*? You were born with super-powers?"

She shook her head. "Not born with them, no. They have to be developed. There are techniques for such things... from ancient Tibet, you know."

"Techniques? Such as what?"

"Such as meditation and yoga... and the exercises in the *Kama Sutra*."

For a few moments I mulled that over in silence, then I suddenly remembered what sort of exercises the *Kama Sutra* described. Obviously she wasn't as prim and spinsterish as she looked. I endeavoured, with great difficulty, to visualize her doing it.

"You can stop that right now." She glared at me venomously through her glasses and her upturned little nostrils.

I groaned. "You mean you're a mind reader as well?"

"Sometimes," she said.
I was starting to feel distinctly inferior, when I remembered that after all I had the upper hand.

"Never mind all these fancy tricks of yours—the fact remains that Len Millet died, and the prime suspect purchased digitalis from this establishment."

Jessica bit her lip. "You're right," she admitted. "Something very strange is going on here. We're going to have to look into it... and quickly—for the sake of my reputation  if nothing else."

"We can't do anything until after dark," I reminded her. "The answer to all this lies in Stanley Badd's backyard, and that's not a place we're going to get into in broad daylight."

Jessica pondered for a few moments. "I'm giving one of my Aikido classes this evening at St Mary's church hall. It finishes at nine o'clock. Come and meet me then and we'll go on from there to Mr Badd's house."

"You teach Aikido?" The word sounded vaguely familiar. "That's the ancient Japanese art of flower-arranging, isn't it?"

"No—you're thinking of Ikebana. Aikido is a Japanese martial art... for self defence, you know."

"Like kick-boxing, you mean?" I couldn't visualize her doing that, either.

"Um, sort of—you'll see."

I arrived at the church hall a few minutes before nine o'clock. There was a notice on the door: *"Tonight at 7pm: Aikido for Self-Defence with Jessica Peace-Lily, Black Belt Seventh Dan"*. I pushed on the door and went inside.

It wasn't a big class in terms of numbers: just half a dozen students. But they were big students—all young men, and all tough-looking. The shortest of them was a head taller than Jessica, and the largest must have weighed twice what she did. The students were all dressed in white karate-style suits, with belts of various colours. Jessica was dressed in a karate suit too, but hers was black—with a black belt.

As I entered the room, the students appeared to be lining up along one end of the mat ready to charge at Jessica. And that's exactly what they did—one after the other. And one after the other, they went down like ninepins. Some were felled with a high kick, others with a twirl of the arm. In some cases she didn't even seem to make physical contact.

I shrugged my shoulders. So she could knock people down without even touching them... so what? What else would you expect from someone with psychokinetic powers? The students might be impressed by it, but I certainly wasn't.

The class finished a few minutes later, and Jessica came over to me. "Okay, loser—let's do this thing. Lead the way."

"Right you are," I said. I took a step towards the door, then stopped and looked back at her. "What do you mean, loser?"

She didn't say anything.

Under cover of darkness, I sneaked along the path at the side of Stanley Badd's cottage. Jessica, still wearing her black karate suit, followed close behind. We stopped at the door of the corrugated iron workshop.

I examined the door. It was fastened securely with a heavy padlock. "Locked tight," I whispered. "How are we going to get in?"

Jessica stepped forward. She took the padlock in her hand and fixed an intent gaze on it. "Shut up—I need to concentrate."

I shut up. Jessica concentrated. After a few moments, the padlock clicked open.

"Psychokinesis," Jessica explained, "isn't as easy as it looks. Particularly when you're working on something you can't see, like the tumblers inside a lock."

We went inside the workshop and switched on the light. The place was full to overflowing with all kinds of junk. There were several partly dismantled microwave ovens, TV sets of every vintage, and a massive jumble of wires, cables and other oddments. The workbench was dominated by a large coil of wire, surrounded by a mass of apparatus including a computer, an oscilloscope, and numerous metal boxes covered in knobs and dials. A few of the small brown bottles—the kind used for homeopathic chemicals—were scattered about the bench.

"Hmm, I wonder what all this is?" Jessica was studying the apparatus intently.

"Oh, it's just some electronic gizmo," I told her, showing off my superior technical knowledge. Women may be all right when it comes to things like psychokinesis and telepathy and aikido, but they're never any good at science.

"Let's see," Jessica said thoughtfully. "There's a Tesla coil, a high-frequency signal generator, a series of cascaded magnetrons, and a pair of microwave horns. It must be some kind of rudimentary scalar wave projector."

So much for masculine superiority. "Well, yes—of course. That goes without saying." I began to wish I'd learnt to smoke a pipe... I bet she couldn't do that.

"The microwave horns are pointing out through the window," Jessica continued. "The beams converge on the house next door. This must be how he did it, though I don't quite see how homeopathy fits in."

There was a sudden sound behind us, and we turned to see a tall lugubrious figure standing in the doorway. He was dressed in pyjamas and an old bathrobe, and had what appeared to be a large metal saucepan on his head. He was pointing a double-barrelled shotgun at us.

"Stanley Badd?" I presumed.

"The very same," he said. "And I compliment your partner on her shrewd assessment of my little constructional project."

"His *business* partner," Jessica corrected hastily, putting what I felt was an unnecessarily strong emphasis on the word 'business'. Behind her steel-rimmed glasses, a venomous look came into her eyes. "What you're doing here is wicked—using homeopathic remedies to murder the innocent."

"No-one will miss the man or the cat—I was doing the world a service by getting rid of them." Stanley puffed out his chest. "I'm a heroic figure, really. You need to look at the bigger picture. For more than fifty years, scalar waves have been under the exclusive control of the government—the secret weapon they use to keep the people in their place. The government gets inside our minds and makes us do things against our will—unless we take precautions, of course." He tapped the saucepan on his head. "Metal shielding keeps the scalar waves out."

"Like a lunatic's tinfoil helmet," Jessica said.

"That may well be," Stanley sneered. "But I'm no lunatic. I've discovered the secret of scalar waves for myself, and now it's time to get my own back."

Stanley went over to the workbench and sat by the computer console. He was careful to keep the shotgun pointing at us. "It's all a matter of modulation," he continued. "To provoke a physical effect on the human body, you need to modulate the scalar waves with a suitable chemical signature. This is where the homeopathic mixtures come in. Although the chemical is no longer present, its vibrational signature remains in the solution indefinitely—the water memory effect. That's why homeopathy works, and why I was able to project its effects via electromagnetic waves into the house next door."

He booted up the computer and began to type with his left hand, all the time keeping us covered with the gun. "To get more subtle mind-control effects, you can use computer-generated digital modulations. You can make people do anything you want—buy things they don't need, vote for people they don't like, watch mindless drivel on the TV..."
"Can you make people fall in love?" I asked.

"Easiest thing in the world." Stanley waved his hand dismissively. "That was the first program I ever wrote. Anything that breaks down people's better judgment. That's what the government's been doing to us for half a century. In the early years, they were forced to project their mind-control programs from a distance, which of course diluted their effect considerably. What they really needed was some way of persuading their victims to hold a microwave source right up against their skulls. For decades they struggled with the problem— after all, even the ignorant masses weren't *that* stupid. Then finally they hit on the solution. They invented mobile phones, and all over the world people fell straight into their hands."

"Mobile technology is a capitalist plot to make money out of the weak-minded and gullible, through advertising hype and ruthless marketeering," Jessica said solemnly.

"I've got the latest state-of-the-art model," I said, proudly displaying my affordably priced but feature-laden smartphone.

"That proves my point," Jessica said.

"And mine," Stanley nodded vigorously. Then he lapsed into silence, continuing with his one-handed typing for several minutes.

I couldn't stand the suspense. "Are you going to kill us, too?" I asked.

"Oh, good heavens, no." Stanley looked horrified at the thought. "You haven't done me any harm. Not like that old bugger next door—him and that damned cat of his. No, I'm just going to play around with your minds a bit, to make sure you no longer pose a threat to me."

"You'll never get away with this," I told him. "You don't know who you're dealing with. My mild-mannered assistant here is a telepathic super-powered master of the martial arts. She's going to make mincemeat out of you the second you drop your guard."

"I doubt it." Stanley turned his lugubrious gaze on me. "Take a look at her."

I glanced at Jessica, then did a double-take. She was looking back at me with what can only be described as a blissfully dumb expression. Her glasses had slipped down her nose and were lying crookedly across her face. She stuck her tongue out at me and giggled.

"What have you done to her?" I asked, horrified.

"Oh, nothing to worry about," Stanley said breezily. "It's simply that the room is now thoroughly irradiated with scalar waves. I'm using a standard government-issue dumbing-down program. It drastically reduces attention span, reasoning power and other higher brain functions."

For a few minutes I mulled over this explanation in silence. Then I thought of something. "If that's the case, why is the program only affecting her—and not you or me?"

"As I explained earlier, I've taken precautions for my own protection." Stanley tapped the saucepan on his head. "As for yourself... well, the program works its way down the IQ scale. Your friend here obviously has a higher IQ than you do, which is why it's taken effect on her first. But never fear—it will catch up with you eventually."

Stanley rose to his feet, and crossed over to a battered metal cupboard at the far end of the workshop. He kept his eyes and the shotgun firmly on myself as he started to rummage around inside the cupboard.

"I'm going to leave the two of you here for the rest of the night," he explained. "By morning the program should have run to completion. It will then be safe for me to let you go."

Stanley came over with several pieces of rope, and proceeded to tie up our wrists and ankles. When he was sure we were both thoroughly bound, he went out and closed the door behind him. Once again we were alone in the workshop.

Everything depended on me, I realized. Jessica was completely out of it, and it was probably only a matter of minutes before Stanley's dumbing-down program clicked down to my IQ and finally took its effect on me. I started to think frantically.

I was still thinking frantically several hours later when the sun came up. It seemed that for some reason I was immune to the dumbing-down program. But even after racking my brains for all that time, I hadn't been able to come up with a way out. Stanley had left me with my mobile phone, but I couldn't reach it because my hands were tied behind my back. If Jessica had been her normal self, she could have used psychokinesis to loosen the ropes... but as it was she just sat there with a foolish grin on her face, humming inanely.

After a while Stanley reappeared. You can say what you like about my IQ (or lack of it), but at least I had the brains to pretend the program had worked. I adopted the same blissfully dumb expression as Jessica.

Stanley untied me, and then moved over to Jessica. The moment his back was turned I jumped up, whipped the saucepan off his head and hit him with it as hard as I could. He fell to his knees, dazed. I quickly tied him up with the ropes he'd used on me, then finished untying Jessica. Now came the tricky part—how was I going to get her back to normal?

I went over to Stanley's computer and looked at the screen. The cursor was flashing against a button labelled *"Dumbing down"*. Next to it there was another button labelled *"Undo"*. I moved the cursor onto it, but just as I was about to click on it, I hesitated. I was thinking about something Stanley had said earlier.

Carefully, I scrolled up to the top of the list. Sure enough, the first button was labelled *"Fall in love"*. Triumphantly I placed the cursor over it. Then I paused. Perhaps I ought to think this through. Did I really want to get involved with a mind-reading, kick-boxing, *Kama Sutra* specialist? I shook my head, and moved the cursor back down the list. With some relief, I clicked the button to undo the dumbing-down program.

A few minutes later Jessica blinked, straightened her glasses, and glared at me. "About time too, dipstick," she said.

My jaw dropped. "What do you mean?"

"My higher brain functions may have been scrambled, but that doesn't mean I was oblivious to what was going on," she explained. "It's just that I was powerless to do anything about it. As indeed were you, although the machine had nothing to do with that."

She came over and looked at the computer screen. "Now, what are we going to do with Mr Badd here?" She took control of the mouse, scrolling up and down the list. "Ah, this looks just the thing." She clicked on a button labelled *"Tell the truth, the whole truth, and nothing but the truth"*.

"I was just about to suggest that myself." I spoke quickly, to get the words out before the truth program took effect. "What do we do now?"

"Now we make an anonymous call to the police. By the time they get here we'll be gone, and Stanley will be just about ready to make a full confession."

"Good thinking," I said. I took out my mobile phone and held it out to her. "Do you want to borrow this?"

Jessica shuddered. "No—you make the call. I don't want to touch that thing."

"Why not?" I asked. "Because mobile phones are a capitalist plot to extract money from gullible people? Or because they're a government-controlled mind-control device?"

"Because it's your phone, and I'm sure that if I touched it I'd catch some dreadful disease off it."

# THE MYSTIC FAYRE AFFAIR

I opened the vestry door and poked my head in. "Oops, sorry." I covered my eyes. The large, buxom woman inside was dressed in green paint and very little else.

She glanced round at me. "Hi there, sonny. The blessings of the Goddess be upon you." She was adjusting what little there was of her costume. It consisted of an under-engineered leather thong, in a matching shade of green.

I looked at my clipboard. "Ms Shakti O'Shaughnessy? You're doing the 'Dance of Nature' piece? You're on in five minutes. The Peruvian Feng Shui people are just winding up their demonstration."

I shut the door and breathed a sigh of relief. The things a struggling student has to endure just to earn a bit of extra cash at weekends! I shuddered again at the thought of all that Rubensesque green flesh.

In its heyday, All Souls—which lies on the edge of Clifton Down in Bristol—had been a dignified church of the High Victorian Gothic variety. But it was deconsecrated in the 1990s, and soon transformed into a trendy New Age venue. A typical month saw an eclectic mixture of classes, workshops, meetings and events, all organized by a rather oily individual named Barry Axon. Barry was a connoisseur of cheap student labour—hence my involvement in the enterprise. At this particular Mystic Fayre, I was gopher-in-chief. It was my job to look after the various speakers and performers, and make sure they had everything they needed.

At the east end of the church, where the altar used to be, there was a raised wooden stage. Fifty chairs had been laid out in front of it, but less than half of them were occupied at any one time. The punters seemed more interested in the Mystic Fayre's commercial attractions, which were to be found in what used to be the nave of the church.

The punters were, in my opinion, entirely justified in their preferences. From what I'd seen of the stage performances, they were uniformly dire. I glanced at my watch, then consulted the schedule. I wasn't likely to be needed again for another half hour. I could afford to wander round and sample the attractions of the nave.

The north aisle was occupied by stalls selling everything from relaxing CDs and inspirational books to kaftans, crystals and incense. The south aisle was given over to a range of 'taster' demonstrations: Tarot readings, Indian head massage, aromatherapy. I had a good leisurely look round... taking care, of course, to keep my meagre supply of cash firmly in my pocket.

I stopped in front of one of the demonstration stands. 'Try our unique Sensory Deprivation Chamber!' I read. 'A ten minute mystical experience you'll never forget! Special price £5, today only!'

I watched as a rather nervous young man eased himself into the heavily padded interior of a coffin-like contraption made of white fibreglass. The operator carefully placed blacked-out goggles over his victim's eyes, followed by heavy duty ear defenders. Then he closed the lid. I looked at my watch—it was time I was getting back to my post. I left the punter to his mystical experience.

I crossed the nave, passed through a stone archway into the north transept and headed over towards the vestry in the corner. Before I could reach it, however, the vestry door was flung open and a flustered-looking individual burst out: a tall gentleman—in his sixties, I judged— with wayward hair and a tweed jacket. He cast about madly, saw me approaching with my clipboard, and hurried over to me.

"Are you in charge here? Look, there's been a theft... a very valuable item. Priceless, in fact." He looked around wildly. "Where's Miranda? She's at the bottom of all this."

I blinked at him. "I beg your pardon? What is it that's gone missing, exactly? I'm sure there must be a simple explanation."

"There's a simple explanation, all right. That demented little bluestocking Miranda Perks is trying to get one up on me, that's what's happened. She's gone and walked off with the Celestial Green Phallus of Poontang!"

"The Celestial Green what?" I wasn't sure I'd heard correctly.

"Phallus, man... phallus! The Celestial Green Phallus of Poontang. It's a... well, it's green, and it's about twelve inches long." He gestured vaguely. "But it's priceless... utterly priceless. And it's very fragile and delicate. Made of the finest porcelain of the Ming dynasty. It belongs to the department of Ethnography here in Bristol. You can't imagine the trouble I had to go through, just to get it out on loan for the weekend. It was going to be the star exhibit in my talk."

"Your talk?" I felt the conversation was finally getting somewhere.

"My talk on the Masculine Cross." He puffed out his chest. "I'm the Number One world authority on the subject—I've been studying it for more than thirty years. But my reputation will be ruined... ruined... if I don't get the Celestial Green Phallus back in one piece."

I raised my clipboard and ran a finger down the schedule. "Masculine Cross... ah, yes—I see. You must be Cyril Prendergast. But I'm afraid I still don't understand. What do you need the phallus for, if your talk is on the subject of a masculine cross?"

Cyril rolled his eyes. "Oh, the ignorance of the young! 'Masculine Cross' is an another term for phallus, my dear boy... a very ancient term. It's the one true archetypal symbol... the foundation of all human civilization—all the great world religions, all true art, all forms of architecture. The whole world is ruled by the phallus."

Before I could answer, a loud noise diverted my attention towards the stage. Shakti O'Shaughnessy—still in green body-paint, and now with a large third eye drawn on her forehead—was in the middle of what I assume was meant to be an ancient Indo-Celtic ritual of some kind. She had just struck a large gong, and was now performing a yogic style obeisance in front of a green-draped altar.

I tore my attention from the stage and turned back to Cyril. "Look, we need to think this through methodically. Are you quite certain the Celestial Phallus was here in the first place? When was the last time you saw it?"

"Of course it was here!" He ran a hand through his unruly white hair. "I brought it in myself yesterday evening, and placed it in the secure cabinet in the vestry. I watched Mr Axon lock it up a few minutes later. He gave me a key."

"But there are other keys as well," I pointed out. "People have been using the cabinet all morning... the other speakers, and even some of the stallholders."

Cyril was nodding furiously. "Absolutely—that's what I've been saying all along. Miranda Perks has a key... she's one of the other speakers. She's taken the Celestial Phallus to sabotage my talk."

I looked down the list of speakers. "Ah, yes... Miranda Perks. She's speaking this afternoon— her talk's called 'The Cave of Venus'."

"I'm sure it is. Miranda has this misguided notion that worship of the female genitalia lies at the heart of all human civilization. It's irrational nonsense, of course. She sees all the evidence of phallic worship, and wilfully misinterprets it." Cyril shook his head sadly. "And now, as if that wasn't enough, she's taken my star exhibit and vanished into thin air."

I tried to calm him down. "I'm sure you're jumping to conclusions. Miranda may not even be here yet... her talk isn't for another three hours. There's probably a perfectly innocent explanation. Maybe one of the stallholders picked up the phallus by mistake, and it's got mixed up with their stock."

Cyril didn't need a second prompt. He set off briskly in the direction of the stalls in the north aisle. I followed close behind.

The first few stalls were laden with books, CDs, Tarot packs and inspirational calendars. Cyril didn't give them a second glance. He homed straight in on a stall selling an impressive array of decorative items: Buddhas, Celtic crosses, crystal balls, Egyptian scarabs. He knelt down and started rummaging through the cardboard boxes under the table.

I grinned sheepishly at the vendor—a young man sporting an emo-style fringe, a nose stud and a tight black nylon vest.

"Can I help in any way?" he asked.

"We're looking for a phallus, about a foot long," I informed him.

"Aren't we all?" He flicked the hair out of his eyes. "I don't think I've got anything quite like that."

Cyril stood up. "Come on, it's not here." He dragged me on towards the next vendor.

"Hope you find what you're looking for," the stallholder called after us. "Remember to leave a bit for me!"

Several hectic minutes later we'd finished our search of the north aisle, with no success. We crossed the nave of the church—passing under the great west window, with its stained glass depiction of the Last Judgment—to the south aisle. Maybe the phallus had got mixed up in the eclectic jumble of displays and demonstrations spread out there.

After minutes of fruitless search, we came to the 'Sensory Deprivation' stand. The operator was just releasing another of his victims. He clicked open the coffin lid, and a rather dazed-looking figure staggered out of it: a short, mousy-haired woman of thirty-something, dressed in a smart blue trouser-suit. As soon as the goggles and ear-defenders were removed, she plopped a pair of wire-rimmed glasses on her small nose and peered around.

"Miranda—it's you!" Cyril confronted the woman belligerently. "What have you done with my phallus?"

She blinked at him uncomprehendingly. "I haven't done anything with your phallus." She glanced briefly down at his crotch, then wrinkled her nose. "I'm sure I wouldn't want to."

"You know perfectly well what I'm talking about... the Celestial Green Phallus of Poontang. What have you done with it?"

A flicker of understanding appeared in her eyes. "Green? A little thing, about so big?" She indicated an approximate length of twelve inches with her hands.

"That's it! Now tell me where you've hidden it!"

"I haven't hidden it anywhere." Miranda straightened her glasses. "The Irish Priestess has got it. She was in a state this morning because she'd forgotten one of her props—an essential part of her sacred ritual. I found that thing in the cabinet, and asked if it would do as a substitute. She was very grateful. The shape and colour were exactly right, she said... and it seemed to be sturdy enough for her purposes."

By this point Cyril was no longer listening. He had rushed off madly in the direction of the stage. Miranda blinked after him with a 'What did I say?' expression on her face.

I looked at her. "Sturdy enough? Miranda—that 'thing', as you call it, is made of the finest Chinese porcelain! It dates from the Ming dynasty. It's a museum piece... it must be worth a fortune!"

She put her hand to her mouth in horror, then sprang into action. She ran full tilt after Cyril. I followed close on her heels.

The three of us arrived in front of the stage at pretty much the same time. It was obvious even to our uninitiated eyes that Shakti O'Shaughnessy's Dance of Nature was rapidly approaching its climax. She was gyrating her massive, green-painted hips in a wild frenzy of pagan energy. As she did so, she was inching closer and closer to her makeshift altar. Suddenly, with a grand flourish, she whipped away the altar's green cloth covering... to reveal the object standing proudly erect beneath it. A distinctly green object, about twelve inches in length—

"Is that...?" I began.

"The Celestial Green Phallus of Poontang!" Cyril virtually wailed in anguish. He looked on impotently, pulling at his hair.

The sudden commotion was enough to wake up the audience. They leaned forward in their seats expectantly.

On the stage, Shakti picked up the phallus—none too gently, I might add—and jammed it into the front of her leather thong. She began a series of disturbingly violent thrusts with her pelvis.

As I watched open-mouthed, the inevitable happened. The phallus worked its way loose and launched itself into a ballistic trajectory across the stage.

Before I could grasp what was happening, Miranda bounded into action. She leapt up onto the stage, did a quick combat roll, and deftly caught the phallus as it tumbled in mid-air. A fraction of a second later and it would have smashed to pieces on the floor of the stage.

The audience burst into spontaneous applause. Shakti looked bewildered for a moment, then appeared to decide it was a good enough ending for her performance—even if it hadn't been in strict accordance with the ancient Indo-Celtic tradition. She bowed graciously.

Miranda rolled off the stage and held out the phallus to Cyril. "This is yours, I believe?" She wrinkled her nose in disgust. "That's the first time I've ever had to handle one of these things... and I hope it's the last!"

# MISS PERCEPTION
## A Comedy of Errors in Five Acts

## - 1 -

### A is for Android

Georgina was travelling on the Circle Line from Paddington to Euston Square on her way to work. She glanced around suspiciously at her fellow commuters, probing their minds carefully. In a city teeming with perverts, space aliens and foreign spies, she couldn't afford to let her guard down for a moment.

Georgina was an android—a synthetically created replica of a human being. To all external appearances, she was a perfectly normal Earth female in her early twenties: dark-haired, short in stature, and perhaps slightly on the chubby side. But inside she was different. She had a vastly superior intellect, and extrasensory powers. She heard voices in her head telling her what to do.

### B is for Bookstore

Georgina worked in a large bookstore in the Bloomsbury area of London. Her favourite department was SCI-FI AND FANTASY, but today they had put her in RELIGION AND SPIRITUALITY. It was a good thing they had, too—because something very odd was going on over by the shelf labelled 'Bibles'. Georgina observed the proceedings carefully.

### C is for Conspiracy

A tall black man had been standing there for several minutes, scrutinizing one bible in particular. Then he put the book back on the shelf and headed for the door, without purchasing anything. On the way out, he met another tall black man, and a brief whisper passed between the two. They exchanged a strange kind of handshake. Georgina knew instantly what it meant: they were members of the sinister organization known as the Illuminati!

The second black man sauntered up to the bible shelf, scanned his eyes along it, and picked up the same bible that the first man had been looking at. Then he came over to Georgina's till.

*D is for Detective work*

The voices in Georgina's head told her what to do. When the man presented his credit card, Georgina frowned and told him she needed another form of ID—one with the man's address on it. The tall, sullen-looking man fumbled in his coat pocket and, rather reluctantly, showed her an envelope that was addressed to him: *D. Blake Esq., Flat 359, Cavendish Towers, Islington.* The transaction was completed, and the man left with his newly purchased bible.

In her lunch break, Georgina took the tube and headed for Flat 359, Cavendish Towers, Islington.

*E is for Encounter*

She knocked on the door. It was opened by the tall, sullen-looking black man—whose name she now knew to be D. Blake Esq. He looked distinctly surprised to see her—horrified, almost. *As well he might*, she thought. *Illuminati scum!* Brushing his objections aside, she pushed her way into his flat. He glanced both ways along the corridor, then closed the door and faced her.

The voices instructed Georgina to get a DNA sample, and told her how to go about it. She took out a condom. "Unzip your trousers and put this on," she told him. Looking bewildered at first, then strangely relieved, the black man did so. She knelt down in front of him and carefully extracted the necessary sample.

*F is for Fantasy Role Play*

The girl left, and Darius Blake breathed a sigh of relief. When the bookstore assistant had turned up on his doorstep, he'd really thought the game was up. He'd never liked the trick with the hollowed-out, substitute bible—it had been a crazy idea all along. There were easier ways of transferring five hundred grams of pharmaceutical grade heroin. But they hadn't been rumbled, after all. The crazy white bitch just wanted some quick kicks with a black dude—some weird kind of fantasy role play.

- 2 -

*G is for Going undercover*

Georgina was back at her flat near Paddington station. She took out the condom containing the Illuminati's DNA sample, and put it to one side for later analysis. There was more urgent work to do first. Skilfully, she put on one of her disguises—blonde wig, heavy make-up, short skirt and thigh-high boots. She looked just like one of the many streetwalkers who frequented this part of the city after dark!

### H is for Hotel

The Regal Hotel was located directly opposite the block of flats where Georgina lived. It was a strange kind of hotel, which charged an hourly rate for rooms, not a nightly rate. It was used almost exclusively by young ladies of the night, who took their clients there. Her disguise stood her in good stead: the desk clerk didn't bat an eyelid when she requested an hour's stay in room sixteen.

Georgina always took room sixteen, and with good reason. Months ago, she had discovered— behind the broken television—a small peephole into room fifteen next door. And some strange things went on in room fifteen... some very strange things.

### I is for Incubus

As she peered through the tiny hole, Georgina saw a street girl enter room fifteen with a client in tow. The girl was a petite, brown-skinned oriental—a Thai, Georgina guessed. The client was also a woman—a successful businesswoman by the look of her, dressed in expensive-looking clothes.

Prostitute and client proceeded to undress. And then came the surprise... although it wasn't a surprise to Georgina, because she had seen it before. The client-woman was a real woman, but the prostitute-woman was a counterfeit. She possessed a male generative organ. She slipped on a condom, and proceeded to copulate with her businesswoman client.

*An incubus!* a voice in Georgina's head informed her. *A sinister species of extraterrestrial— one that adopts human form in order to mate with unsuspecting Earth-women!*

### J is for Justified

As soon as the incubus and its client had left, Georgina crept around to room fifteen. She pushed open the unlocked door and darted inside to retrieve the discarded condom, with its precious sample of incubus-DNA. Then she headed for the stairs. Her hour's stay in the Regal Hotel had been justified indeed!

### K is for Katoey

Bo-Bo smiled with satisfaction as he examined the wad of banknotes the punter had given him. Bo-Bo was a Katoey—commonly but inaccurately translated    as 'lady-boy'. Biologically, he was one-hundred-percent male. But a few years ago, in his native Thailand, he had taken a course of hormone treatment that had left him with certain superficial female characteristics.

Then he had come over to London—where people such as himself could earn thousands of pounds in a single night.

## - 3 -

### *L is for Laboratory*

Georgina was back in her own flat. It contained a small but well-equipped chemical laboratory. She quickly got to work analysing the pair of DNA samples she had collected—the first from a member of the Illuminati, the second from an Incubus-alien.

### *M is for Memorandum*

```
(1) Illuminati suspect. I followed the suspect
to its hideout and obtained a D.N.A. sample by
subterfuge. Analysis of D.N.A. indicates
beyond any possibility of doubt that suspect
is of extraterrestrial origin.
(2) Incubus suspect. I observed the suspect
mating with an Earth woman. I then secured the
D.N.A. sample produced during this mating.
Analysis of D.N.A. indicates beyond any shadow
of doubt that suspect is of extraterrestrial
origin.
```

### *N is for Neighbourhood Watch*

The night was now well advanced. Georgina was sitting at her window, observing the rear elevation of the Regal Hotel through powerful binoculars. The top floor windows were all brightly illuminated, and uncurtained. The goings-on inside were clearly visible... and they were very strange goings-on indeed.

### *O is for Outer Space*

Georgina had seen aliens before, of course—but she only knew they were aliens because the voices in her head told her they were. All the aliens she had encountered so far looked exactly like Earth people. But these aliens, on the top floor of the Regal Hotel... they really looked like aliens! They had big grey heads, large eyes and no visible noses. There was only one human-looking person present: a fat, bald, middle-aged man who seemed to be telling the aliens what to do.

It was all very weird. She would have to get back into her streetwalker disguise and investigate this at close quarters.

### *P is for Pornography*

The rooms on the top floor of the Regal Hotel were no longer available to the public. The rooms, in fact, were no longer rooms—just a single big room. The dividing walls had been knocked down two years ago. The top floor of the hotel was now a film studio: the home of W2BLUE Productions Unlimited. Harvey Stone—fat, bald and middle-aged—was the owner, executive producer, cameraman and sound recordist of W2BLUE... as well as being the manager of the Regal Hotel.

At the moment, Harvey Stone was fuming. His latest epic, *Space Thrusters*, was behind schedule. The three young studs were all here—dressed in their grey alien heads and little else. The cameras, lights and microphones were all in place. But he was missing one leading lady. The actress who played the Earth girl hadn't turned up for the big final scene! Harvey had half a mind to grab the first street girl he saw and give her the starring role instead.

## - 4 -

### *Q is for Quest*

Georgina, dressed once more as a Lady of the Night, made her way to the Regal Hotel. She anticipated some difficulty in gaining admittance to the top floor, and the negative attitude of the desk clerk when she made the request did nothing to encourage her. But when he phoned upstairs, his manner changed completely. "The boss says go on up—he says you just saved his life."

### *R is for Reptoids*

Georgina entered the brightly lit room on the top floor of the hotel. The room contained three reptoid aliens, plus the fat, middle-aged man she had seen through the window. He introduced himself as Harvey. Strangely, he seemed to be in charge—constantly telling the reptoids what to do. *A dirty alien collaborator*, Georgina thought to herself. *But he doesn't know I'm an android, and that I've infiltrated his little conspiracy. I'll turn the tables on him yet!*

### *S is for Surgical Procedure*

Georgina watched as one of the three reptoids was instructed to lie on its back on a stainless steel examination table. The alien was naked, and in an obvious state of arousal. Harvey turned his attention to her. "Take off your clothes and straddle Marcus," he instructed her. "Then grab hold of the two other lads, one in each hand."

It was obvious to Georgina what all this was leading up to. They were intending to perform some strange kind of surgical procedure on her.

### *T is for Teleportation*

A warning voice screamed inside Georgina's head. *"Don't let it happen! If they inject their DNA into you, all will be lost!"* She decided it was time for an emergency teleportation.

Georgina teleported out of the room.

*U is for Unhinged*

"Talk about primadonnas!" Harvey groaned, attempting to pull out what remained of his hair. "One minute she's up for it, the next minute she scarpers like a cat out of hell. That girl is seriously unhinged!"

## - 5 -

*V is for Voices*

The next day was a Saturday. There was a big Mind-Body-Spirit festival in South Kensington, and the voices told Georgina to go to it. So she did.

*W is for Workshop*

Georgina walked around the crowded hall, studying the displays carefully. There were demonstrations of acupuncture, yoga and hypnotherapy; and stalls selling incense, crystals and Tarot cards. Georgina was suspicious of everything and everybody.

She spotted a small side room, with a notice outside saying: *WORKSHOP ON ZEN BUDDHISM, presented by the Venerable Ryogaku.* The voices told her to go inside.

*X is for Xenocrat*

Inside the room, a small audience—perhaps half a dozen people—sat facing a tall figure on a raised platform. It was this figure that instantly grabbed Georgina's attention. It was a tall, elderly, oriental man, dressed in a long black robe. He had a shaven head, a small, pointed beard, and green, cat-like eyes. She recognized him immediately. He might call himself the Venerable Ryogaku, but in truth he was none other than the insidious Doctor Fu Manchu! Fu Manchu—the sworn enemy of the Western world, who was slowly but surely taking over the whole planet through sinister mind control!

*Y is for Yellow Peril*

Fu Manchu stopped speaking: he was evidently in the middle of a lecture of some kind. He looked straight at Georgina, and said "Young lady—you have just joined us. Your mind will be clear of preconceptions. Let me ask you a few questions."

Her heart pounded. She knew they would be trick questions, designed to subvert her will to his. She decided she wouldn't even listen to the questions—just say the first thing that came into her head. When asked "Why did Bodhidharma travel East?" she replied "My bottom is itching." When asked "What is the sound of one hand clapping?" she replied "I am a soulless android." When asked "Does a dog have the Buddha-nature?" she didn't reply at all—she had teleported out of there.

*Z is for Zen Buddhism*

A broad smile spread across the Venerable Ryogaku's face. That young lady had the true spirit of Zen! Rarely had he encountered anyone with such laudable detachment from the everyday world. Why, it had taken him thirty years in a Buddhist monastery to achieve such enlightenment!

# THE MYTHOLOGIST

I think I'd seen the fellow lurking around the college grounds a few times before. I'd always had the feeling he'd been staring in my direction, but then he'd look away just as I turned toward him. I didn't give it much thought—I guess I'm something of a local celebrity now, and I've become accustomed to little things like this. But then one day he strode right up to me as I was crossing the quad on the way to my rooms.

"Doctor Raphson!" he exclaimed. "I need to speak to you. Do you think you could spare me a few minutes of your time?" He was red-faced and out of breath, clutching a briefcase in one hand and a dog-eared paperback book in the other.

The fellow looked harmless enough—he had the manner of a lifelong academic—but on this occasion I was in a hurry to correct some proofs and return them to the printers. "I'm afraid you've caught me at a bad moment," I said. "Perhaps we could arrange to meet later on?" I reached into my jacket pocket for my diary.

"It's about your time machine," he said. "I know all about it."

I put my diary away. I'd read the man wrong—he was obviously a crank. I excused myself and tried to move on, but he blocked my way.

"It's all in here," he said, waving the book in my face. I recognized it, of course—it was my own *Escape from Ragnarok*. The second paperback edition, published a couple of years ago. But the book was about space travel, not time travel. I made a second attempt to get past him, and then a sudden thought flashed into my head. It was only a tiny possibility, but if I was right it was something that called for immediate action. I had to put a stop to this before it got out of hand.

"Very well," I said. "Come up to my rooms and we'll talk there. But we'll have to make it brief."

As we walked through the cloisters and ascended the stone staircase, he introduced himself. His name was Charles Horndyke, and he was a lecturer in Mediaeval Literature here in

Oxford. He belonged to one of the newer colleges of the university—"nowhere near as prestigious as your college," Horndyke had said regretfully. He was old and grey-haired—pretty close to retirement, I judged.

Once inside my rooms, I ushered him into one of the well-worn but comfortable leather armchairs the college had provided me with. After a few moments in the kitchen I provided him with a mug of coffee. "Now, what's all this nonsense about a time machine?" I asked.

"It isn't nonsense, as you well know." Horndyke's eyes roamed over the oak panelling and gilt-framed pictures with unconcealed envy. "To the outside world, Clayton Raphson is simply a charismatic space scientist with a talent for writing money-spinning popularizations. But I've discovered your secret—I know you've invented a time machine. It allows you to alter the course of history." He leaned forward confidentially. "You choose to keep your invention secret. Very well—I'll respect that secrecy, so long as you grant me use of your time machine for my own purposes."

By this time I'd got a fair idea what was on Horndyke's mind, but I feigned incredulity all the same. "You're out of your mind," I told him. "As far as I know, time travel is an impossibility. Certainly I don't have a time machine, and I don't know anyone who has. Wherever did you get this ridiculous idea?"

"From this book." Horndyke tapped his battered copy of *Escape from Ragnarok*. "On the surface, it's an impassioned plea in favour of interstellar colonization. You say it's the next logical step in human evolution—and essential if the species is to survive in the long term. That's a favorite theme of yours, of course, and I'm not doubting your sincerity. But to support your case you quote the old Norse legend of Thor and the Rettungs—and this is what proves to me that you must have a time machine."

I shrugged. "All it proves is that I'm an amateur mythologist," I said. "I study myths in my spare time. I came across that particular legend, and its imagery suited my theme perfectly. I even used it in the book's title—*Escape from Ragnarok*."

"Mythologist, indeed!" Horndyke snorted. "I've studied mythology all my life—it's my job. The Norse pantheon is my speciality. Perhaps that's why I've seen through you when no-one else has. This legend of yours—the legend of Thor and the Rettungs—there's something very odd about it. Something very odd indeed."

"Really? I would have thought it was simple enough," I said. "Shortly before Ragnarok—the long-prophesied end of all things—the god Thor takes pity on a particular group of humans. This is the clan known as the Rettungs, a wise and peaceful people. To ensure that the Rettungs are saved when the rest of Earth is destroyed, Thor builds a great ship for them and sends them off to the stars to begin a new life. A charming little tale—what's odd about that?"
"Many things," Horndyke said. "To start with, it just doesn't fit in with the rest of the Scandinavian mythos. It's an upbeat, moralistic story in what is otherwise a bleak and desolate literature. And it's hopelessly anachronistic. The idea that inhabitable worlds might exist

around other stars is a post-Copernican development—a thing of the fifteenth or sixteenth centuries at the earliest. The Norse legends go back a thousand years before that." The grey-haired man shifted uncomfortably. "But strangest of all is the fact that I'd never heard of the Rettungs until I read your book."

I smiled. "You have to admit the legend matches my theme perfectly," I said. "If it didn't exist, I would have had to invent it. Maybe that's what I did—maybe I made the whole thing up."

"I think that's exactly what you did." Horndyke nodded vigorously. "And that would be no big deal in itself, except for one thing. You must have invented the myth in the past as well as in the present. I've been doing some research, you see, and the legend of Thor and the Rettungs turns up in a number of old sources."

I waited while Horndyke extracted various books and papers from his briefcase. He set them out neatly on the coffee table.

"Imagine my surprise when I discovered an account of the legend here, in Thomas Bulfinch's *The Age of Fable*, written in 1855." Horndyke tapped one of the books in front of him. It was a recent paperback reprinting of Bulfinch's classic. "I first read Bulfinch as a child," Horndyke went on. "I'm certain there was nothing about the Rettungs in it then. And it's not just Bulfinch—the legend appears, in a slightly altered form, in Jacob Grimm's *Deutsche Mythologie* of 1835 and many other places. I traced it back to four lines in the *Voluspa* of the Elder Edda, first written down in Iceland in the thirteenth century and based on an oral tradition dating from many centuries before that."

Horndyke passed a sheet of paper to me. On it were four lines of verse:

> *Into space the great ship soars*
> *And speeds away from Earth;*
> *Forewarned by mighty Thor*
> *The Rettungs to their star-home flee.*

"That's from the popular translation by Auden and Taylor," Horndyke said. "Something very similar appears in the classic version by Henry Adams Bellows from 1936, and in Simrock's German edition of 1831. And going further back..."

"I get the picture," I said, cutting him short. "You think I invented the legend to fit my message, and then somehow went back in time to alter the historical records to agree with my version."

"So you admit it!" Horndyke said. "Now, if you'd be so good as to explain your time machine to me. I believe I have a use for it."

I held up my hands. "Slow down a moment," I said. "I'm not admitting anything. The sources you consulted—were they all recent editions? Or digitized versions? This printout from the Edda looks like it came from the internet archive."

Horndyke slumped visibly. "Most of my research was online, or using relatively recent reprints," he admitted. "But not all—I consulted some older books in the Bodleian library."

"But I also have access to the Bodleian," I pointed out. I looked at Horndyke—he seemed to be totally deflated. I felt a pang of sympathy for the fellow. "You said you had a use for a time machine. What would that be?"

Horndyke looked up. "I retire next year," he said. "My career has been adequate but not spectacular. Along the way I've made a number of decisions—perhaps not always the right ones. There was one occasion in particular—almost fifty years ago now—when I feel sure that I took a wrong turning. If only I could go back and change the past—just that one little thing..." He tailed off. There was hint of moistness in his eyes.

The man was an interesting case, that much was certain. To be so dogged in one's beliefs—even to the point of carrying the burden of a young man's mistake through all his adult life. It was going to be difficult to cut through all that and explain what was, after all, a pretty mundane truth. "Let's see," I said. "Do you ever have cause to visit the University's central administration offices in Wellington Square?"

"Occasionally," Horndyke said. "What of it?"

"There's a quotation pinned to the noticeboard there," I said. "Attributed to one Petronius Arbiter. It goes something like this: *'I was to learn later in life that we tend to meet any new situation by reorganizing, and a wonderful method it can be for creating the illusion of progress while producing confusion, inefficiency and demoralization.'* Does that ring any bells?"

"I believe I've seen it—not just there but in other places as well," Horndyke said. "It's quite a common quotation—it sums up the timeless fatuousness of bureaucracy. What are you getting at?"

"The quotation is a hoax," I said. "It's true that a man named Petronius Arbiter really did exist—he was a satirist in the Roman empire at the time of Nero. A lot of his writings have survived, but that simply isn't one of them. The quotation was invented—probably not even as a deliberate hoax—by someone trying to make a point back in the 1940s or 50s. The precise origin is obscure, but it's almost certain that the quotation didn't exist prior to that date. Yet as soon as it appeared it struck a chord in the world's collective consciousness. It cropped up more and more frequently, until now it's everywhere. Wherever there's gratuitous bureaucracy, you'll find that quotation pinned up on a noticeboard."

Horndyke looked doubtful. "Maybe it's a hoax and maybe it isn't," he said. "But what's this got to do with your time machine? You're changing the subject."

"I'm trying to make a point by analogy," I said patiently. "The significance of the Petronius quote is not that it's a hoax, but the astonishing—almost religious—fervour with which people are prepared to defend its authenticity. These are people who know little or nothing about the Roman empire, let alone the works of Petronius Arbiter. Yet they object vehemently to anyone who suggests the quotation is anything but genuine. These people are confusing the truth—factual truth, with a lower case 't'—with Truth—deep, inner Truth, with a capital 'T'. They intuitively recognize the inner Truth of the quotation, and that's enough for them. It's True, even if it never happened."

Horndyke looked thoughtful. "That's an interesting notion," he conceded. "But I still don't see the connection. What does this have to do with your fabrication of the Rettung legend?"

"It's the same thing exactly," I said. "Tell me, what do your colleagues say about the legend of Thor and the Rettungs?"

Horndyke's eyes narrowed. "The idiots say the legend has always existed," he said. "They write about it in their own books and articles. They like the story—they believe it. Fools... all of them."

I sat back. "I think I've proved my case," I said.

"You haven't," Horndyke said. "By your own admission, the Petronius quote can't be traced back before the middle of the twentieth century. I've traced the Rettung legend back to the middle ages, or even earlier."

I was stumped. I'd told Horndyke the truth, and he just wasn't listening. I could have gone on to tell him every last detail of my *modus operandi*—but I didn't want to. With hindsight, I was rather ashamed of my efforts to fabricate a myth for my own purposes. It's not that I'd broken the law, in the strictly legal sense—but some of my actions were less than ethical. I was worried that Horndyke would carry out his earlier veiled threat, and divulge his suspicions to a wider audience.

I had to think rapidly. "If you give me your word that you won't speak of this to anyone else, then I'll tell you the whole story," I told him. "You're going to be the first person to hear it— and, I hope, the last. But I should warn you that you won't like what I'm going to say."

Horndyke's eyes flashed. "The truth at last!" he said. "Yes, yes—I give you my word. Please proceed."

"I have constructed a device..." I was thinking furiously as I went along. "It's probably not what most people would think of when they imagine a time machine. It's not a vehicle that travels through the fourth dimension, like something out of H.G. Wells' story. But my device has two apertures—one aperture here in the present, and the other in the past. The aperture that opens into the past has a very narrow focus, and is governed entirely by the equations of quantum chronodynamics. I can go into details if you'd like..."

Horndyke shook his head, as I'd hoped he would. I have no idea what the equations of quantum chronodynamics are, or even if they exist at all.

"A few years ago I found myself in luck. The past-time focus was centred on a point in Iceland in the year 1265. As you know, that particular date was something of bottleneck in the history of Norse mythology. Before that point, there were countless different oral legends. After that point there was an ever-multiplying number of written texts. But at that time, there was just one text, the Elder Edda, from which all the later texts derive. So that was the only thing I had to change. I sent my own version of the Edda back in time."

Horndyke could scarcely control his excitement. "So I was right," he said. "You can change the past!"

"Yes, but there's a problem," I told him. "The equations of quantum chronodynamics determine where the past-time focus is located. When I used the device, that focus was in thirteenth century Iceland. Most of the time it's out in the vacuum of space. At the moment it's half-way between the Earth and the Moon, some time back in the Jurassic period. It will be another sixty years before it coincides with the surface of the Earth again." I held up my hands in mock despair. "And there you have it—the whole story. I said you wouldn't like it."
Horndyke slumped back in his chair. He looked very tired. After a while, he began to collect his books and papers together and put them back in his briefcase.

I shook hands with Horndyke and told him—genuinely—that I was sorry I hadn't been able to help him. He made his own way out, leaving me to ponder what had happened. It was ironic that he'd been so easily satisfied with a lie, after it had proved impossible to convince him of the truth. It was yet another example of what I'd told him earlier. Human beings aren't interested in the truth with a small 't'—factual truth. Only in the grand, deep, inner Truth, which echoes their beliefs even if it has no grounding in reality. Truth with a capital 'T'. Or perhaps it's so big it's all in capitals, like this: TRUTH.

I told Horndyke the truth when I said I didn't have a time machine. I can't change the past, and I don't think anyone can. But maybe the TRUTH is different. After all, I succeeded pretty well in changing the record of the past. So perhaps I have got a time machine, after all.

# PSYKICK KWEST

## - 1 -

The bookstore stood in one of the side streets to the south of King's Cross station. Behind its broad, plate-glass window, with its coating of London grime, was an impressive array of works on every esoteric subject imaginable: from Acupuncture and Alien Abductions to Zen Buddhism and the signs of the Zodiac. Above the window, a large sign proclaimed the shop's name: *PSYKICK KWEST*.

Eric Runestone was the proprietor of the Psykick Kwest bookstore. He was a broad, stocky man in his mid-thirties, with a bushy beard and long hair fringing a bald patch. The top three buttons of his shirt were unfastened, affording female customers a tantalizing glimpse of his hirsute chest.

Behind the counter, Eric glanced at his watch. It was after four o'clock—he needed to get on with the poster if it was to be up in time to catch the homeward bound commuters. There was no-one to serve at the moment, so he turned his attention to the computer. He typed for a few minutes, then stood back and surveyed his work on the screen. *Perfect!* He pressed 'Print', and the inkjet behind him clicked and whirred into action.

**HERE TONITE AT 7.30**
**LEKTURE**
***RECALLING PAST LIVES***
**with**
**LOBSANG KHANDRO WANGDAK**
**enlitened master from tibet**

Eric went over to the window and stuck the poster onto it with blu-tak, peering outside as he did so. Walking past was a tall, dark-haired young woman dressed in shiny black leggings and a leather jacket. She saw the poster, stopped in her tracks, and appeared to read it. *Way to go!* Eric thought. *A punter already—and a hot-looking chick, at that.*

*Past lives—that's just my kind of thing,* Abigail Novak thought to herself. She was a very spiritual woman, despite her high-powered job as a legal secretary. She made a mental note to attend the lecture. But first she had to go back to her flat in Highbury and get changed for her twice-a-week yoga class.

Abigail thrust her way through the crowds and went down the steps into the bustling tube station. As she made her way to the ticket barrier, she felt a tingle in the back of her neck and looked around. Her instinct had been correct. Over there, leaning against the wall... a scruffy little man was staring at her through his thick glasses. A real creep by the look of him: greasy hair tied back in a pony tail, too-small black jeans, too-big T-shirt. The T-shirt had the image of a grey alien head on it. Obviously he was some kind of pervert, on the lookout for a streetwalker.

She went over to him, and glared down at him angrily. She towered over him—in her high-heeled boots, she was taller than him by at least six inches. "Okay, squirt—I know what you're thinking," she told him. "You can forget it right now. I'm a lesbian—I don't do it with men. The only time a man gets inside me is when I eat one for breakfast."

The little man looked up at her and blinked through his thick glasses. "F.B.I.," he told her. "Special Agent Travis Tate. I've made a record of this conversation, but for now you're free to go. Please move along."

Abigail snorted in disgust and hurried towards the ticket barrier. She'd be really pissed off if that loony had made her late for yoga.

Travis Tate watched the tall woman until he lost sight of her in the thronging mass of commuters. Contrary to what he had told her, he was not, in fact, an F.B.I. agent. He was an unemployed lounger, conspiracy theorist, and—for want of a better term—girl-watcher. He found that it paid to keep his eyes on suspicious-looking people. In a world of alien abductions and government conspiracies, no-one could be trusted.

His eyes latched onto another figure—one that was coming from the direction of the tube and making for the steps leading to the outside world. This one—like the previous specimen—appeared to be a human female, although the proportions and outward trappings were quite different. *This one is shorter in stature,* he said into his mental tape recorder, *and the mammary glands and gluteus maximus are distinctly larger. The hair is pink and spiky, and the subject is wearing red-framed spectacles. Subject is dressed in an ankle-length dress made from velvet, or some synthetic substitute thereof.*

He pulled away from the wall and slipped unobtrusively into the crowd, surreptitiously following the pink-haired girl as she ascended the steps leading to Euston Road. She then proceeded in a southerly direction, and Travis tailed her at a safe distance. After a while she stopped in front of a bookstore, and Travis made a mental note of the name: *PSYKICK KWEST*. She spent a minute or two reading a notice that was posted in the window, and then entered the shop.

Travis sauntered up to the shop window and read the notice for himself. *Hmm, a lecture*, he thought. *Obviously pink-hair is planning to attend it. I shall go too, in order to make closer observations.* He followed her into the shop.

Sally Moon had been aware for some time that the pervy-looking man was following her—she could feel his eyes on her large, velvet clad bottom. Sometimes she wished her bottom wasn't *quite* so big, or *quite* so attractive to the opposite sex. Men automatically assumed her only interest was fornication, when really she had lots of other interests as well. She'd finished college earlier that year, and was still trying to decide what to do for a living... because there were just so many things she was *capable* of doing.

Seeing the poster about the Past Lives lecture brought another possibility to her mind. You could earn good money as a past-life regression hypnotist, and she was certainly caring and sensitive enough for the job. She had a latent psychic talent, as well, and that was bound to come in useful. She made a definite decision to attend the lecture and find out more.

The pervy man came into the bookshop and looked straight at her. Then he mumbled something to himself, and headed over to a shelf labelled ALIEN TECHNOLOGY.

Sally went as far away from pervy-man as she could get. She found herself facing a shelf labelled TAROT. *Of course!* she thought. *Tarot—I'd make an absolutely brilliant tarot card reader!* She started to flick through some of the more colourful books on the subject.

## - 2 -

As Lobsang Khandro Wangdak finished his lecture, there was a smattering of applause from the meagre audience. Just four people on this occasion—possibly the worst turnout he had ever seen. Besides the bookshop proprietor, there was one other man—a scruffy individual who virtually had the word LOSER tattooed on his forehead—and two not-bad-looking females: a tall one with dark hair, and a short one with pink hair.

Lobsang Khandro Wangdak was short and plump, with a round face and yellowish, oily-looking skin. It was easy to pass himself off as a Tibetan, in a city where no-one knew what a Tibetan looked like. In actual fact he came from no further afield than Dorking. His real name was Kenny Waddle... but whoever heard of an enlightened master called Kenny Waddle?

"Now I give practical demonstration." Kenny—or rather Lobsang Khandro Wangdak—never used definite or indefinite articles. The omission, he felt, added greatly to his standing as a Master of the Mystic East.

Fumblingly, he began to set up his apparatus in the cramped space of the bookstore. It consisted of a metal stand, approximately five feet high, surmounted by an electric motor. He picked up a large wooden disc and screwed it onto the shaft of the motor. The disc was painted with a colourful, oriental-looking design.

"Is Great Mandala of Infinity." Lobsang pointed at the disc and its painted design. "Great Mandala of Infinity will guide you in hypnotic regression—will guide you to past lives. Great Mandala can be tuned to any desired time-zone—today he is tuned twelve thousand years into past."

Lobsang plugged the contraption into the mains and the mandala-disc began to rotate slowly. "Look deep into Great Mandala of Infinity," he instructed.

The four members of the audience stared intently at the rotating disc.

After waiting a few minutes for the mild hypnosis to take effect, Lobsang addressed them again. "Each of you: tell me what you see."

"I see the great temple of Stonehenge, back when it was new." Eric Runestone scratched his balding head. "Hundreds of people are gathered around it—I think there's some kind of ceremony or ritual going on."

"I see a primeval forest of peace and love and wisdom." Abigail Novak crossed her long, lycra-clad legs. "Obviously this is back in a time when the world was ruled by women, before men screwed things up."

"I see the vast technopolis of ancient Atlantis," Travis Tate said, blinking short-sightedly at the rotating mandala. "A great spaceship is landing—it is the long-awaited return of the sky gods."

"I see the temple of the oracle in ancient Greece," Sally Moon adjusted the red-framed spectacles on her nose. "In this past life, that's where I work—I'm a vestal virgin in the temple."

"Excellent!" Lobsang Khandro Wangdak rubbed his hands. "Now, let yourselves relax, and become fully immersed in life of twelve thousand years ago. Just keep looking into Great Mandala of Infinity." It was all bullshit, he knew—a mixture of self-hypnosis and wish-fulfilment—but the punters lapped it up.

Eric was the Arch-Druid. Not one of the decadent, namby-pamby druids of Roman times, but a real druid of twelve thousand years ago. His muscular body was naked except for a wolfskin loincloth. He looked a lot like Conan the Barbarian.

Eric turned to the white-bearded leader of the elders. "Bring me the witch-girl," he ordered.

The nervous old man pushed forward a diminutive figure wrapped in a long white gown. The gown had a hood which concealed her features.

"She is the accursed offspring of a witch and a sabre-toothed cat," the elder said. "She has brought us bad luck since she was born, twenty years ago this very day."

"She will bring us bad luck no longer—I will see to that." Eric—the Arch-Druid—turned to the girl and addressed her. "Remove your robe, wench."

The girl complied. Her slim, lithe body was covered with tawny fur—like the big cat that had fathered her. Her face, also covered in tawny fur, looked up expectantly with large, green eyes. "Please cure me, sir," she pleaded.

"Turn around," Eric commanded.

The furry girl did so. Emerging from her rear, just above her buttocks, was a long, cat-like tail. Eric ceremoniously removed his loincloth. He took hold of the girl's tail and raised it up...

Abigail was summoned to the office of the Sister Superior. The 'office' was a glade in the Forest of Peace. This was in the time before the male of the species had fouled things up by inventing buildings... or clothes, for that matter. Both Abigail and the Sister Superior were healthily naked, tanned and muscular.

"Go, slave." The Sister Superior addressed the male slave that had brought Abigail. Like all men of this time, he was a poor specimen—weedy-looking and barely five feet tall. Abigail, by contrast, was over six feet, while the Sister Superior was half a foot taller still.

"You have transgressed," the Sister Superior said calmly. "You know very well that men are to be used for procreation only. You were observed performing a forbidden act on one of the slaves."

Abigail shifted nervously. "But it was all very spiritual," she pleaded. "I was giving thanks for the bountiful seed of the Goddess."

"You transgressed our laws, nevertheless." The tall woman was unforgiving. "You know the consequence of that."

The Sister Superior reached for the Great Rod of Punishment—a heavy wooden shaft three inches in diameter and six feet long. "Now, sister—bend over and present your buttocks."

Travis watched open-mouthed as the huge spaceship landed softly in Autothon Park, that broad green oasis in the middle of the high-tech city of Atlantis. He had managed to worm his way to the front of the vast, expectant crowd.

The huge door of the spaceship opened with a soft hiss. Travis waited impatiently for his first glimpse of the space-gods.

A moment later a figure emerged. It was, as it turned out, not a space god but a space goddess. She was ten feet tall, clad in a form-fitting silver suit that showed her vast, conical breasts to best advantage.

"Who is the wisest among you?" The voice of the space goddess boomed out over the hushed crowd. "We wish to perform some tests."

"Me! Me! I'm the wisest!" Travis jumped up and down to attract her attention.

She looked down at him, then beckoned him to enter the spaceship.

"Remove your clothing," she instructed when they were inside. "Then lie down on the examination table."

Travis did as he was told, then blinked as he saw the three-foot long metal contraption that the space goddess had taken from a locker.

"Prepare yourself for the anal probe," she said.

Sally was seated in her booth inside the Temple of the Oracle. She was one of a dozen vestal virgins who told fortunes there.

Sally's latest punter, like most of them, was a fat, middle-aged woman. "Place your hand on the table," Sally instructed her. "Ah, yes—I see it clearly. You will meet the man of your dreams next week. That will be two drachmas, thank you."

The woman paid up and left the booth.

"Next!" Sally took a moment to lean down and put the two coins in her purse.

When she looked up, the next punter was already sitting at the table facing her. This one was a man—strongly built, with a flat nose, large ears, long curly hair and a full beard.

"Place your hand on the table," Sally said mechanically.

"Bollocks to that," the punter said. "I don't want my palm read. I want to ravish you. I'm a satyr, you see—that's what I do. I ravish virgins." He stood up.

The satyr had the haunches and cloven hooves of a goat. Sprouting from his hairy loins was the biggest thing Sally had ever seen (and she'd seen quite a few—'virgin' being a job description and not a biological fact).

"Oh, Zeus!" Sally exclaimed. "What are you going to do with that?"

The satyr leered at her. "I'll give you three guesses."

Lobsang Khandro Wangdak switched off the mandala-machine and snapped his finger. "Enough! Past-life demonstration now over. Please, each of you—tell me what you experienced in world of twelve thousand years ago."

"As I shafted the young cat-girl, I had the orgasm of my life!" Eric said.

"As the Great Rod of Punishment slapped down on my buttocks, I had the orgasm of my life!" Abigail said.

"As the ten-foot high space goddess administered the anal probe, I had the orgasm of my life!" Travis said.

"As I was ravished by the rampant satyr, I had the orgasm of my life!" Sally said.

# THE MIND WHISPERERS

D ylan Horn emerged gloomily from the Amusement Arcade. A fierce onshore gale was sending a mixture of rain and sea-spray lashing across the grey, almost-deserted Esplanade. Dylan shuddered at the sight of it. For the last three hours he had been immersed in a video game—until financial strictures forced him reluctantly back into the real world. In the pocket of his jeans, all that remained of his holiday spending money was a solitary two-pound coin.

He kicked vainly at a polystyrene burger box. Hunching against the wind, he turned dejectedly towards the cheap B&B that constituted his current accommodation. It wasn't much to look forward to. If only reality was as exciting and eventful as the world inside the video game!

Dylan had only walked a short distance when he almost tripped over something lying on the rain-swept pavement. He looked down—it was a sign-board that must have blown over in the wind. The crudely painted inscription read *'Let Mystic Zelma Tell Your Fortune. Only £2. Number 248, The Esplanade'*.

He looked around. Just ahead of him, there was a shabby-looking doorway with the number 248 inscribed on the fanlight.

Well, why not? After all, he did have two pounds left in his pocket. Dylan made a decision. He went in through the open door, and pushed through the beaded curtain that lay beyond. He was in Mystic Zelma's consulting room.

Zelma (if that was her real name) turned out to be a thin, skanky-looking woman of thirty-something, with a stud in her nose. She looked at Dylan with a bored expression. "Two pounds, please."

He handed over his one remaining coin. "That's all I've got left. This had better be good."

"Oh, it will be." She still sounded bored. "I use Egyptian Chakra Cards. I invented them myself." She produced a pack of colourfully, if rather artlessly, illustrated cards. She shuffled them a few times, then began to lay them out on the table.

Suddenly, as Dylan watched, a funny look came across Zelma's face. She froze in mid-movement. A second later, the cards dropped from her hands. She sat bolt upright, her face screwed up in concentration. It was almost as if she was possessed by some outside force.

Zelma began to speak, apparently starting in mid-sentence. Her voice was several tones lower than it had been a moment ago. "...then you must pass through the Unholy Sanctum of Pleasure and enter the Temple of Mysteries..."

"I already did that," Dylan said. It was part of the *Castle of Madness* role-playing game—the one he had been immersed in all afternoon. His failure to progress beyond the First Citadel of the Unbaptized was the proximate cause of his current state of insolvency.

Zelma was still talking, seemingly oblivious to his reply: "...and approach the Shadowy Idol of Nothingness. Insert the Seven Fragments of the Unthinkable Amulet of Garak into their correct places. In this way you will unlock an ancient volume called '*The Meditations of Comprehension*'..."

"Yes, yes—I know." Dylan was growing impatient. "I decoded all the diagrams in the book, which showed how to get into the First Citadel of the Unbaptized. But that's where I got stuck. I..."

Mystic Zelma wasn't listening. "...Slit open the binding and you will find secreted there a map containing a five-digit access code and a set of GPS coordinates. These figures relate to the local headquarters of the Satanic Crime Cartel. That's where they're holding me captive. You must hurry, Anastasia..."

"Say what?" Dylan was more than a little confused. He began to think the woman was insane. "They didn't have GPS coordinates in mediaeval Transylvania. And what's the Satanic Crime Cartel? And—who the heck is Anastasia?"

But Zelma was in no fit state to answer any of these questions. She had slumped forward across the table, scattering dozens of Egyptian Chakra cards onto the floor.

Dylan had a lot more questions, but it was obvious he wasn't going to get any answers from Zelma. But then again... why waste time asking questions? He wasn't one to look a gift horse in the mouth. Mystic Zelma—insane or not—had given him an insight into a level of the game he hadn't reached yet. He felt sure he was onto something big... maybe even the hidden jackpot!

But there was a small problem. He needed money to get back into the game, and money was the one thing he didn't have. He looked around the room. Hmm... Mystic Zelma's purse was right there on the seat behind her, and its owner was currently out cold. There was nothing wrong with borrowing a bit of cash from her—he could easily pay her back tomorrow out of his winnings. He could even afford to give her a bit extra as well. After all, it was her tip-off that put him on the right track.

Dylan scrabbled in the purse and took out half a dozen pound coins. That ought to be enough—no need to be greedy. He left the banknotes and the credit card... although he did take a quick glance at the latter. He saw, with some surprise, that the fortune teller's name really was Zelma—Ms Zelma Dean, in fact.

The tall figure of Anastasia Carr moved briskly along the Esplanade, then swung lithely and confidently into the Amusement Arcade. Suddenly she stopped in her tracks and frowned in puzzlement. A small, unshaven, slouch-shouldered young man was making a bee-line for the machine labelled *Castle of Madness*. It was no-one she had ever seen before... an unknown factor that had not been included in her calculations.

Anastasia Carr scowled; she didn't like unknown factors. Something like this could jeopardize the whole mission. She would have to play things by ear. She resumed her forward movement.

Dylan Horn was making a bee-line for the *Castle of Madness*. Just as he got to the machine, he became aware of a tall, purposeful figure converging from another direction. He looked up to see an improbably statuesque blonde in a black leather catsuit. She seemed intent on butting in ahead of him.

"I was here first," he informed her. "You wait your turn." He put a number of coins in the machine and turned his attention to the screen.

For a few seconds the woman hovered over him, looking as though she was seriously contemplating an act of violence. She clenched and unclenched her fists, glaring at him. Then she suddenly appeared to relent—apparently she'd decided to wait her turn after all. She stood with her arms folded, watching his every move.

Dylan found the woman's behaviour rather puzzling—he wasn't sure if it was the game or himself that she was interested in. Probably himself, he decided: some women could scent a financially successful male a mile off.

Immersing himself in the game, Dylan headed straight for the Unholy Sanctum of Pleasure, then quickly passed through into the Temple of Mysteries. He went up to the Shadowy Idol of Nothingness, and inserted the Seven Fragments of the Unthinkable Amulet of Garak into their appropriate niches. With a puff of smoke, an ancient leather-bound volume appeared: '*The Meditations of Comprehension*'.

Remembering the words of Mystic Zelma, Dylan carefully slit open the binding. To his satisfaction, he discovered that there was indeed a slip of paper there... a subtlety he'd missed the previous time he played the game.

The blonde woman was breathing down his neck, apparently trying to see the screen over his shoulder.

"Don't cheat," he told her. "It's not nice. If you want to know what it says, you can ruddy well play the game yourself... AFTER I've finished with it." He carefully shielded the screen with his hands.

What was it Zelma had said in her trance? Something about a map with a five-digit access code and a set of GPS coordinates. Well, the five-digit code was there, all right—and it was easy enough for him to memorize: 61616. But where were the mysterious coordinates?

Using the cursor, Dylan turned the map over to look at the other side. Yes, there it was: a set of figures... small and faint, but just about readable. He peered at the numbers.

"But they don't make sense!" He was completely baffled. He'd been expecting to see a set of coordinates in the standard format used in the game... but this set of figures was in a completely different format. He was so mystified he forgot to shield the screen from the prying eyes of the woman.

She seized her chance. Leaning forward, she took in the mysterious coordinates with a single glance. Then she pulled out a handheld GPS unit and typed rapidly into it.

"What are you doing?"

The woman looked down at him contemptuously. "Keep out of things you don't understand, you little squirt."

"What do you mean, things I don't understand? I understand everything there is to know about this game."

"These numbers aren't part of the game—they're real. Now, tell me the access code and I'll get out of your way. You can go on playing the game to your heart's content."

Dylan began to see the light. Perhaps this game had a new twist in it, with the prize money hidden somewhere in the real world. Of course—that's what the GPS coordinates must refer to! He opened his mouth to speak.

Anastasia Carr glared fiercely at the little man. "Oh, I haven't got time for this!" She grabbed him by the scruff of his neck and dragged him out of the Amusement Arcade.

After a brief glance at the GPS, she turned onto the wet and windswept Esplanade, still with the spluttering little nonentity in tow.

They headed away from the town centre, in the direction of the high cliffs overlooking the sea. The gale battered away at them as they struggled up the muddy path leading to the top of the cliffs. Every so often they passed signs saying: *'DANGER: Keep clear of the edge. These cliffs are liable to erosion. Landslips may occur at any time.'*

As they approached the top of the cliff, Anastasia glanced at her wrist chronometer. Fifteen minutes had passed since they had left the Amusement Arcade. She checked the GPS unit, and managed to pinpoint their destination. It was a small ruined chapel, perched precariously on the edge of the cliff.

She hauled her weedy companion the last few yards, and they crossed the threshold into what was left of the chapel. Then they descended the slippery, weather-beaten stone steps to the entrance of the crypt. In jarring contrast to the surrounding ruins, the door to the crypt was a modern-looking, high security affair constructed of heavy steel plating.

Anastasia turned to the little man. "Quick, key in the access code."

Dylan had no idea why the tall blonde woman was taking the game so seriously, but he was as keen as she was to get inside the crypt and claim his prize. He was even prepared to share it with her, since he would never have found the place without her GPS gizmo. He used the keypad next to the door to enter the correct access code: 61616.

The door swung open and the two of them went inside.

The crypt was small and austerely furnished, with all the appearance of a security vault. In the middle of the room, tied to a steel-framed chair, was a man—a ludicrously good-looking man, dressed in a spotless tuxedo. He looked up as the woman entered the room.

"Anastasia—what kept you?"

Anastasia! The name gave Dylan a start. It was the name Mystic Zelma had mentioned when she was in her trance!

Anastasia pushed Dylan roughly across the room and pointed a futuristic-looking gun at him. "This little twerp is what kept me," she said. "I've no idea who he is, but he's mixed up in this somehow. He knew just where to find the Cartel's secret data inside the arcade game."

Dylan blinked at her. "I don't know what you're talking about. My name's Dylan Horn, and I'm here on holiday. I was having a great time this morning playing *Castle of Madness*... until I got stuck on one level. I got to the First Citadel of the Unbaptized, but then I couldn't get any further. And then I ran out of money. So I went to a fortune teller called Mystic Zelma, and she told me exactly what I needed to do."

A thoughtful expression came over the man's face. "Fortune teller, eh? A clairvoyant, you mean? I suppose it could have happened like that. When I regained consciousness, I was tied up and helpless here. Straight away I sent out a telepathic message, and your fortune teller must have picked it up by mistake. The message was meant for Anastasia here."

Dylan looked at him blankly.

"Perhaps we should introduce ourselves," the man continued. "My name is Blade—Lazarus Blade." He indicated Anastasia, who had put away her gun and was now busy untying him. "And this is Anastasia Carr, my partner. The two of us have certain special talents, which we have pledged to use in the battle against crime. I do not refer to commonplace crime, but to crime of the most fiendish and insidious kind. Our arch-enemies call themselves the Satanic Crime Cartel. This crypt was, until very recently, their headquarters in this district. But when I arrived here they had just finished removing the last piece of incriminating evidence."

"The Satanic Crime Cartel? Is that some kind of underworld organization?"

Lazarus Blade gave a dry chuckle. "It is indeed... in more ways than one. Superficially, the Satanic Crime Cartel is just another criminal gang—albeit a very powerful one, controlling a string of gambling and drug-dealing rackets all over the world. The Amusement Arcade in the town is one of their many fronts. But the real power of the Cartel derives from a more literal underworld—a vast network of subterranean caverns in which dwell a hideously ancient species of decadent, degenerated beings called the Dero. The Dero are inhuman, and never show themselves on the surface. But they have a number of human puppets under their control, and among these puppets are the leaders of the Satanic Crime Cartel."

Dylan shook his head. "I'm having a hard time believing all this—it sounds like something out of a video game. Things like that just don't happen in the real world."

Blade shook his head sadly. "Too many people think along those lines. It is difficult to persuade people of the truth. More than sixty years ago, an American named Richard Shaver published a string of writings on the subject, and he was reviled for them. Because of the shameful treatment he was subjected to, those people who know the truth—people such as Anastasia and myself—have learned to be very circumspect in what we say about it in public... very circumspect indeed."

"I still can't believe you're for real," Dylan said. "I mean, you don't even talk normally. You sound like something out of a 1930s newsreel."
Blade was silent for a few seconds, then appeared to come to a decision. "I confess that my diction may be somewhat dated. The fact is, you see, that I am quite a bit older than you might imagine. The truth is..."

He was interrupted in mid-sentence by a sound from outside the room. A second later the thick steel door flew open. Standing on the threshold was a heavy-set, balding man of late middle age.

Anastasia gasped. "Victor Stone, Grand Master of the Satanic Crime Cartel!"

"Quite right, Ms Carr." The newcomer paused to take a large swig from a hip flask, then wiped his fleshy mouth with the back of his hand. "What a pleasant surprise to find you here! I expected only to find Mr Blade. And what's this? I see you've released him from his fetters. Never mind—that is of no great concern to me. Once this door is closed, it cannot be opened from the inside. So both of you..."

"Ahem," Dylan said.

"My mistake," Stone corrected himself. "All THREE of you. I see you've brought a pet monkey along. All three of you, I say, are doomed. Nothing will save you this time. Explosive charges have been put in place which—in just ten short minutes—will plunge this chapel two hundred feet into the sea. Doubtless it will be seen as a tragic accident... cliffs liable to erosion, and all that. Landslips may occur at any time, you know."

"You fiend!" Lazarus Blade snarled.

Victor Stone's only reply was an evil-sounding laugh, ending abruptly in a hiccup. He turned and left the room, slamming the heavy steel door behind him.

Dylan blinked at the closed door. "Is he for real? He looked like an old drunk to me."

"He drinks, that's true... but don't underestimate the man," Blade replied. "Victor Stone is controlled by the Dero, and he is completely ruthless. We have followed his trail for months, and it is critical that we capture him before he wreaks further destruction. But before we can do that, we must find a way out of here."

Anastasia scratched her nose, then casually looked at her wrist chronometer. "Six minutes till the explosive charges go off. Ho-hum. Any ideas?"

Lazarus remained silent, apparently deep in thought.

"What about Zelma Dean?" Dylan suggested. "You know—Mystic Zelma, the clairvoyant? Can't you send her a telepathic message or something? She could fetch help."

Lazarus looked up at him. "It's a good enough idea, but..."
"But there isn't time," Anastasia finished flatly. "It took us fifteen minutes to get here from the Esplanade, and..."

Suddenly the door burst open.

"I thought I heard voices in here."

They looked up to see Mystic Zelma standing in the doorway.

133

Dylan rushed over to her. "Zelma! What are you doing here?"

"I had a sudden premonition these cliffs were going to collapse, so I thought I'd better check to see if there was anyone messing around in this old crypt. People do, you know, from time to time."

Two minutes later, as the four of them stood well back from the edge of the cliff, Mystic Zelma's premonition proved to be spot on. With an explosive boom, the old chapel fell into the sea.

Before the dust had settled, Lazarus Blade swung towards the path leading back down to the town. "Come, Anastasia, while the trail is still hot—we must pursue Victor Stone and the rest of the Satanic Crime Cartel."

Dylan rushed to catch up with the rapidly departing crimefighters. "Um, what about Zelma and me... I mean, ah, our expenses and that?"

He was more than satisfied with the reply.

# SECRETS OF THE GREEN GOD

The creature had four arms and three eyes, and it was green. Surrounded by the relics of past centuries, it stood motionless, frozen in its cosmic dance of creation and destruction. Arthur leaned forward for a closer look. Inside the glass display case, there was a faded paper label: *Shiva Nataraja, copper alloy, India, 20th century. $1000.00.* Expensive, but irresistible. Arthur beckoned the sales assistant.

"That Indian figurine," he said. "I'll take it."

"A fine choice," the assistant said, unlocking the display case. "You're a collector?"

"No, not really," Arthur said. "But it reminds me of home. It reminds me of Earth."

Arthur paid the assistant and left the antiques store, clutching his new acquisition. He made his way through the crowded shopping area to the transport ship's docking bay, and the connecting tunnel leading back to the space station.

Rita Sanchez, head of security on DSD-2, was on duty in the station's reception area. Given the sensitive business of Dynamic System Design Incorporated, it paid to keep close track of all personnel and goods entering or leaving the space station.

"Hello, Mr Krim—bought anything interesting?"

"Just an ornament," Arthur said, handing over the six-limbed figurine. "A hundred years old, or so—not a real antique, but it'll brighten up my living quarters. The Indian god Shiva, the Lord of the Dance. It's quite attractive, don't you think?"

"Elegant," Rita said, passing the statuette through her scanner. The machine beeped. "And bugged," she added. "But that's not surprising, considering the business we're in. Half the stuff that comes on board has got a hot link back to some competitor or other. Still, not to worry. It's easily dealt with."

Rita scraped a small sliver of metal from the base of the statuette and dropped the bug into the disintegrator. "Looked like the work of LeGrand Corp," she said. "They never stop trying." She passed the figurine back to Arthur. "But then neither do we, I guess. Enjoy."

Arthur turned toward the elevator, only to be intercepted almost immediately by a tall young man. Arthur vaguely recognized him as another of the thousand-odd employees on the DSD-2 station. A scientist, he thought—someone from the research labs.

"Excuse me," the young man said. "I couldn't help overhearing." He looked distinctly excited. "That copper statuette—it is copper, isn't it? It had a LeGrand bug? I'm Peter van Houten, by the way. DSD Industrial Intelligence Division, advanced research group."

"Pleased to meet you," Arthur said, somewhat taken aback. "Arthur Krim, project librarian." He passed the verdigris-coated figurine to van Houten, trying to remember what the label had said. "Yes, it's copper, I think—copper alloy."

"Terrific!" van Houten said. "Can you spare a few minutes? This little statuette could be of considerable value to the company, if my guess is right."

Van Houten moved off towards the research labs, taking Arthur's figurine with him. Seeing no alternative, Arthur followed. "Yes, it is quite valuable," he said. "A thousand dollars, I paid for it. Still, it's a lot cheaper than an original. And it's an investment. Twentieth century reproductions are rising in price all the time. They're becoming collectible."

Van Houten didn't appear to be listening. He glanced back at Arthur and asked: "Do you know anything about the BSR research project?"

"No—I'm just an archives man," Arthur said. "I know a bit about DSD's history and current products, but the research side is a closed book."

"It's a new breakthrough in industrial espionage," van Houten said. "And as far as we know, none of our competitors are anywhere near us. It does away with the need for active devices altogether—it's a completely passive system. This statuette, for example—if it's been at a LeGrand site, it can tell us more about them than their bug would ever have told them about us."

They reached the lab, and van Houten made towards one particularly complicated piece of apparatus involving several computer monitors, keyboards, and assorted boxes and wires. It was all way beyond Arthur. Van Houten ushered Arthur to a seat.

"The important thing about this statuette is that it's copper," van Houten said, busily connecting the Shiva figurine into the apparatus. "That means it's a good conductor—the outer electrons can move freely throughout the crystalline lattice."

"Yes," Arthur said, totally out of his depth.

"And it's an ornament—the sort of thing that might be left in the same place for long stretches of time. On a quantum level, the object has time to come into equilibrium with its environment... at least, those parts of the environment that remain constant during that time. The lattice-wide wave functions of the conduction electrons adapt to reflect the surroundings. And the memory of past configurations remains intact. But it's encoded in a horrendously non-linear way—and with so many degrees of freedom—that for all practical purposes it's inaccessible."

"Until now?" Arthur hazarded.

"That's right," van Houten nodded. "Until now!" He flicked a few switches. "BSR stands for Bloch State Reconstruction. We make a large number of simultaneous measurements, typically several billion—the conductivity tensor, and other macroscopic properties—and combine them with real-time computer predictions to create a virtual-reality model of the past environment. Of course, the model has statistical validity only—it's not a true image of any particular instant in the past, and it doesn't contain any transient information like the coming and going of individuals. But we've performed several impressive tests of the method."

Van Houten typed rapidly at a keyboard, and a blurred image appeared on one of the computer screens. "But your statuette offers greater possibilities than any of our previous test objects. It's considerably bigger for one thing, and..."

"What's that, there on the screen?" Arthur asked. The view had been shifting as van Houten made adjustments, but now it had steadied. It showed the interior of a small grey room with rough stucco walls and stone floor.

"Damn," van Houten said. "That's not what I was expecting. I'll try and widen the field of view."

"Can you do that?" Arthur asked. "If the statuette was inside that tiny room..."

"You're forgetting," van Houten said. "This isn't a simple image—not like you'd get on a photographic film. The collective wave-function contains information on the location of all fixed objects within a radius of... well, of several meters, or tens of meters, or hundreds of meters depending on how long the object was in place. A complete three-dimensional map, irrespective of intervening walls or whatever. The computer uses the 3D map to reconstruct a pseudo-image from a particular viewpoint at a particular time."

The view on the screen scrambled chaotically, and van Houten suddenly snapped his fingers. He was looking at some numbers on another screen. "Okay—I think I know what's wrong," he said. He fiddled with the machine again, and another image formed. This time it was clearer—a modern office lobby, with potted palms and a receptionist's desk, an elevator bank, and a corridor running off to one side. Over the desk, a large *LeGrand Corp* logo was clearly visible.

"Bingo!" shouted van Houten. "Obviously one of LeGrand's big offices on Earth—possibly even their HQ in Paris. And the image is so clear... the statue must have been there for years. We'll get a complete site plan out of this!"

"Uh—but my statuette..." Arthur said.

"Oh, don't worry, Mr Krim. It'll only take a few hours to upload the information we need.

Then you can have it back, safe and sound. And I'm sure the company will recognize your contribution to the project, and reimburse you accordingly."

"Right, thanks," Arthur said. He thought for a moment. "But what was that first image we saw?"

"Oh that," van Houten said. "I thought you said the object was a twentieth century reproduction, so I set the machine to display its surroundings some hundred years after manufacture. Then I checked the diagnostics and realized we were looking at the middle of the twelfth century. It's a genuine antique, isn't it?"

# THE ALCHEMIST'S CURSE

**B**OOM!

It sounded like an explosion. And it came from the room next to mine.

Staircase 13, besides being the oldest corner of Old Court, was also the noisiest... thanks to the moron on the floor below, his state-of-the-art sound system and his predilection for Heavy Metal music. So I almost missed the explosion—and I doubt that anyone else noticed it at all. Anyone, that is, with the exception of Thompson: the first-year Physics student who occupied the room next to mine. Thompson was the only other inhabitant on the top floor of Staircase 13.

With a sigh, I put down the copy of Dryden's *Annus Mirabilis* I'd been reading. I glanced at my watch: it was 11 pm. The relentless thud of Satanic Death Metal continued unabated below... but there was no hint of alarums and excursions. If someone was going to investigate the explosion it would have to be me.

So I played the reluctant hero. I went out onto the landing—and instantly recoiled at the stench of smoke. It wasn't just the recreational smoke that habitually wafted up from the floor below, but thick, acrid smoke emanating from Thompson's slightly open door. I pushed it fully open and went inside. The room was filled with choking smoke and dust. Through the haze I could make out a gaping hole in the plasterwork of the opposite wall.

As I stepped into the room my foot kicked something lying on the floor. I bent to pick it up—it was a human skull. "Thompson..." I muttered, revolving the skull in my hands and inspecting it thoughtfully. The lower mandible was crudely fastened to the upper jaw by means of a rusty piece of wire.

"Beardsley, old man—" Thompson emerged from under the desk, coughing and looking rather sheepish. "Cold fusion, you know... just a little experiment of mine. Formula's not quite right..." Absent-mindedly he started to brush the dust from his clothes.

"The formula is most definitely not right," I concurred. "You've positively wrecked the place, old boy. The Bursar won't be pleased when he finds out. These rooms are four hundred years old, don't you know?"

"If it wasn't for these little setbacks science would never make any progress." Thompson fumbled around for his glasses, found them, and put them on. "Anyway, nobody was hurt..."

"Nobody hurt? What about old wire-jaw here? I'd say he looks distinctly traumatized." I tossed the skull to Thompson, who made a clumsy catch.

Thompson turned the skull over and looked at the teeth. "Hmm... no fillings or bridge-work. Must have been deceased for several centuries, I'd say. Where'd you find him, old bean?"

"Tripped over the thing when I rushed in here to see what that bang was about." I used my foot to indicate the approximate spot on the floor, then looked up. By this time the smoke and dust had largely dissipated, and I pointed at the hole in the wall. "It must have come from behind the plasterwork over there, on the wrong side of your cold fission experiment."

"Cold fusion," Thompson corrected. "Fission would have made a bang that everyone in Cambridge could hear, even with that damned racket going on downstairs."

The floorboards were, as ever, vibrating to the discordant strains of Satangöre's Greatest Hits.

"The noise gets on your nerves too, does it?" I asked. "Never mind, our nemesis will get his comeuppance one of these days."

We went over and inspected the hole in the wall. A portion of the ancient-looking plaster and lath had been blown in, revealing a cavity about a cubic foot in size. A few dusty objects were visible inside.

Thompson peered eagerly at the objects, then sniffed in disgust. "Just a load of old junk. I thought it might be hidden treasure." He scooped out the items one by one, unceremoniously dumping them on the floor. "A few more bones, a couple of feathers, a chunk of quartz crystal... and what's this? Looks like an old piece of parchment. Literary stuff—that's more your line, Beardsley."

I took the sheet from him and scratched my head over it. It was written in a strange, crabbed handwriting that took some getting used to. But it was English... English of the very period I was studying this term. After a few minutes I was confident enough of my decipherment to read it out loud:

> *"By the Hande of mee, Magister Lucius Littlerood, this XVI day of*
> *Aprille in the Year of Our Lorde 1666. Confessing due Feare*
> *and Humilitie before the all-seeing Eye of Almighty GOD, I with*
> *greatest Reluctance, being forc'd of grimme Necessitie in this my*

*darkest Houre, do call on the Loathsome and despis'd Legions of Hell to aid mee in this one Deed, to witt: to bring Miserie and Pestilence and DEATH to the execrable and thrice-damn'd Satan-worshipping son of a ha'penny whore who doth inhabit the Roomes below mine and doth forever distract me from my Worke to uncover ye Secret of Gold-Fusion, by makynge the most unholy NOYSE of misbegotten merrie-making at all hours of ye Daie and Nichte; all the while he smoketh what is most assuredly not honest Tobacco but a Narcotic Intoxicant from the Apothecaries of Hell. Ye Skull, Bones &c being placed in this cavity to marke my Solemn Covenant as it is laid down in Clavicula Salomonis.*

*AMEN."*

As I finished reciting the words there was a second bang, this time from the floor below, and the thudding music stopped abruptly. The next morning, our bedmaker discovered the room's occupant dead on the floor—electrocuted by a sudden and unaccountable short circuit in his state-of-the-art sound system.

# Collector's Item
### *A Ballad of Victorian Times*

The sky grew dark, the rain came down.
Schwartz darted through the door
of some small musty-smelling shop
he'd never seen before.

Then old Schwartz gasped as he beheld
the books that lined the store:
all leather-bound and marked in scripts
of dusty days of yore.

A happy find, this back-street shop!
His feeble pulses raced.
For Schwartz a book collector was
of esoteric taste.

"Old grimoires, demonologies,
and books of secret lore
are items I collect," he told
the store's proprietor.

"This just came in," the man told Schwartz.
"It might be just the thing.
It's from an auctioned-off estate:
*'Balaam the Demon-King'*."

'Balaam'! The book of boundless power!
'Balaam'... within his reach!
He'd thought it lost three centuries...
the wonders it could teach!

The work of Stryfe the sorcerer,
who dared dark depths explore:

Stryfe wrote the book of great Balaam...
and then was seen no more!

"I think I may have heard of it,"
Schwartz barely croaked it out.
"You said a dead man left the book:
how happened that about?"

"Not dead, but simply disappeared,"
the bookshop owner said.
"Sir Arthur Knowles ten years ago
just vanished from his bed."

The man went on: "He came back home
from farthest Bangalore;
he took a book and went upstairs...
and then was seen no more!"

The shop-man passed across a book.
Schwartz took the thing and saw
'twas wrapped in yellowed newspaper:
'The Times of Bangalore'!

"The price?" Schwartz asked offhandedly.
"I'll buy it if it's cheap."
The shop-man shrugged. "Three guineas cash,
and then it's yours to keep."

Schwartz paid, and left. The rain had stopped.
Saint Martin's struck the hour.
He hurried home, and clasped it tight:
the book of boundless power!

He locked his door and studied then
the cover of the thing.
In antique script he traced the words:
'Balaam, the Demon-King'.

He opened up the book and saw
an incantation there.
Forthwith he spoke the words aloud:
"Balaam, arise from air!"

A flash of lightning! Then appeared
a creature like a goat.

"I am Balaam," the creature said,
and grabbed Schwartz by the throat.

Schwartz learned the truth that Stryfe had known,
as had Sir Arthur Knowles:
Balaam was a collector too,
and he collected souls.

"His name was Schwartz. The Yard was here:
they traced him to my door.
He even bought a book from me...
and then was seen no more!"

# THE VANISHING CURATE

The express from London rolled to a stop with a hissing of steam. "Taunton!" the guard shouted. "Change here for Minehead, Yeovil and Bristol!"

Among the passengers decanting onto Platform Five was Inspector Franks of Scotland Yard. A quick glance at his battered copy of Bradshaw's timetable confirmed his next move. He crossed over to Platform Four, where the stopping train to Minehead was standing ready for its scheduled departure at 3.15 pm. Franks selected one of the First Class compartments and stepped into it. One of the best things about his job, in his opinion, was being able to travel all over the country in First Class railway carriages!

Another passenger from the London train got into the compartment with Franks. This struck the detective as slightly odd, because there were three other compartments in the First Class section and as far as he had seen they were all empty. He was even more surprised when his companion—a tall and rather arrogant-looking young man—spoke up.

"Just on my way home from jolly old London, don't you know?" The man paused to top up his pipe and relight it. "Been there on business since first thing yesterday morning. Absolute bore, but there it is."

Franks nodded politely. He was on the point of replying with some innocuous comment of his own, but before he could do so the man had unfurled his copy of the *Times* and was already immersed in reading it. The conversation, apparently, was at an end.

Just under an hour later, the train pulled into a small station which—according to the sign-board—went by the name of Washford. This was Franks's destination! He took his overnight bag from the rack, and was surprised to see his companion do the same. Apparently the mystery traveller was a resident of Washford, or somewhere close by. The man stepped down onto the platform as if he owned it, and Franks followed a few steps behind.

Outside the station there was a row of taxis and private cars standing in the dusty afternoon sunshine. The haughty-looking young man got into a cab and was driven off. Franks looked around for a "dark blue 1924 Morris Oxford", as it had been proudly described to him. These small-town bobbies were doing all right for themselves if they could afford a brand-new car!

The vehicle was easy enough to spot, as was its driver in his police uniform. The latter introduced himself as Sergeant Butter, and held the door open for his esteemed colleague from the Yard.

"We'll go straight to the police station at Old Cleeve." The sergeant had to shout over the noise of the engine. "It's only about a mile from here. Then I'll fill you in on the details of the case."

A quarter of an hour later the two men were sitting comfortably in the office of the small police station, smoking what Franks was certain were the sergeant's very best cigars.

"I should start with an apology for bringing you all the way out here on such a trivial matter, Inspector..."

Franks waved the comment aside. "You don't have to apologize for bringing me to the Somerset coast on a sunny day in July. If you've ever tried breathing the atmosphere in London at this time of year you'll know what I mean. I'm at your service to help in any way I can."

"That's very generous, Sir. But I'm afraid the case really is trivial, all the same. A fully grown man of sound mind and body who was only reported missing this morning. But the man in question is the curate—the vicar's assistant—and the vicar was most insistent that we should get Scotland Yard onto this without delay. The Reverend Brigandine doesn't think much of my detecting abilities, you see."

Franks blew a smoke ring. "You don't get much in the way of crime around these parts, I imagine?"

"We don't, and that's a fact." Sergeant Butter shook his head to emphasize the point. "The odd burglary, of course... and there was a car reported stolen yesterday. Most of the local crimes turn out to be the work of the same few miscreants. There's one ne'er-do-well who's constantly in and out of the cells for one thing or another. His name's Andrew Baker: just a young fellow, about twenty-five or twenty-six. Last thing we had him in for was indecent exposure... he flashed his private parts at a young lady as she was crossing the park on her way home from work. He was dressed as Charlie Chaplin... considers himself something of a master of disguise, does young Baker. But the girl recognized his voice when he asked her if she wanted to be a movie star."

"Charlie Chaplin!" Franks chuckled. "You have to give the lad credit for imagination, if nothing else. Any other major crimes lately?"

The Sergeant's face became serious. "Yes and no. We had a reported rape, but then the alleged victim withdrew her accusation. The girl is a chamber-maid, and there's reason to believe the rapist paid her handsomely to change her story. But as things stand there's nothing we can do about it. Peter Smethwick—that's the fellow's name—has a lot of influence in the community. You've seen him, although you probably weren't aware of it at the time."

Franks looked puzzled for a moment, then clicked his fingers. "Ah, you must be referring to the young gentleman who left the railway station ahead of me. A superior being if ever there was one... or I'm sure that's how he thinks of himself."

"Exactly." The sergeant nodded. "Young Smethwick acts like he owns the place. His father is one of our wealthiest landowners, and on his mother's side he's some kind of nephew or second cousin of Reverend Brigandine."

"Reverend Brigandine... you mentioned him a moment ago. He's your vicar—the one who reported the missing curate? Perhaps you can fill in some of the details for me."

"Certainly, Sir. Would you like another cigar, by the way?"

Franks shook his head. "They're very fine cigars, but like all cigars they have a relaxing effect on the brain. The situation calls for mental stimulation, so if you don't mind I'll switch to smoking cigarettes." He proceeded to light up a cheap gasper, and the sergeant did the same— with obvious relief at not having to dig any further into his box of cigars.

"The curate's name is Trat." The sergeant paused while he took a long drag on his cigarette. "A fine young man, who takes his job very seriously. Sees himself as a crusader against evil. It started when he came back from the Great War... some of the things he witnessed in the trenches, you know. Reverend Brigandine's getting on in years, and he lets Trat take the church service more often than not. It was Trat that took the service this last Sunday, two days ago now... and that was a day few people who were there will forget in a hurry."

"Something happened?" the inspector prompted.

"I'll say it did. The curate didn't mince his words. His sermon was all about evil, as per usual, but this time it was aimed at one person in particular: Peter Smethwick. Trat all but accused him of buying his way out of a rape charge, and told him he'd never buy his way out of Hell. People who saw Smethwick afterwards tell me he was livid with rage—he even threatened to kill Trat with his bare hands."

Franks looked alarmed. "And do you think that's what happened?"

Sergeant Butter shook his head. "It's impossible. The timing is all wrong. Trat was seen by several people yesterday afternoon, and reported missing at ten this morning. All that time Smethwick was away in London."

Franks nodded thoughtfully. "Yes, he was careful to make that point when I saw him on the train. It was the only thing he said to me, in fact. But about those witnesses yesterday... you're sure it was Trat they saw? Did they speak to him? Is there any chance they could have been mistaken?"

"No chance at all. I didn't find anyone who saw him close enough to speak to, but Curate Trat is an unmistakeable figure all the same. Always wears a wide-brimmed shovel hat, and walks with a pronounced limp. He was injured by a landmine in 1917... it blew off half his foot, and left shrapnel lodged in his calf muscle. He uses a walking stick most of the time."

There was a thoughtful pause while Inspector Franks lit another cigarette. "So if Smethwick is out of it, do you have any other indications as to what might have happened to Trat?"

The sergeant shrugged. "Not really. When the vicar went to Trat's cottage this morning and found him missing, he called me. We searched the place, and everything seemed to be in order... but there was no sign of the man himself. His shovel hat was hanging on a peg in the hallway, and his walking stick was propped up inside the door. That's what alarmed the vicar: he couldn't imagine Trat leaving the house voluntarily without his hat and stick."

Franks ruminated for a while. "There doesn't seem much to go on," he admitted.

The sergeant shook his head glumly. Then he looked up. "Wait a moment... I haven't told you about the Irishman yet!"

"The Irishman?"

"The Irishman," the sergeant repeated. "He was in the Lamb and Flag yesterday evening. Just went in there and sat in the corner drinking pints of Guinness. No-one had seen him before, and no-one has seen him since. He said he was staying at Curate Trat's place. According to witnesses he spent the whole evening railing against the Church of England."

"A strangely tactless thing to do, under the circumstances. Do you have a clear description of this mysterious Irishman?"

"I do indeed." Sergeant Butter consulted his notebook. "He had bright red hair and a bright red beard, and he was wearing a bright green suit and a bright green hat. And he, ah, spoke with an Irish accent, of course."

"Of course," Franks agreed. "Now it strikes me that..."
Just at that moment the phone rang. The sergeant begged the inspector to excuse him and picked up the receiver.

For several minutes Inspector Franks of Scotland Yard had to content himself with listening to the sergeant say things like "Yes, I see" and "Is that so?" while he scribbled furiously in his notebook, an ever more baffled expression on his face. Then finally he said "Thank you very much for calling, Sir. We'll send someone over to take a formal statement tomorrow," and hung up the receiver.

"New information?" Franks inquired.

"I'll say it's new information. This changes everything. The call was from..." The sergeant glanced down at his notes. "... Reverend Sacheverell, the vicar of Blandford Forum. That's a town in Dorset about seventy miles from here. Turns out their vicar's of an age with Curate Trat... they were at university together before the war. Sacheverell hadn't seen hide or hair of Trat for more than ten years, then suddenly he turns up outside his house at the wheel of a car."

"A car? You didn't mention that Trat owns a car."

"He doesn't. My guess is that it was the same car that was reported stolen yesterday... the description seems to match, anyway. But the story gets better. Sacheverell was working in his garden this afternoon when Trat pulled up outside. He didn't get out of the car, but he shouted across that he had just killed an Irishman who uttered one blasphemy too many. He said he'd left the body in his cottage, and was on his way to France. Before Sacheverell could ask any questions, he'd driven off."

Franks rubbed his chin thoughtfully. "And Sacheverell was positive the man was Trat?"

"Well, he couldn't be absolutely sure, not having seen him since before the war. But he said the man announced himself as Trat, spoke with a Somerset accent like Trat, and wore a wide-brimmed shovel hat like the one Trat always wears."

"But you said the hat was hanging on a peg in Trat's cottage," the inspector pointed out.

"That's true." Sergeant Butter nodded slowly. "We should go there straight away... and not just to look for a wide-brimmed hat. If this latest information is correct, there's a dead Irishman waiting to be found as well. I'll call the vicar and ask him to meet us there in ten minutes. He'll be able to let us in."

Reverend Brigandine turned out to be a tall, white-haired gentleman of about seventy. He met the two policemen at the gate of Trat's cottage, where the sergeant introduced him to Inspector Franks.

"So good of you to come down from Scotland Yard, Inspector." The evening sunlight glinted off the vicar's spectacles. "I do hope nothing untoward has happened. Mr Trat has proved to

be such a good man over these last few years. Only a few days ago I made a revision to my will, you know. Under the new terms, he will receive my entire estate when I pass away."
Franks looked interested. "Is that so? Was this a sudden decision on your part?"

"The idea had been brewing for some time. Under its original terms my legacy would have gone to my next of kin, that dreadful Smethwick boy. I was never happy about that, and after the terrible business over that poor young girl, I decided it was time to take action."

The vicar unlocked the door and they went into the cottage. The sergeant pointed out the shovel hat and walking stick in the hallway. "Exactly as they were this morning," he observed. The vicar sniffed the air. "But there is a distinctly unpleasant odour that I didn't notice earlier."

The sergeant sniffed as well. "Smells like putrid meat. It must have been left out in the kitchen, and it's gone off in the hot weather."

They went through the narrow passage and opened the door into the kitchen. As soon as they did so they were assailed by the most appalling smell, like hitting a solid wall of nauseating putrefaction. All three of them started retching uncontrollably.

"Quick... open the windows and let some fresh air in!" Franks strode across to the back door and flung it wide open.

It was several minutes before the air had cleared enough for them to breathe properly. When they had regained their senses, they looked around in consternation. The kitchen was neat and tidy and sparkling clean.

The sergeant was the first to find his voice. "Where's the stench coming from? It all looks exactly as it did this morning. Nothing has changed!"

"In a physical sense, I'm sure that's true," Franks commented. "Whatever is causing the foul smell was here when you searched the place this morning. It's simply that hours of unrelenting summer heat have hastened the process of decay. Look... what about these jars?"
The detective was examining a shelf laden with half a dozen large earthenware jars. He carefully took one down and placed it on the kitchen table. He removed the cork lid, then recoiled in disgust as the smell hit him.

Sergeant Butter saw a chance to score a point for the local police force. Covering his mouth and nose with a handkerchief, he peered inside the jar. "It looks like a joint of meat," he reported to the others. "It's just gone off, that's all. Nothing too dreadful."

With a grimace, he put his hand in the jar, lifted out the contents and plopped it on the table. It wasn't a joint of meat. It was a human forearm and hand.

"My God!" The sergeant staggered back in horror. "It looks like we've found our mysterious Irishman, after all."

"I wouldn't be too sure about that," Franks said cautiously. "In any event, we shouldn't touch anything else for the moment. It's time to call the coroner."

By midnight, they had completed their gruesome inventory. The earthenware jars all contained various parts of butchered limbs. The victim's torso had been found crammed into a suitcase in the bedroom, while the skull was found in a metal bucket in the cellar. The flesh had been almost completely dissolved with acid.

The three men—Inspector Franks, Sergeant Butter and the Coroner—stood outside the cottage, smoking cigarettes in the warm summer's night. The vicar had long since retired from the scene, completely baffled and thoroughly distraught by the evening's discoveries.

"So one thing's clear, at least." It was Franks who broke the ruminative silence.

"Yes, the body is Trat's." The coroner was a short, plump man, with a surprisingly jovial disposition given his profession. "The matter was put beyond doubt as soon as we found the lower right leg. The two lateral metatarsals missing and healed over; the shrapnel lodged in the gastrocnemius muscle. An exact match to Trat's medical records from the war. The murderer tried to hide the victim's identity by cutting up the body, but it didn't work."

Sergeant Butter nodded. "It's obvious now that the Irishman killed Trat, and then tried to make it look like it happened the other way around. The man claiming to be Trat who confessed to the murder in Blandford Forum must have been an impostor... none other than the Irishman himself."

"Ah, the mysterious Irishman." Franks took a last drag on his cigarette, then threw it to the ground and crushed it with his foot. "I've always had problems with the Irishman, you know." The Sergeant darted a glance at him. "What do you mean?"

"The description, for one thing. It sounds like a cartoon Irishman... an Irishman pictured by someone who has never met a real Irishman. You may not get many Irish visitors in this part of the world, but we see enough of them in London. And very few of them have bright red hair and beards, let alone wear bright green suits and hats. More to the point, the Irish aren't fools, and they know which side their bread's buttered on. No Irishman would voice critical opinions of the Church of England while enjoying the hospitality of a Church of England clergyman."

"So you think the Irishman was an impostor too?" It was the coroner who spoke this time. "A deliberate red herring, as it were?"

"Quite." Franks nodded vigorously. "The Irishman was deliberately thrown into the mix to sow confusion and conceal the identity of the true murderer. It's my opinion that the Irishman yesterday evening, and the man claiming to be Trat this afternoon, were one and the same person."

"But who?" The sergeant was looking increasingly baffled.

"I would have thought the answer was obvious. Didn't you tell me one of your habitual offenders fancied himself as a master of disguise? I forget the young man's name... the one who dressed up as Charlie Chaplin and offered to audition a young lady for the movies."

"Andrew Baker, the lad's name is. But surely you're not suggesting he's the murderer?"

Franks shook his head. "I doubt it. The plot is too complex to be the work of just one person. I imagine Baker was paid well for his actions by the man who is the brains behind the affair: the real murderer."

"And that is...?" Sergeant Butter prompted.

"Peter Smethwick, of course. The arrogant young man I met on the train this afternoon. He had a double motive: Trat had just usurped his inheritance from Reverend Brigandine, and then the curate went on to humiliate him in front of the congregation on Sunday. An ego like Smethwick's would have been pushed to breaking point."

"But it's impossible," the Sergeant objected. "The murder took place on Monday evening, and Smethwick only returned from London this afternoon. He has a watertight alibi."

Franks nodded. "He has an alibi, certainly. When he encountered me on the train he was only too eager to inform me of the fact. He had no idea I was from Scotland Yard, of course... I was just a useful independent witness. He went out of his way to buttonhole me, shunning several empty compartments in order to do so. When a man is so eager to establish an alibi, I am automatically suspicious of it."

"Maybe so," the sergeant said. "But it's an alibi nevertheless."

"Yes, but it's a worthless one. It's an alibi for Monday evening, when we are supposed to believe the murder was committed. But that's not the case. The murder took place a day earlier, on Sunday evening."

"But Trat was seen alive on Monday! There were several..." Sergeant Butter stopped abruptly as a look of enlightenment came over his face. "Oh, I see what you mean, Sir. The people who said they saw Trat on Monday... that wasn't Trat at all. It was young Baker in disguise!"

"Exactly," Franks agreed. "And young Baker, as an accessory to murder, will be old Baker before he gets out of prison. But that's not something young Smethwick will need to worry about. He'll hang before the year is out... and I doubt very much that anyone will mourn his passing."

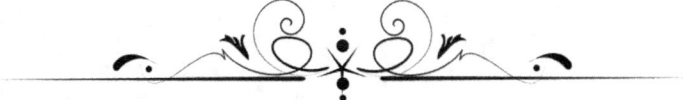

# MUSEUM OF THE FUTURE

## *Take 1: A hundred years from now*
*Originally published in "The Idle Spinster's Companion", Spring 1912*

The day, which was destined to be so memorable, started perfectly normally. Dorothy Photon took the fast tube from Windsor (one of the inner suburbs) straight into the centre of London. A smart young lady of the professional class, Dorothy worked as an Assistant Archivist in the Egyptian wing of the British Museum (yes, the British Museum will still exist in the year 2012!).

The twenty-five mile journey along the Extended Piccadilly Line took a mere fifteen minutes: a pleasant enough trip, though marred from time to time by the grimy beggars who shuffled through the carriages in search of alms. By way of diversion, Dorothy turned her attention to the news-reel that was playing on the lowered blinds of the underground carriage.

The main news story, to which Dorothy paid scant attention (having heard much the same tidings on countless previous occasions), concerned the Seventh Afghan War. Seemingly endless clashes were carrying on between the brave troops of the British-German-Spanish coalition and the retrograde imperialist forces of the Russian Empire. The latter, of course, posed the only serious threat to civilization—and had done so for almost a century, ever since France was overrun by Germany in the Short War of 1913 (a war in which Britain had sensibly remained neutral).

Dorothy pricked up her ears when the topic switched to the latest Voyage to Mars. This was an event she had been following avidly! The picture showed a group of earnest looking women who, the narrator explained, had just returned from Sri Krishnamurti's mountain fastness in Tibet, from whence they had travelled, by means of astral projection while in a yogic trance, to the Red Planet. The women were shown being congratulated by none other than the British Prime Minister herself!

Dorothy knew, as a keen student of history, that at one time the idea of a female Prime Minister would have been unthinkable. But not any longer! "What a truly emancipated age we live in," she thought to herself. Idly, she brushed aside a noxious-smelling urchin that had thrust an upturned bonnet under her nose, in solicitation for what it called "a coupla pennies, miss".

Presently the tube train pulled into Holborn station, at which stop Dorothy alighted. She took the fast automatic elevator to the surface, then walked the short distance to the British Museum. That venerable old edifice, now well into its second century, was surrounded on all sides by towering buildings of striking modernity. Alongside the architecture of 2012, even '*Art Nouveau*' would have looked positively *vieux*!

As Dorothy sat down at her desk a servant came over, bowed respectfully, and handed her a silver foil telegram. Curious, Dorothy read the message: *"EGYPTIAN DEPT BRIT MUS EXPECT INCOMING SHIPMENT ARRIVING BY NOON AIRSHIP STOP"*.

There were still several hours until the delivery was due, so Dorothy set to work cataloguing a batch of artefacts that had arrived from Egypt a few days ago. These days, cataloguing ancient relics was a simple matter of psychometry. Dorothy held the object to her forehead, closed her eyes, and instantly an image formed itself in her mind of the object in its original surroundings. On the few occasions that she was stumped—as for example by some unusual hieroglyphs on one particular artefact—then she could always rely on the ultimate information source: the Psychic Telephone. A quick telepathic conversation with the Egyptian Museum in Cairo, and the answer was hers!

In the Britain of 2012, psychic talents were taken for granted; they played an important part in all aspects of everyday life. As a general rule, women were more psychically sensitive than men, which was why a young woman like Dorothy found herself working in what had hitherto been an exclusively male domain. This feminine revolution could be traced back to the early years of the twentieth century, when a small number of talented and inspirational women such as Madame Blavatsky had pioneered the development of psychic techniques.

Just on the stroke of noon, a huge shadow darkened the window of the room Dorothy was working in. It was the airship, delivering the day's mail and other supplies. This was such an everyday occurrence in 2012 that Dorothy didn't even go over to the window to look at it!

A few minutes later, a servant came in to inform her that the mysterious shipment was awaiting her inspection. Dorothy rushed down to the receiving area and found a big crate waiting for her. She summoned a couple of workmen, and with the aid of crowbars the crate was soon opened to reveal... a brightly painted mummy case!

As Dorothy stared at the mummy case, there was a clicking sound, and the lid started to swing open. Before she knew what was happening, the coffin was lying open and its occupant had stepped out of it! But this was no ancient Egyptian mummy. It was, without a shadow of doubt, a Russian aristocrat: an unmistakable figure in a tailed coat, black cravat and waxed moustache. And the fiend was holding a bomb!

"Victory to the Russian Motherland! Watch helplessly as I strike a deadly blow at the heart of the British Empire!" The man fumbled with the bomb as he attempted to light the fuse.

Suddenly the man froze as if paralyzed, and the unlit bomb dropped harmlessly to the ground. Dorothy had used her finely honed mental powers to launch a psychic attack! The Russian aristocrat was completely in her power!

She looked scornfully at her captive. "We don't call it the British Empire any more," she informed him. "Empire-building is a thing of the past. Britain is a very modern, emancipated nation in the year 2012!"

## Take 2: Eighty years from now
*Originally published in "Shocking Science Quarterly", Spring 1932*

The day started just like any other. In the skies above London, there were all the usual traffic jams. Doug Neutrino cursed under his breath as he navigated his air-car through the packed skyways leading into the centre of the city. Doug was as an Assistant Floorwalker in the Egyptian department of the British Museum. Or, as his father would have it, he was an unambitious loser who would never amount to anything. Doug's father owned a small industrial corporation.

In the sky-lane above Knightsbridge, traffic ground to a halt again. Doug saw the driver of the air car ahead of him lean over the side of his machine and peer down towards the ground below. Following suit, Doug cast his eyes downwards as well. He could see why the traffic had stopped. On the street below, a full-scale blaster fight was in progress: a bunch of gangsters exchanging deadly ray-fire with blue-clad police officers. Within seconds the battle was over... the two parties had annihilated each other. A street cleaning robot whirred into action, and a few minutes later the traffic began to move again.

As he turned into the sky-lane above Oxford Street, Doug came within sight and sound of the giant full-colour news screens that towered above that thoroughfare. *"Huge gains on Wall Street!"* a screen blared out. *"Slight fall in Frankfurt market!"* it added, with equal glee. Footage was shown of the two most powerful men in the world: a beaming president in Washington, and a stony-faced chancellor in Berlin.

In the world of 2012, war was a thing of the past: the last one had finished almost a hundred years ago, in 1918. But an end to war didn't mean an end to international rivalry. Britain had been the 49th state of the U.S.A. since 1935—and, boy, was she proud of it! The newsmen never missed a chance to put down Britain's geographical neighbour and biggest competitor, Greater Germany (as the continent of Europe was now known).

Doug glanced down at another of the big screens, and almost lost control of his air-car. The screen showed a hideous green monster with bulging eyes and writhing tentacles. Then the camera angle changed, and he saw that the creature was safely behind bars: inside a cage on the tarmac in front of a gleaming, towering rocket-ship. These were the latest pictures from the Goddard Spaceport, where the Mars expedition had just returned with its sample of Martian life.

Arriving at the British Museum, Doug descended to street level and landed his air-car. He jumped out and handed his keys to a parking robot that came hurrying over. With hardly a glance at the towering skyscrapers on the other side of the street, he turned towards the old stone building of the Museum. It looked ancient... and of course it was. The customers liked it that way.

Doug made his way to the Egyptian floor, where the sales robots were already at their stations behind the counters. The doors of the Museum would be opening any minute now! Doug hurried to his booth in the corner. On the desk, the red light was flashing over the video phone: a message was waiting for him. Doug punched the button and the face of a robot operator appeared. "Message for you, sir or madam," the robot intoned. "Incoming shipment for the Egyptian department arriving by the noon rocket. End of message."

A bell rang and he jumped up, cursing under his breath. Time to go out on the floor and start being pleasantly obsequious to the customers!

Doug was vaguely aware that there had been a time, way back in the 20th century, when the exhibits in the Museum had not been for sale. In those days, they had been there for display only. But Progress marches on, and in the 21st century Commerce was king! The Museum's patrons were among the richest businessmen in the country.

But Doug was not just an ordinary salesman. He was an expert on the history of Egyptian artefacts. He prided himself that, right off the top of his head, he could answer almost any question that a prospective customer might ask. On the rare occasions that he was stumped, for example if he was asked the meaning of some obscure hieroglyphic inscription, he could always fall back on the ultimate information source: the Museum's vast microfilm library.

Shortly after the noon bell rang, a robot came up to Doug and informed him that the expected rocket shipment had arrived. Doug took the robot with him to the receiving area, where he found a large crate waiting for him. He instructed the robot to open the crate, and in a matter of moments its contents lay revealed. It was a brightly painted mummy case!

As Doug gaped at the mummy case, there was a sudden click and the lid swung open. Something stirred inside. The mummy lived! Before Doug had time to react, the mummy had leapt to its feet and was pointing a ray gun at him. But it wasn't a mummy after all. This was no bandage-wrapped cadaver... it was an ordinary-looking businessman with a moustache and pin-striped suit!

"So, British pig-dog! Soon vill I blast your Egyptian collection to atoms! Denn vill dere be only one Egyptian collection in der World, und dat vill be der Altes Museum in Berlin! Haha!" The man—obviously some kind of deranged German nationalist—waved his ray-gun menacingly.

"Look behind you," Doug suggested.

"Ha! Dat is der oldest trick in der book! Behind me is only der robot, und robots, dey is programmed never to harm der human person!"

The robot slugged the German on the back of the head, knocking him out cold.

"I ain't a robot," the robot explained, pulling off its head to reveal a grinning human face.

"Well, I'll be!" Doug shook his head. "If it isn't Sammy, the Museum's very own Private Eye!"

## Take 3: Sixty years from now
*Originally published in "Bleak Futures Weekly", 15 March 1952*

One depressing day followed another in the nightmare world of 2012. Donovan Meson trudged along the seemingly endless ramps and passageways that led from his dwelling on Sublevel 23 to the administrative centre of New London. A third-generation Normal whose IQ was too high for military service, Donovan worked as an Assistant Preservation Operative in the Pre-War section of the British Museum.

New London was nowhere near old London; it was hundreds of feet below what had once been Wiltshire... but was now a barren, war-ravaged wilderness. Donovan encountered very few other Normals as he tramped through the dusty, dimly-lit corridors. Normals made up a small minority in the world of 2012; the great majority of humankind were mutants. There were vacant-eyed alpha-mutants, inanely giggling beta-mutants and silent, sinister gamma-mutants. Even the animals were mutants. Donovan kicked out at an ugly, hairless, metre-long rat as it tried to bite his ankle.

At precisely 0900 hours, the public address system crackled into life. *"This is a public service announcement,"* the speaker said. *"At 0858 GMT today, the Third World War entered its twenty-one thousand, two hundred and forty-fifth day. Unbowed by almost sixty years of continuous nuclear warfare, Western Civilization continues its great struggle against the Soviet menace. We should always keep in mind the heart-warming maxim that our great-grandfathers taught us: it is better to be Dead than to be Red."*

There was a brief burst of patriotic music, then the voice continued: *"As we all know, this is a War that is being fought in Space as well as on the surface of the Earth. The government is pleased to announce that in Space, just as on Earth, the West has the upper hand. As of today, West-Civ controls two hundred and twenty three orbiting nuclear battle-stations, as opposed to a paltry two hundred and twenty-two controlled by the Soviets. Victory is in sight!"*

After walking for what seemed like hours, Donovan ascended the last access ramp leading to the Museum. At the steel-studded entrance portal, a security officer checked his identification, scrutinized him carefully, and then pressed a button. The heavy doors slid open with a hydraulic hiss. Donovan stepped inside. The Museum was a single vast cavern, hewn out of bare rock.

Donovan trudged past endless steel racks crammed with pre-war artefacts. Finally he came to the back of the cavern, where he had a small, formica-lined cubicle—a workspace he shared with one of the Sigma mutants. The Sigma was a singularly dim-witted specimen of devolved humanity... but one that was useful in certain situations.

As Donovan entered the cubicle, the mutant gestured stupidly at a shiny canister lying on the desk. Donovan picked it up: it was a message canister that had been piped down the tube from the surface station. He cracked it open and read the message: *"Expect valuable shipment arriving 1200 hours by unmanned rocket drone."*

Putting the message to one side, Donovan readied himself for the drab tedium of another day's work. It was his job to catalogue the artefacts, and preserve those among them that were deemed useful to the war effort. Gloomily he picked up his clipboard and proceeded to where he had left off yesterday: Aisle 15 – Rack 63 – Shelf 9 – Bin 24.

The small plastic bin contained a collection of ceramic shards, which to Donovan's eye looked ancient... and hence valueless. But some of the shards bore markings, and these might prove to be important if he could get them decoded. That meant consulting the ultimate information source: the Computer.

He carried the bin over to the nearest Computer Terminal. This was connected by a mass of conduits to a vast artificial brain, composed of billions of valves and clattering relays, which occupied the whole of Sublevels 55 to 63. He held the shards one at a time in front of the camera lens, then waited patiently until the paper printout clicked out of its slot. *"ANCIENT EGYPTIAN HIEROGLYPHS: NO MILITARY VALUE: MAY BE DESTROYED."*

Later, when he was back in his office writing up the destruction record, a buzzer sounded to indicate the arrival of the rocket drone. "Come on, Siggy—we're going on a trip to the surface," he said, addressing the Sigma mutant. He carefully zipped himself into a lead-lined radiation suit... a safety precaution that the mutant, being fully radiated already, didn't need. They took the express lift to the surface, and stepped out onto the barren, desolate landscape that was twenty-first century Britain.

Although it was the middle of the day, the sky was almost completely dark: obscured from horizon to horizon by the perpetual thick black clouds of nuclear winter. Occasionally the sky would light up with the brief flash of a distant hydrogen bomb. A few metres from the lift-head they found the rocket pod lying on the dusty ground: a gleaming, coffin-sized cylinder.

Donovan bent down and pressed a button on the surface of the pod. A panel slid open, and something leapt out of the pod. It was a human being! Before Donovan had time to react, the man was standing in front of him, pointing a needle-gun.

"Good, I see that you are a Normal like myself," the visitor said in an icily calm voice. "We are not so very different, physically. How easy it will be for me to take your place! At last, an agent of the Supreme Soviet will infiltrate to the very heart of the decadent West!" The man started to squeeze the trigger.

Things happened very quickly. Something that looked like a long red snake flicked out and knocked the needle-gun from the Soviet agent's hand. Then the snake—now impossibly long—flicked back and wound itself rapidly round the agent's arms and legs, immobilizing him.

"Good work, Siggy," Donovan said. "I've always maintained that Sigma mutants are useful in certain situations. You never know when you're going to need a prehensile tongue!"

---

## Take 4: Forty years from now
*Originally published in "The Chromium Placenta: An Anthology of Relevant Fiction", Spring 1972*

The start of another bright, happy, liberated day in the year 2012! In her trendy suburban pad-apt, Dodo Quark wriggled into a tight-fitting antigrav suit in preparation for the short hop into the centre of town. A statuesque brunette (whose figure was at least partly natural), Dodo worked as an Assistant Hostess at the British Museum.

She checked her hair in the mirror, then launched herself out of the window.

"Out of my way, sky-hogs!" Dodo yelled at two young men who were—as far as she could tell—attempting to copulate in mid-air. They were doing it directly in line with her trajectory. "Oof!" She was flipped in an involuntary somersault as her antigrav field collided with that of the two young men. Regaining her breath she looked back and saw they were still at it, apparently unaware of the collision. It was obvious they were high on something. "Acid head morons!" Dodo yelled back at them.

Realizing it was time for the morning newscast, Dodo switched on her satellite wrist video.

The tiny screen swirled into psychedelic life, and a moment later small but powerful speakers chimed out stereophonically: *"Well, my chicks and dudes, things are looking just cool and groovy all over the fantabulous Free World. I guess that's all the news you need to know.*

*Mayhap there's some politics going on somewhere, but here in your friendly neighbourhood newsroom we're just too busy enjoying ourselves to grok that kind of thing. Not like those squares over on the other side of the planet! They call it the Soviet Union, and everything there is cold and grey and solemnly serious, and all they ever talk about is politics..."*

There was a pause, and Dodo glanced down at the tiny screen attached to her wrist. The anchorman—who was conservatively dressed in an orange poncho and flared trousers—was consulting a note that had been handed to him. *"Breaking news, for those of you still hanging in there! Hot in from our reporter-dude in Aldrin City on the little old Moon. Seems the Mars Mission has just landed back at Armstrong Field in the Sea of Tranquillity. Took them eight months to get there and eight months to get back, and they didn't find any bug-eyed monsters or canals or anything. What's the point of that? Astronauts are all a bunch of squares, if you want my opinion..."*

Dodo clicked off the wrist video as she descended towards the British Museum. She zeroed in on the 32nd floor—the Egyptian floor, where she worked—and flew in through the entrance window. This particular building, Dodo knew, had not always housed the British Museum. When it was built, way back in the 1960s, it had been called the Post Office Tower. But when a new, bigger Post Office Tower was built twenty years later, the British Museum had moved in here. It was suitably old-fashioned!

As Dodo wriggled out of her antigrav suit, the senior floor hostess came over to her. She was a matronly woman of fifty-something, conservatively dressed in a lime-green microskirt and seethru blouse. "Hi there, sweetie, how's it hanging? Grok this: a message just came through on the old fax machine. A hyperliner shipment is hauling in around about noon-time. I'm gonna need you to check it out for me."

"Sure thing," Dodo nodded. "But right now I gotta run—I spy a punter heading this way. And he looks loaded!"

The 'punter' was a shiny-suited gentleman of Japanese appearance. He looked like he had a question he wanted to ask. Well, he could ask away! Dodo prided herself on her knowledge of the Museum and all its displays. A pleasure palace for the idle rich it may have been—but it was a factually based pleasure palace!

Dodo beamed her most winning smile at the man. "Good morning, Sir. How may I be of assistance?"

The man gave an apologetic little cough. "I was just wondering, Miss... might I perhaps have the pleasure of bonking your brains out in the style of the ancient Egyptians?"

Dodo shook her head. "I'm afraid not, Sir. But feel free to use any of our fully-functional androids for that purpose. Take your pick." She waved her arms, indicating the numerous androids of assorted shapes, sizes and genders that were lounging around the exhibits.

During the course of the morning, Dodo was called on to answer a seemingly endless stream of queries... not all of them concerned with interactive experiences of the copulatory kind. She was only stumped once, when someone asked a question about an obscure hieroglyphic inscription. On this occasion, she had to refer to the ultimate information source: the Museum's talking computer, HANK 9000. Like all computers, HANK was a relentlessly factual machine. It insisted on pointing out, gratuitously and unnecessarily, that her backside looked big in the fluorescent purple micro-suit she was wearing today.

Finally noon came around. It was time for Dodo to deal with the mysterious hyperliner shipment. She sent a couple of androids to bring it down from the receiving area on the roof, wondering in the meantime what on earth it could be. She didn't have to wait long... a few minutes later the androids staggered in and plonked down the new acquisition in the middle of the floor. It was a brightly painted mummy case!

As Dodo stood gawping at the mummy case, there was a sudden click and the lid flipped open. Something stirred inside. "Eek, a living mummy!" she shrieked. Before she knew what was happening, a figure had leapt from the coffin and was waving a menacing-looking hypodermic at her.

On second thoughts, she decided it wasn't a mummy after all. It was just a pasty-faced, underfed-looking man in shapeless grey pyjamas.

The newcomer looked Dodo up and down, scowling at her scanty attire. "So this is the much-vaunted Free World! You call yourselves liberated... pah! I see only decadence, and the symbols of decadence. In the East we do not tolerate such things. I will destroy this building and all that it symbolizes. But first, I must incapacitate you with the paralyzing drug."

The man lunged forward with his hypodermic, plunging it into the part of Dodo's anatomy that was closest to him. "So... now you are paralyzed! You cannot move!"

The man turned away, intent on nefarious action. As soon as he had his back to her, Dodo flashed into action. Grabbing a Nineteenth Dynasty canopic jar from a nearby stand, she bashed the man over the head with it. He fell senseless to the ground.

Dodo glanced down at her chest, grimaced, and plucked the hypodermic out of her left bosom. Then she addressed the inert form at her feet: "Western decadence has its benefits," she informed him. "I bet you never even heard of silicone breast implants in the solemnly serious Soviet Union!"

# Take 5: Twenty years from now
*Originally published in CYBER / ESCAPE, March 1992*

T
he day that ended so ominously started like any other. Dorian Higgs-Boson sped along the streets of London in his little red zero-emissions eco-car. Dorian was a rising member of the New Technocracy: a Digital Assistant in the Egyptian wing of the British Museum.

Traffic was flowing freely along the South Circular... as it had every day since the final defeat of the Illuminati in 1999. Never-ending roadworks had been part of Homo Reptiloid's scheme to keep Homo Sapiens under its heel... as, indeed, had been the suppression of energy-efficient technologies such as those used in Dorian's eco-car. It was ages since he'd seen a vehicle powered by fossil fuel...

As if on cue, at that very moment an ancient, gaudily painted VW camper van pulled out in front of him, belching black smoke from its rattling exhaust. Dorian swore when he saw the inscription scrawled across the van's rear: *'The Children of Aquarius'*. It was one of the irrational, technophobic cults that had sprung up with the new millennium. Dorian scowled: he had no time for such mystical nonsense.

He leaned forward and toggled the channels on the car's digital audio receiver: *"... classic track from way back in 2001... <click> ... the latest news, every hour, on the hour..."* Dorian had dim childhood memories of a time when news broadcasts had headlined stories of wars, famines and international tensions. That, of course, had been in the days before Global Peace and Prosperity. Now the news started with what old-style news reporters would have thought of as 'the quirky stories that go at the end': news of NASA space missions, the latest technological innovations, and such like.

*"Today's top story comes from Cydonia on Mars, close to the huge enigmatic monument known as the Face on Mars. NASA archaeologists have discovered further relics left by the ancient Martian civilization. There was a time, before the fall of the Illuminati, when NASA kept all Martian discoveries a closely guarded secret. But today things are different, and a NASA spokesperson has stated that full results will be posted on the internet as and when they are available. A similar openness prevails at Area 51 here on Earth, where yesterday's press conference revealed a new batch of previously classified..."*

Dorian clicked off the receiver, sounded his horn, put his foot down, and overtook the camper van. A few minutes later he arrived at the British Museum. He headed straight to his office.

Dorian bootstrapped his computer, and as the screen flickered into life he saw that he had received a new electronic mail message, or 'e-mail' as it was popularly known. The message must have been sent by another technocrat like himself—since ordinary people, lacking the necessary degrees in software engineering, were incapable of mastering the complex SMTP syntax of dots and hashes and backslashes. Gone were the days when the computer-literate were targets of mass ridicule, dismissed as socially inept geeks. In the twenty-first century, the techno-literate were the new elite, while the digitally ignorant masses were restricted to manual labour and similarly degrading roles.

In this case, however, the e-mail turned out to be an automated one sent by the IP server. It stated, in appropriately obscure technical jargon, that a large FTP file was on its way and that (due to limitations of bandwidth) delivery was not expected to be completed before 1200 hours.

Dorian's desktop machine was a state-of-the art multitasking computer, which allowed him to get on with his routine work while he waited for the file transfer to complete. He carefully donned the headset and cybergloves of the virtual interface. This allowed him to interact directly with the hyperdimensional matrix of abstract information that constituted the Museum's relational database. His current assignment involved the development of information-rich drilldowns which would provide an enhanced Virtual Reality experience for Museum visitors.

Dorian was adept at his work, and he progressed with lightning speed. He felt more at home in cyberspace than he did in the real world. On the rare occasions that he was stumped by something—such as the meaning of an unusual hieroglyphic inscription—he could always fall back on the ultimate information source: the so-called 'internet'. Ah, the wonders of Usenet, Gopher and Telnet!

Dorian was engrossed in his work when a cyberspace notification popped up in his field of vision. The FTP download was complete. Curious about the contents of such a large file, he actuated it with a deft flick of his cyberglove. Instantly, a three dimensional image materialized in cyberspace. It was a brightly decorated mummy case!

The mummy case, appearing to float weightlessly, performed a slow pirouette about its axis. Then suddenly, as Dorian watched open-mouthed, it burst into a million glittering fragments. In its place was a vista of ancient Egypt... but not the ancient Egypt that Dorian knew from scholarly study. This was an impossible fantasy world—complete with magic carpets, animal-headed space gods and jewel-studded golden pyramids! There could be no mistake: this was ancient Egypt as it was envisioned by the Children of Aquarius!

A long-robed, white-bearded guru popped into existence. *"The age of materialism is over,"* the CGI-generated figure intoned. *"The Age of Aquarius has dawned. With the passing of the old millennium, the..."*

The guru's speech was cut off abruptly as Dorian triggered the computer's electronic countermeasure defences. The intrusive vision wavered briefly and then disappeared: the sanity of cyberspace had been restored. Shaken, Dorian tore off the headset and cybergloves, and headed straight for the office of the SysAdmin.

"Obviously it was a malicious program of the 'trojan horse' variety," the SysAdmin observed, when Dorian had finished his report. "But what worries me most is its source: the Children of Aquarius. These people are notoriously technophobic, yet they have clearly mastered the basics of computer programming and FTP transfer. The implication is as ominous as it is inescapable. The internet is now being used by the ignorant masses."

# NOTES ON THE STORIES

**The Guardian of the Tomb**
This is a retelling of the legend of Rennes-le-Chateau in the style of M. R. James's *Ghost Stories of an Antiquary*. It's fiction, so I've taken a few Dan Brown-esque liberties with the facts... but then most of the "facts" were made up in the first place. In reality, M. R. James had probably never even heard of Rennes-le-Chateau—certainly not the legend in its modern form, which was largely fabricated in the 1950s and 60s.

**The Balloon Factory**
This is a satire on conspiracy theories of the Roswell variety. It's a lot easier to believe in extraterrestrials than to try and get your head round the ever-changing world of international politics—which all too often provides the dull-as-ditchwater truth behind government secrecy. There really was a secretive "Balloon Factory" on Farnborough Common in the early years of the twentieth century. As well as building giant airships, the factory saw the birth of heavier-than-air aviation in this country. It was renamed the Royal Aircraft Factory in 1912.

**The Call of Cool-O**
Stylistically, it's difficult to think of two writers more different than H. P. Lovecraft and Philip K. Dick. But thematically, there are similarities. Dick had a life-long fascination with Gnosticism: the notion that demented and/or evil demi-gods long ago usurped the benevolent true God. Surely there are parallels here to the Lovecraftian Cthulhu mythos? That was the thinking behind this story, which is a re-telling of "The Call of Cthulhu" in an exaggeratedly Dickian style.

**Flowers of the Future**
One of the things you learn as you grow older is that fashions change. Not just fashions in music and clothes, but fashions in philosophy, science, politics... even the fundamental beliefs that society holds to be self-evident. I'm convinced that if someone could see the future, or even visit it, they simply wouldn't understand it. That's what this short piece is about.

**The Gravity Engine**
This story inverts certain historical facts for satirical effect. In the real world, Michael Faraday (1791 – 1867) was a scientific genius who discovered the intimate connections between electricity, magnetism and motion. In the 1840s, after he had done the work for which he is remembered, Faraday tried unsuccessfully to find a connection between electricity and gravity, using experiments similar to the one described in this story.

Much of the story's background is based in fact: there was a Great Exhibition in London in 1851, Robert Stephenson was living in Gloucester Square at the time, and the Surrey Shot Tower was a major landmark on the South Bank. But there's no such thing as an electro-calorimeter. In reality, electric current is measured with a galvanometer, but that works by electromagnetism so I couldn't use it in the story!

**Loss of Power**

Several of the stories in this book are about individuals who get too deeply engrossed in a fantasy world. During the 19th century, King Ludwig II of Bavaria was the arch-fantasist, building the fairy-tale castle of Neuschwanstein and immersing himself in the world of Wagner's operas. But not to the extent of the character in this story...

**A Case for Crane**

Although it's not essential, it's best to visualize this story as taking place in the 1970s—before the days of video games and the internet, when television was everyone's favourite escape mechanism. The show itself, "A Case for Crane", is meant to date from the 70s, which was the golden age of cop shows.

I'm not a chess player, and the game that is featured in the story came out of a library book. I assume the moves are all legal and logical... but it doesn't really matter if they're not.

**The Rendlesham Magi**

Britain's most notorious UFO case, the Rendlesham Forest incident, took place in 1980 over the Christmas period. Given the comparative nearness of Rendlesham to Cambridge University, I couldn't resist transforming it into this story about Wise Men following a star.

**The Case of the Purloined Poe**

This story uses a couple of the characters I created for my series about SOLVED—The Secret Oxford League of Volunteer Extracurricular Detectives. The earlier stories are collected in a self-published book called *The Case of the Invisible College and Other Mysteries*... but the present story stands on its own, so you don't have to buy the book (although I'd be pleased if you did). You might, however, like to find a pencil and paper and spend a few minutes working out what "Pierce Stormson" is an anagram of.

The details about the Poe manuscript are taken from the John Dickson Carr novel mentioned in the story. As far as I know, these details are completely fictitious.

**Homicidal Homeopathy**

This story was written in the year 2000 as part of a short series I did for a webzine called *Nuketown*. Four years later, it was incorporated into a rather sleazy, slapstick novella called *Kundalini Conspiracy*. With the benefit of another eight years of hindsight, I feel that "Homicidal Homeopathy" stands better on its own—so, in a slightly updated form, here it is.

The technobabble in the story—about Tesla coils, scalar waves and water memory—is all genuine pseudo-science. I mean, it's all nonsense... but it's nonsense I got off the internet, without having to make it up.

**The Mystic Fayre Affair**

A Victorian gentleman named Hargrave Jennings came up with the unorthodox notion that all the world's religions are corrupt version of the one true religion, which is worship of the "male generative organ"—or the Masculine Cross, as Jennings called it. So while this story might come across like a scene from a 1960s *Carry On* film, it actually has a firm basis in serious scholarship. Honestly.

### Miss Perception

This satire takes on two easy targets: paranoid conspiracy theorists, and the highly structured literary style affected by J. G. Ballard and other New Wave writers in the 1960s and 70s. I used to enjoy reading these when I was a teenager—and not just because they had sex in them. You may wonder, when reading the story, whether Georgina is genuinely mad—or simply chooses to live in a fantasy world because she prefers it. I wondered the same thing.

### The Mythologist

Anyone who has worked in a large bureaucratic organization will be familiar with the ubiquitous office-wall quotation attributed to "Petronius Arbiter". I used to be impressed by this, until I discovered that it was a myth. But then I made a much more interesting discovery. Whenever I told people it was a myth, they didn't want to believe me. That's what led me to write this story.

### Psykick Kwest

It's a universal truth that people are always thinking about sex—especially if they're given the opportunity to fantasize imaginatively. And what better opportunity for imaginative fantasizing than past-life regression hypnosis?

### The Mind Whisperers

"Truth is stranger than fiction", they say. Back in the 1940s, the science fiction magazine *Amazing Stories* ran a series of articles by Richard Shaver, describing a race of huge, slobbering, mentally retarded cave-dwellers who were the true masters of the world. It was presented as fact, but of course it was really fiction. The truth is never as strange as fiction... but wouldn't it be cool if it was?

### Secrets of the Green God

One of the exercises on a creative writing course I attended was to write a "narrative hook". The result was this story—a sci-fi version of the Stone-Tape concept, which was referred to in passing in "The Case of the Purloined Poe".

### The Alchemist's Curse

I'm an alumnus of both Oxford and Cambridge universities. I was an undergraduate at Cambridge, and later on I had a postdoctoral fellowship at Oxford. Early in 2012 the Oxford Alumni magazine ran a creative writing competition with a length limit of 1000 words. "The Alchemist's Curse" was my submission, but it didn't even make the runner-up list. It's printed here with just one small alteration: I've moved the setting from Oxford to Cambridge!

### Collector's Item

"Ballad" is one of those words that has changed its meaning over the years. In Victorian times (and earlier), it referred to a narrative poem with lines alternating between eight syllables and six syllables, with only the six-syllable lines rhyming. This creates a distinctly hypnotic effect ideal for the telling of spooky tales. It's a shame the form went out of fashion—and an even greater shame that the word has now come to mean a sentimental love song.

### The Vanishing Curate

Stylistically, with its 1920s setting, this story is a loose pastiche of my all-time favourite mystery writer, Freeman Wills Crofts. However, many of the plot details and characters are based on a real-life murder case that took place three hundred years earlier in 1624, which was recounted (and quite possibly embellished) in a four-page broadsheet of the time entitled "Crying Murther at Old Cleeve".

## Museum of the Future

I like reading old science fiction stories, because of what you can learn from them about the past. All too often early sci-fi writings are dismissed on the grounds that their predictions about the future were all wrong. But that misses the point. Science fiction authors rarely make a serious attempt to predict the future—instead they use the "future" as a metaphor for their own present. That's what I tried to illustrate in this story... five times over!

![Still on the track of unknown animals — photograph of researchers paddling a canoe on a lake, with The Centre for Fortean Zoology logo (www.cfz.org.uk)]

# STILL ON THE TRACK OF UNKNOWN ANIMALS

T he Centre for Fortean Zoology, or CFZ, is a non profit-making organisation founded in 1992 with the aim of being a clearing house for information, and coordinating research into mystery animals around the world.

We also study out of place animals, rare and aberrant animal behaviour, and Zooform Phenomena; little-understood "things" that appear to be animals, but which are in fact nothing of the sort, and not even alive (at least in the way we understand the term).

Not only are we the biggest organisation of our type in the world, but - or so we like to think - we are the best. We are certainly the only truly global cryptozoological research organisation, and we carry out our investigations using a strictly scientific set of guidelines. We are expanding all the time and looking to recruit new members to help us in our research into mysterious animals and strange creatures across the globe.

Why should you join us? Because, if you are genuinely interested in trying to solve the last great mysteries of Mother Nature, there is nobody better than us with whom to do it.

Members get a four-issue subscription to our journal *Animals & Men*. Each issue contains nearly 100 pages packed with news, articles, letters, research papers, field reports, and even a gossip column! The magazine is Royal Octavo in format with a full colour cover. You also have access to one of the world's largest collections of resource material dealing with cryptozoology and allied disciplines, and people from the CFZ membership regularly take part in fieldwork and expeditions around the world.

The CFZ is managed by a three-man board of trustees, with a non-profit making trust registered with HM Government Stamp Office. The board of trustees is supported by a Permanent Directorate of full and part-time staff, and advised by a Consultancy Board of specialists - many of whom are world-renowned experts in their particular field. We have regional representatives across the UK, the USA, and many other parts of the world, and are affiliated with

You'll find that the people at the CFZ are friendly and approachable. We have a thriving forum on the website which is the hub of an ever-growing electronic community. You will soon find your feet. Many members of the CFZ Permanent Directorate started off as ordinary members, and now work full-time chasing monsters around the world.

Write to us, e-mail us, or telephone us. The list of future projects on the website is not exhaustive. If you have a good idea for an investigation, please tell us. We may well be able to help.

We are always looking for volunteers to join us. If you see a project that interests you, do not hesitate to get in touch with us. Under certain circumstances we can help provide funding for your trip. If you look on the future projects section of the website, you can see some of the projects that we have pencilled in for the next few years.

In 2003 and 2004 we sent three-man expeditions to Sumatra looking for Orang-Pendek - a semi-legendary bipedal ape. The same three went to Mongolia in 2005. All three members started off merely subscribers to the CFZ magazine. Next time it could be you!

We have no magic sources of income. All our funds come from donations, membership fees, and sales of our publications and merchandise. We are always looking for corporate sponsorship, and other sources of revenue. If you have any ideas for fund-raising please let us know. However, unlike other cryptozoological organisations in the past, we do not live in an intellectual ivory tower. We are not afraid to get our hands dirty, and furthermore we are not one of those organisations where the membership have to raise money so that a privileged few can go on expensive foreign trips. Our research teams, both in the UK and abroad, consist of a mixture of experienced and inexperienced personnel. We are truly a community, and work on the premise that the benefits of CFZ membership are open to all.

Reports of our investigations are published on our website as soon as they are available. Preliminary reports are posted within days of the project finishing.

Each year we publish a 200 page yearbook

We have a thriving YouTube channel, CFZtv, which has well over two hundred self-made documentaries, lecture appearances, and episodes of our monthly webTV show. We have a daily online magazine, which has over a million hits each year.

Each year since 2000 we have held our annual convention - the Weird Weekend. It is three days of lectures, workshops, and excursions. But most importantly it is a chance for members of the CFZ to meet each other, and to talk with the members of the permanent directorate in a relaxed and informal setting and preferably with a pint of beer in one hand. Since 2006 - the Weird Weekend has been bigger and better and held on the third weekend in August in the idyllic rural location of Woolsery in North Devon.

Since relocating to North Devon in 2005 we have become ever more closely involved with other community organisations, and we hope that this trend will continue. We have also

worked closely with Police Forces across the UK as consultants for animal mutilation cases, and we intend to forge closer links with the coastguard and other community services. We want to work closely with those who regularly travel into the Bristol Channel, so that if the recent trend of exotic animal visitors to our coastal waters continues, we can be out there as soon as possible.

Apart from having been the only Fortean Zoological organisation in the world to have consistently published material on all aspects of the subject for over a decade, we have achieved the following concrete results:

• Disproved the myth relating to the headless so-called sea-serpent carcass of Durgan beach in Cornwall 1975
• Disproved the story

of the 1988 puma skull of Lustleigh Cleave

- Carried out the only in-depth research ever into the mythos of the Cornish Owlman.
- Made the first records of a tropical species of lamprey
- Made the first records of a luminous cave gnat larva in Thailand
- Discovered a possible new species of British mammal - the beech marten
- In 1994-6 carried out the first archival fortean zoological survey of Hong Kong
- In the year 2000, CFZ theories were confirmed when a new species of lizard was added to the British List
- Identified the monster of Martin Mere in Lancashire as a giant wels catfish
- Expanded the known range of Armitage's skink in the Gambia by 80%
- Obtained photographic evidence of the remains of Europe's largest known pike
- Carried out the first ever in-depth study of the ninki-nanka
- Carried out the first attempt to breed Puerto Rican cave snails in captivity
- Were the first European explorers to visit the `lost valley` in Sumatra
- Published the first ever evidence for a new tribe of pygmies in Guyana
- Published the first evidence for a new species of caiman in Guyana

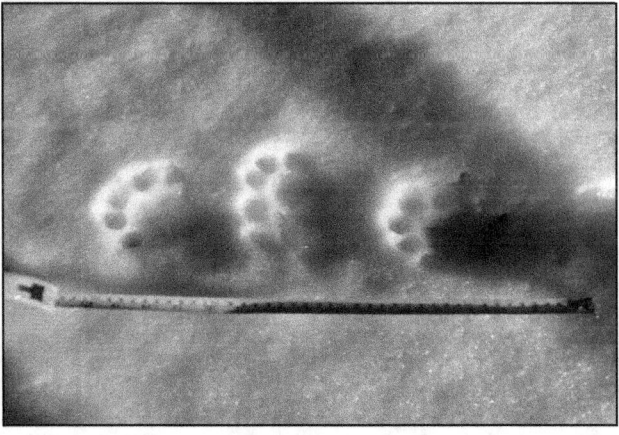

on a monster-haunted lake in Ireland for the first time
• Had a sighting of orang pendek in Sumatra in 2009
• Found leopard hair, subsequently identified by DNA analysis, from rural North Devon in 2010
• Brought back hairs which appear to be from an unknown primate in Sumatra
• Published some of the best evidence ever for the almasty in southern Russia

CFZ Expeditions and Investigations include:

• 1998 Puerto Rico, Florida, Mexico (Chupacabras)
• 1999 Nevada (Bigfoot)
• 2000 Thailand (Naga)
• 2002 Martin Mere (Giant catfish)
• 2002 Cleveland (Wallaby mutilation)
• 2003 Bolam Lake (BHM Reports)

- 2003 Sumatra (Orang Pendek)
- 2003 Texas (Bigfoot; giant snapping turtles)
- 2004 Sumatra (Orang Pendek; cigau, a sabre-toothed cat)
- 2004 Illinois  (Black panthers; cicada swarm)
- 2004 Texas (Mystery blue dog)
- Loch Morar (Monster)
- 2004 Puerto Rico (Chupacabras; carnivorous cave snails)
- 2005 Belize (Affiliate expedition for hairy dwarfs)
- 2005 Loch Ness (Monster)
- 2005 Mongolia (Allghoi Khorkhoi aka Mongolian death worm)

- 2006 Gambia (Gambo - Gambian sea monster , Ninki Nanka and  Armitage's skink
- 2006 Llangorse Lake (Giant pike, giant eels)
- 2006 Windermere (Giant eels)
- 2007  Coniston Water (Giant eels)
- 2007 Guyana  (Giant anaconda,  didi, water tiger)
- 2008 Russia (Almasty)
- 2009 Sumatra (Orang pendek)
- 2009 Republic of Ireland (Lake Monster)
- 2010 Texas (Blue Dogs)
- 2010 India (Mande Burung)
- 2011 Sumatra (Orang-pendek)

For details of current membership fees, current expeditions and investigations, and voluntary posts within the CFZ that need your help, please do not hesitate to contact us.

The Centre for Fortean Zoology,
Myrtle Cottage,
Woolfardisworthy,
Bideford, North Devon
EX39 5QR

Telephone 01237 431413
Fax+44 (0)7006-074-925
**eMail** info@cfz.org.uk

**Websites:**

www.cfz.org.uk
www.weirdweekend.org

# THE WORLD'S WEIRDEST PUBLISHING COMPANY

**ANIMALS & MEN** ISSUES 16-20
THE JOURNAL OF THE CENTRE FOR FORTEAN ZOOLOGY
NEW HORIZONS
Edited by Jon Downes

**BIG CATS** LOOSE IN BRITAIN

**PREDATOR DEATHMATCH**
NICK MOLEY
WITH ILLUSTRATIONS BY ANTHONY WALLIS

PHENOMENA
Edited by Jonathan Downes and Richard Freeman
FOREWORD BY Dr. KARL SHUKER

**A DAINTREE DIARY**
Tales from Travels Daintree tropical North Queensland
**CARL PORTMAN**

STAR STEEDS
THE COLLECTED POEMS
Dr Karl P. N. Shuker

**STRANGELYSTRANGE** ly normal
an anthology of writings by
**ANDY ROBERTS**

# HOW TO START A PUBLISHING EMPIRE

Unlike most mainstream publishers, we have a non-commercial remit, and our mission statement claims that "we publish books because they deserve to be published, not because we think that we can make money out of them". Our motto is the Latin Tag *Pro bona causa facimus* (we do it for good reason), a slogan taken from a children's book *The Case of the Silver Egg* by the late Desmond Skirrow.

WIKIPEDIA: "The first book published was in 1988. *Take this Brother may it Serve you Well* was a guide to Beatles bootlegs by Jonathan Downes. It sold quite well, but was hampered by very poor production values, being photocopied, and held together by a plastic clip binder. In 1988 A5 clip binders were hard to get hold of, so the publishers took A4 binders and cut them in half with a hacksaw. It now reaches surprisingly high prices second hand.

The production quality improved slightly over the years, and after 1999 all the books produced were ringbound with laminated colour covers. In 2004, however, they signed an agreement with Lightning Source, and all books are now produced perfect bound, with full colour covers."

Until 2010 all our books, the majority of which are/were on the subject of mystery animals and allied disciplines, were published by `CFZ Press`, the publishing arm of the Centre for Fortean Zoology (CFZ), and we urged our readers and followers to draw a discreet veil over the books that we published that were completely off topic to the CFZ.

However, in 2010 we decided that enough was enough and launched a second imprint, `Fortean Words` which aims to cover a wide range of non animal-related esoteric subjects. Other imprints will be launched as and when we feel like it, however the basic ethos of the company remains the same: Our job is to publish books and magazines that we feel are worth publishing, whether or not they are going to sell. Money is, after all - as my dear old Mama once told me - a rather vulgar subject, and she would be rolling in her grave if she thought that her eldest son was somehow in `trade`.

Luckily, so far our tastes have turned out not to be that rarified after all, and we have sold far more books than anyone ever thought that we would, so there is a moral in there somewhere…

Jon Downes,
Woolsery, North Devon
July 2010

**CFZ PRESS**

# Other Books in Print

*Wildman!* by Redfern, Nick
*Globsters* by Newton, Michael
*Cats of Magic, Mythology and Mystery* Shuker, by Karl P. N
*Those Amazing Newfoundland Dogs* by Bondeson, Jan
*The Mystery Animals of Pennsylvania* by Gable, Andrew
*Sea Serpent Carcasses - Scotland from the Stronsa Monster to Loch Ness* by Glen Vaudrey
*The CFZ Yearbook 2012* edited by Jonathan and Corinna Downes
*ORANG PENDEK: Sumatra's Forgotten Ape* by Richard Freeman
*THE MYSTERY ANIMALS OF THE BRITISH ISLES: London* by Neil Arnold
*CFZ EXPEDITION REPORT: India 2010* by Richard Freeman *et al*
*The Cryptid Creatures of Florida* by Scott Marlow
*Dead of Night* by Lee Walker
*The Mystery Animals of the British Isles: The Northern Isles* by Glen Vaudrey
*THE MYSTERY ANIMALS OF THE BRTISH ISLES: Gloucestershire and Worcestershire* by
Paul Williams
*When Bigfoot Attacks* by Michael Newton
*Weird Waters – The Mystery Animals of Scandinavia: Lake and Sea Monsters* by Lars Thomas
*The Inhumanoids* by Barton Nunnelly
*Monstrum! A Wizard's Tale* by Tony "Doc" Shiels
*CFZ Yearbook 2011* edited by Jonathan Downes
*Karl Shuker's Alien Zoo* by Shuker, Dr Karl P.N
*Tetrapod Zoology Book One* by Naish, Dr Darren
*The Mystery Animals of Ireland* by Gary Cunningham and Ronan Coghlan
*Monsters of Texas* by Gerhard, Ken
*The Great Yokai Encyclopaedia* by Freeman, Richard
*NEW HORIZONS: Animals & Men issues 16-20 Collected Editions Vol. 4*
by Downes, Jonathan
*A Daintree Diary -*
*Tales from Travels to the Daintree Rainforest in tropical north Queensland, Australia*
by Portman, Carl
*Strangely Strange but Oddly Normal* by Roberts, Andy

*Centre for Fortean Zoology Yearbook 2010* by Downes, Jonathan
*Predator Deathmatch* by Molloy, Nick
*Star Steeds and other Dreams* by Shuker, Karl
*CHINA: A Yellow Peril?* by Muirhead, Richard
*Mystery Animals of the British Isles: The Western Isles* by Vaudrey, Glen
*Giant Snakes - Unravelling the coils of mystery* by Newton, Michael
*Mystery Animals of the British Isles: Kent* by Arnold, Neil
*Centre for Fortean Zoology Yearbook 2009* by Downes, Jonathan
*CFZ EXPEDITION REPORT: Russia 2008* by Richard Freeman *et al*, Shuker, Karl (fwd)
*Dinosaurs and other Prehistoric Animals on Stamps - A Worldwide catalogue*
by Shuker, Karl P. N
*Dr Shuker's Casebook* by Shuker, Karl P.N
*The Island of Paradise - chupacabra UFO crash retrievals,*
*and accelerated evolution on the island of Puerto Rico* by Downes, Jonathan
*The Mystery Animals of the British Isles: Northumberland and Tyneside* by Hallowell, Michael J
*Centre for Fortean Zoology Yearbook 1997* by Downes, Jonathan (Ed)
*Centre for Fortean Zoology Yearbook 2002* by Downes, Jonathan (Ed)
*Centre for Fortean Zoology Yearbook 2000/1* by Downes, Jonathan (Ed)
*Centre for Fortean Zoology Yearbook 1998* by Downes, Jonathan (Ed)
*Centre for Fortean Zoology Yearbook 2003* by Downes, Jonathan (Ed)
*In the wake of Bernard Heuvelmans* by Woodley, Michael A
*CFZ EXPEDITION REPORT: Guyana 2007* by Richard Freeman *et al*, Shuker, Karl (fwd)
*Centre for Fortean Zoology Yearbook 1999* by Downes, Jonathan (Ed)
*Big Cats in Britain Yearbook 2008* by Fraser, Mark (Ed)
*Centre for Fortean Zoology Yearbook 1996* by Downes, Jonathan (Ed)
*THE CALL OF THE WILD - Animals & Men issues 11-15*
*Collected Editions Vol. 3* by Downes, Jonathan (ed)
*Ethna's Journal* by Downes, C N
*Centre for Fortean Zoology Yearbook 2008* by Downes, J (Ed)
*DARK DORSET -Calendar Custome* by Newland, Robert J
*Extraordinary Animals Revisited* by Shuker, Karl
*MAN-MONKEY - In Search of the British Bigfoot* by Redfern, Nick
*Dark Dorset Tales of Mystery, Wonder and Terror* by Newland, Robert J and Mark North
*Big Cats Loose in Britain* by Matthews, Marcus
*MONSTER! - The A-Z of Zooform Phenomena* by Arnold, Neil
*The Centre for Fortean Zoology 2004 Yearbook* by Downes, Jonathan (Ed)
*The Centre for Fortean Zoology 2007 Yearbook* by Downes, Jonathan (Ed)
*CAT FLAPS! Northern Mystery Cats* by Roberts, Andy
*Big Cats in Britain Yearbook 2007* by Fraser, Mark (Ed)
*BIG BIRD! - Modern sightings of Flying Monsters* by Gerhard, Ken
*THE NUMBER OF THE BEAST - Animals & Men issues 6-10*
*Collected Editions Vol. 1* by Downes, Jonathan (Ed)
*IN THE BEGINNING - Animals & Men issues 1-5 Collected Editions Vol. 1* by Downes, Jonathan
*STRENGTH THROUGH KOI - They saved Hitler's Koi and other stories*

by Downes, Jonathan
*The Smaller Mystery Carnivores of the Westcountry* by Downes, Jonathan
*CFZ EXPEDITION REPORT: Gambia 2006* by Richard Freeman *et al*, Shuker, Karl (fwd)
*The Owlman and Others* by Jonathan Downes
*The Blackdown Mystery* by Downes, Jonathan
*Big Cats in Britain Yearbook 2006* by Fraser, Mark (Ed)
*Fragrant Harbours - Distant Rivers* by Downes, John T
*Only Fools and Goatsuckers* by Downes, Jonathan
*Monster of the Mere* by Jonathan Downes
*Dragons:More than a Myth* by Freeman, Richard Alan
*Granfer's Bible Stories* by Downes, John Tweddell
*Monster Hunter* by Downes, Jonathan

CFZ Classics is a new venture for us. There are many seminal works that are either unavailable today, or not available with the production values which we would like to see. So, following the old adage that if you want to get something done do it yourself, this is exactly what we have done.

Desiderius Erasmus Roterodamus (b. October 18th 1466, d. July 2nd 1536) said: "When I have a little money, I buy books; and if I have any left, I buy food and clothes," and we are much the same. Only, we are in the lucky position of being able to share our books with the wider world. CFZ Classics is a conduit through which we cannot just re-issue titles which we feel still have much to offer the cryptozoological and Fortean research communities of the 21st Century, but we are adding footnotes, supplementary essays, and other material where we deem it appropriate.

*Headhunters of The Amazon* by Fritz W Up de Graff (1902)

# Fortean Words

The Centre for Fortean Zoology has for several years led the field in Fortean publishing. CFZ Press is the only publishing company specialising in books on monsters and mystery animals. CFZ Press has published more books on this subject than any other company in history and has attracted such well known authors as Andy Roberts, Nick Redfern, Michael Newton, Dr Karl Shuker, Neil Arnold, Dr Darren Naish, Jon Downes, Ken Gerhard and Richard Freeman.

Now CFZ Press are launching a new imprint. Fortean Words is a new line of books dealing with Fortean subjects other than cryptozoology, which is - after all - the subject the CFZ are best known for. Fortean Words is being launched with a spectacular multi-volume series called *Haunted Skies* which covers British UFO sightings between 1940 and 2010. Former policeman John Hanson and his long-suffering partner Dawn Holloway have compiled a peerless library of sighting reports, many that have not been made public before.

Other books include a look at the Berwyn Mountains UFO case by renowned Fortean Andy Roberts and a series of forthcoming books by transatlantic researcher Nick Redfern. CFZ Press are dedicated to maintaining the fine quality of their works with Fortean Words. New authors tackling new subjects will always be encouraged, and we hope that our books will continue to be as ground-breaking and popular as ever.

*Haunted Skies Volume One 1940-1959* by John Hanson and Dawn Holloway
*Haunted Skies Volume Two 1960-1965* by John Hanson and Dawn Holloway
*Haunted Skies Volume Three 1965-1967* by John Hanson and Dawn Holloway
*Haunted Skies Volume Four 1968-1971* by John Hanson and Dawn Holloway
*Haunted Skies Volume Five 1972-1974* by John Hanson and Dawn Holloway
*Haunted Skies Volume Six 1975-1977* by John Hanson and Dawn Holloway
*Grave Concerns* by Kai Roberts

*Police and the Paranormal* by Andy Owens
*Dead of Night* by Lee Walker
*Space Girl Dead on Spaghetti Junction* - an anthology by Nick Redfern
*I Fort the Lore* - an anthology by Paul Screeton
*UFO Down - the Berwyn Mountains UFO Crash* by Andy Roberts
*The Grail* by Ronan Coghlan
*UFO Warminster - Cradle of Contract* by Kevin Goodman
*Quest for the Hexham Heads* by Paul Screeton

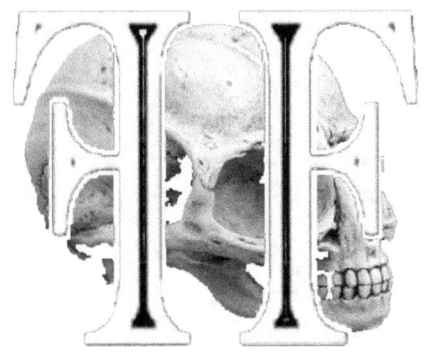

# Fortean Fiction

J ust before Christmas 2011, we launched our third imprint, this time dedicated to - let's see if you guessed it from the title - fictional books with a Fortean or cryptozoological theme. We have published a few fictional books in the past, but now think that because of our rising reputation as publishers of quality Forteana, that a dedicated fiction imprint was the order of the day.

We launched with four titles:

*Green Unpleasant Land* by Richard Freeman
*Left Behind* by Harriet Wadham
*Dark Ness* by Tabitca Cope
*Snap!* By Steven Bredice
*Death on Dartmoor* by Di Francis
*Dark Wear* by Tabitca Cope
*Hyakymonogatari Book 1* by Richard Freeman

www.ingramcontent.com/pod-product-compliance
Lightning Source LLC
Chambersburg PA
CBHW070023260626
47159CB00005B/1934